DEATH
MADN[...]
WAITING FOR YOU?

"Casket Demon" and "The Titan in the Crypt" may remind you that superstition is not meant to be ignored…

Forget the fury of a woman scorned. In "Death has Green Eyes" and "The Third Shadow" you will discover the fury of a woman murdered!

Some ghosts just don't wanna be alone any longer. In "The Rebel's Rest" and "The Three Last Ships" you'll find there may be help for those lonely spooks—but is it "willing" help?

Hectic witchery and sound absconding instruments! "Hatchery of Dreams" and "Horn O' Plenty" will have you grinning and perplexed!

Get ready to indulge in another great series of good 'ol fashioned horror tales! Written by some of the best authors ever to have picked up a pen or banged on a typewriter.

TABLE OF CONTENTS

HORROR GEMS

Volume 3
August Derleth
and others

Edited by
GREGORY LUCE and LEANNE WRAY

ARMCHAIR FICTION
PO Box 4369, Medford, Oregon 97504

THE CLOSING DOOR

By August Derleth

After all, the advice was sound—always have the church cleaned before dark...

WHEN it was finally determined that Henry Bessman was not going to be up and around much any more, the position of sexton to St. Jude's at Clyner, near Horsham, was declared open. Henry Bessman had held it for a long time; he had spent the last third of his relatively long life at it and had maintained the position against all comers. But now at last it had to be relinquished and most likely it would go to Ben Thompson, who had hankered after it for years. Ben had been a thorn in Henry's side for a long while, but now it was time to look past all that. As soon as the vicar stopped by and told the sick man that the board had given the job to Ben Thompson, Henry sent for Ben.

Ben came in haste. Quarrel though they might have done for season after season, they were good enough friends underneath.

"Ain't worse, are you, Henry?" asked Ben, coming into the sick room.

"No, Ben. But I ain't long for this world, and that's a fact. Now you sit here a bit for I've a word to say to you and I don't want to tire me out. You've got the job."

"Yes, they gave it to me, Henry," admitted Ben, somewhat abashed now at his memory of how often he had attempted to wrest the position away from the incumbent.

"You always wanted it," said Henry placidly. "But it wasn't you put me out, and that's a fact. So I'm just as glad you got the job, Ben. Only, I've got a bit of advice for you, and I hope you take it."

"I'm listenin'."

"Try to get the church done before dark."

"You always got the church done before sundown," observed Ben.

"I made sure of it."

"Why?"

"Ah, it might be for no reason at all," answered Henry. "If it's reason you'll have, likely you'll find it. I did."

That was all Henry Bessman would say. Nevertheless, it was of a pattern with certain hints he was wont to throw out during his incumbency. "This ain't the job it looks to be," he used to say darkly. Or, "It's not for you, Ben; there's that in it that's not so nice." Ben had passed these hints over as suggesting difficulties with the vicar; perhaps Henry had not meant to impugn the vicar. It was a strange thing to tell him; Ben thought as he walked home.

Oddly enough, the vicar himself hinted the same thing next day; he put it differently by saying that he always liked to have the church closed and locked by sundown. The vicar was a short, rotund little man, who was disconcertingly absentminded; he habitually spoke in a vague, offhand manner, as if his real thoughts were far from the subject of conversation. One hesitated to interrupt him, and Ben did not.

It did not trouble Ben. Ben was a man of his own mind. He would do his work well, but at his own good time. He appreciated advice, but gave no promise of acting on it. Nevertheless, for a considerable time the church was cleaned and closed by sundown, and before there was any alteration in this practice Henry Bessman died and was buried, and the vicar removed to another parish, giving his place to the Reverend Kilvert McDonal, a tall, ascetic man of middle age who had a habit of frowning gravely and gazing down his nose at all and sundry who approached him.

So it was not for three months after Ben Thompson had been given those curious hints that he was delayed enough to have to finish cleaning the church after sundown. He had had to help dig a grave that afternoon, and it had upset his entire schedule, though Ben did not mind; he supposed the dead could be allowed this call upon the living for their last brief while.

ST. JUDE'S was a country parish church without pretensions, a simple building of stone, almost square, set just up on a small rise from the bank of a creek which at that place had been dammed up a little to form a carp pond. There was not much work to the cleaning of it. It had seventeen rows of pews, with one side aisle and one center aisle. There was a door at the end of the side aisle that led into a small passage giving outside to a path, which led over to the vicarage in the one direction and down to the carp pond in the other direction.

It was this door that gave Ben Thompson trouble.

In all the times he had cleaned the church before, he had never had any difficulty with this door to the passage. He had opened it and shut it, he had left it stand ajar, he had cleaned it and waxed it, and never a jot of trouble had he had with it. But on this June evening, when he was late and in a hurry, the door was a vexation. He wanted it to stand open, but for some unaccountable reason it kept closing. Nor was there a breath of air to lay it to. He would go over, open the door, and walk away a little, when lo! the door would move silently away from the wall and swing to with a soft click.

It had never acted in this manner before, and Ben could not understand it. He was a phlegmatic, easy-going man, not easily disturbed, but readily enough annoyed, and the door soon became a source of annoyance, for he meant it to be open to let a little air through the church and also more light, since daylight was now rapidly fading, and the open front door was scarcely enough to light his way. He made one ineffectual attempt to block the door with one of the fragile chairs available, but the chair was not enough to hold the door; thereafter he made periodic trips to that end of the church and angrily opened the door again and again.

DURING this procedure, the sun went down, and the dusk gave way to early darkness. It was at that hour just between twilight and dark that Ben opened the door for the last time. A kind of glow lay in the water of the carp pond at the end of the walk beyond the church, like the spectre of day, and Ben stood briefly to gaze at it. Then he turned and walked back down the aisle, waiting for the click of the closing door to sound.

But before he heard it, he was impelled to turn and look back. What impelled him to do so he did not know; he was aware of a sudden inexplicable chill that struck his retreating back like a wash of cold air, and at the same moment an unnatural stillness seemed to close over the church. He turned and at that instant saw a curious tableau which had but a brief moment of life before it was lost in the shadows.

For the door was not closing of itself alone. It was being drawn shut by the hand of the vicar—or so at least Ben thought him to be, for he had the same build as the Reverend McDonal, and he walked in similar fashion. But Ben had no time to call out, for of a sudden a dark figure launched itself from the single little pew set beside the door to the passage and flung himself upon the vicar.

Ben dropped his broom and ran up the aisle to give aid to the vicar.

But the vicar was not there. No one was there.

Ben was shaken. He touched the doorknob and found it cold, colder than the June air. An aura of coldness clung to the door and the neighboring pew, quite as if someone from outside had come in. Ben was not too upset to ponder what he had seen. He *had* seen something, of that he was certain. Fancy, hallucination, illusion—these words meant nothing to him. He was stolid and sure of himself. He had seen something, which had the appearance of two men, one of them almost certainly the vicar. And, since he was settled in his mind about this, he locked up the church and went forthwith to call on the Reverend Kilvert McDonal.

The vicar was surprised in the midst of his meditations. If he were to be judged by appearances, he had not been out of the vicarage for some time.

"Ah, Mr. Thompson," he intoned, "you have finally finished at the church."

"That I have, Reverend."

The vicar leaned back and folded his hands as if in prayer. "What then, Mr. Thompson?"

Ben told him graphically.

The vicar murmured soothingly about the hallucinatory quality of the dusk. He explained the closing door by pointing out that very often pressure on the boards of a floor was quite sufficient to cause a door to swing shut; that it failed to happen during the day did not seem to him a point worth taking, for was there not after all a considerable difference in humidity between the night air and the day's, and was it not as well known that humidity affected the expansion and contraction of wood, thus lending variation to such purely material objects as doors and floors?

Ben listened soberly, but he was not entirely convinced. "Will you come and see for yourself tomorrow night, then?" he asked at last.

"If it will ease your mind, Mr. Thompson, I will do so."

"Agreed," said Ben and took his leave. The vicar was not an unimaginative man. He returned to his meditations, but in a little while the sexton's story ate its way through his contemplation. By any standard, it was a queer little tale. It was not the kind of story Ben Thompson might have invented. Perhaps his predecessor had suggested it to him and Ben had then "seen" it.

At this moment, too, as he plodded homeward, Ben was thinking of his predecessor. He had a rather good idea what Henry Bessman had meant, and he reasoned readily that if what he had seen had done Henry no harm, it would do him none either. What, he wondered, would the vicar say?

THE vicar came over to the church just before sundown and sat in the last pew next to the wall. He suggested that Ben go about his work just as always, just as he had done on the previous night, and Ben did so without demur; he would not have liked standing in the darkening church waiting for the door to begin closing once more.

The vicar sat alone and waited, acknowledging to himself that there was a certain comfort in Ben's stolid presence. The air within the church was close; June was hot and humid; outside larks sang their vespers, which mingled with the sleepy cheepings of lesser birds already settling down for the night.

The door, the vicar marked, did just what Ben Thompson said it did. Each time Ben opened it, the door stood for a few seconds as Ben had left it; then slowly, almost imperceptibly, it began to close, precisely as if it were being drawn shut. The vicar watched, fascinated. As the dusk flowed into the church, he began to feel definitely uneasy. For one thing, a kind of cloudlike darkness hovered at the door; for another, a similar tangible darkness coupled with chillness occupied the other end of the pew in which he sat.

At the same time, the vicar was aware of an aura of evil, which seemed to emanate from the far end of the pew. It was uncanny and profoundly disturbing; he was as conscious of it as he was of the diminishing light, and he knew, as Ben Thompson had known, that it was not hallucination or fancy before his eyes.

As the dusk deepened, the dark masses at the door and in the pew took dim, suggestive shape. Two men there—the one coming in, the other lurking half-hidden in the pew. Of this the vicar could be sure. But of what manner of men they were, he could not guess, save that his dark companion in the pew gave off a quaking atmosphere of evil.

But even as he sat musing in this fashion, trying to establish a reason for being of these dark entities, he witnessed the culmination of the drama which was being perpetually reenacted about the closing door of the passage through which he himself had walked countless times. The tall dark figure coming through the door was the object of a sudden, swift attack by the figure in the pew. There was a terrified surge of evil power, an entanglement of figures, then nothing, nothing at all but the silence and the heavy breathing of Ben Thompson, who had also seen once more.

The time had been the same as before—that hour when dusk turns into night.

Ben walked out of the church with the vicar, who went sturdily through the passage, as was his custom. They stood outside under the stars for a moment.

"Do you believe in ghosts, Mr. Thompson?" asked the vicar abruptly.

"I believe in what I see," said Ben, "and what I hear and what I taste, such as you might say."

"A materialist," sighed the Reverend McDonal. "What a pity!"

"Do you?" asked Ben bluntly.

"I do and I don't," replied the vicar cryptically. "I think it would be just as well if the cleaning were got over with before sundown."

"Just as it was with Henry," muttered Ben. "That fellow knew, too."

Each of them went his separate way. Ben was bursting to tell his cronies all about his adventure, but he decided to hold his tongue; the men at the *Fox & Hound* had a way of ridicule about them. But he thought persistently about what he had seen; that the vicar had seen it, too, only confirmed him in his own opinion that he had not been the victim of either illusion or hallucination.

In the night he sat up in bed abruptly, awakened from a sound sleep. He shook his wife awake.

"Marget, d'you remember Reverend Billings?"

"Oh, go to sleep," she muttered.

"I recall him well. A big, tall fellow, like McDonal. He had enemies."

"So do we all," said Marget philosophically. "Try to get some sleep, Ben."

"You remember how he disappeared?"

"Not likely. I wasn't there."

"The hour, the hour, I mean. Was it not sundown or just after?"

"He was seen last just before sundown," said Marget.

"On his way to church."

It all fitted in so well. At that same time one of the vestrymen with whom the vicar had had a bitter quarrel disappeared, too. Neither had ever been seen again, and a shortage in the vestryman's funds led to the belief that he had run off with the money entrusted to his care.

AT THIS hour, after long and dutiful meditation, the Reverend Kilvert McDonal was writing a letter to his bishop, soliciting the rites of exorcism. "There is certainly some evil associated with St. Jude's," he wrote soberly. "Exorcism is plainly indicated, after which the church can be consecrated anew. I earnestly commend this matter to your attention. Above all else, we must keep the matter quiet, lest we arouse the curiosity, and, I fear, the ridicule, of the people."

The bishop was as grave and considerate as the vicar. He came down one day and quietly performed the rites of exorcism. If the vicar had hoped to view an evil spirit in retreat, he was disappointed; nothing at all happened, except there was a bad smell in the church. This lingered unpleasantly for days.

Thereafter, the bishop blessed the church anew.

That night all three of them waited upon the events of dusk, beginning with the closing door. And that evening the door did not close; it stayed just as Ben left it. Only the bishop, who was a saintly man, was not surprised.

It was Ben, however, who was the practical one of the three. He reasoned quite correctly that if there had been ghosts, there must have been something more solid and substantial before them. If old Weller had really hidden himself in that pew and assaulted the Reverend Billings, they must have gone somewhere. Wrestling in the church, in the passage. Outside, too, perhaps.

Well, now, he asked himself, what was the distance to the carp pond?

This was a simple measurement no one had thought to take in the thirty years since the Reverend Billings' disappearance. People had taken it for granted that Weller had gone with the money and that the vicar had gone along, not alone for the purpose of saving Weller's soul.

The carp pond was plainly indicated. In the morning Ben went around early to the pond and, after diligent search, he dragged up the bones of two middle-aged men, the vicar and Weller, Ben had no doubt.

THE END

THE TITAN IN THE CRYPT

By J. G. Warner

The hold that H. P. Lovecraft exerts from beyond the grave on followers of fantasy seems to grow stronger through the years. This story, by a New Orleans newspaperman, grew out of his admiration for Lovecraft, and his determination to keep alive the HPL style by using it in fanciful letters to his friends. This was the only letter written. But it weaves a spell worthy of the master.

Dear Jim,

I am sending this by special delivery so it should get to you by the day after tomorrow. I shall follow it by no more than a day. You must take me in for a time until I get my bearings, and can determine on which side of the balance my mind lies.

I know you would receive me without so much as a preparing letter. I am writing this, rather, to keep my own sanity, which has been pushed to the brink by the final horror that has just befallen me. You are the only person I know who would even listen to such a story as I have to tell. You must believe it and help me escape. You can, if anyone or anything can. But I doubt whether I can get away, ultimately.

You remember Tessier, the fat old furniture dealer. It all began with him. He drank a lot, you know, and talked pretty wildly; you seemed rather interested in him, although it seemed to me that his queer hints and insinuations were only the product of an oversensitive imagination nurtured in New Orleans. Well, Tessier remarked that he knew a lot about things you were interested in—your folklore and mythology, of course—after you left last summer. He never would say just what, but kept telling me to wait. I must say that he got me pretty interested.

Two days ago he called me. He was drunk, worse than usual. It was the last night of Mardi Gras, but I hadn't made any plans, and he insisted that I come to his store. He said that he was finally ready to show me the secret he had been talking about, and kept apologizing and bemoaning the fact that you weren't here. Thank God you weren't.

Well, since I really hadn't anything to do, and it would give me a chance to get rid of Tessier and his dark mutterings, I conceded. I left the apartment and started fighting my way through the wild carnival crowds. It was not more than five blocks from my apartment to Tessier's on Royal, but it took me more than half an hour to get there.

You've never seen the French Quarter on a carnival night, Jim. It's mad; the streets are roped off, crowds so thick you can hardly move. Drunks lurch into you and women tug your sleeve—it's really rather unpleasant unless you're in the mood, and I wasn't. The din was deafening, and the old wrought galleries were sagging beneath the weight of the celebrants dancing on them. The streets are so narrow that the people on the galleries could nearly join hands across the packed street. It was terribly hot and muggy, and a rather unpleasant smell was coming off the Mississippi. It's only a few blocks from Royal, you know, and when the Quarter isn't so noisy you can hear the cow-like lowing of the ships' horns.

I WAS in a decidedly foul mood when I finally got to Tessier's pretentious antique furniture store. You were never there, were you? It's the usual thing for the Rue Royal—lots of glass with all those polished gold buckets and vulgar stone statues piled in careless disarray. The old fool was waiting inside under a little porcelain lamp and when he saw me at the door, he waddled to unlock it.

He was almost overpoweringly drunk, and had the air of a man about to uncover the secrets of the universe. I was suddenly beset by an overwhelming urge to turn around and go home; but before I could act he had bolted the door and was leading me to the rear of his shop.

Tessier looked even worse under the lamp, surrounded by all those ominous big stone nymphs and birds and ancient chairs. A gross, revolting soapstone Buddha two feet high peered down from a filing cabinet at us with a vapidly inscrutable expression. The old antique seller was in really bad shape. He hadn't even attempted to shave for a couple of days and there was a yellow tinge under the normal sickly grayish cast of his hog-jowled face. He acted alternately frightened and excited as he pulled me into a dimly lit back room, like a child hugging itself in some pleasurable yet dreaded anticipation.

"This is the night—the night, you know," he tittered, and began fumbling into some sort of closet. I didn't think this sort of statement was worth an answer, so after a moment he went on.

"You'll find a lot of things to startle you about New Orleans tonight, Paul. You'd never believe it if I told you, and you'd probably have babbled it, so that's why I didn't tell you until tonight, so you can see for yourself.

"But you must never speak to anyone of what you will see down there tonight. Never. You'll see what I mean. God, if they should ever learn I brought you…"

I was growing impatient. "What's all this about, Tessier? And what's that?" He had brought two strange, musty-looking dun-colored robes with loose cowls from the closet.

"Put it on," he said, handing one of the mildewed things to me.

"Paul, you won't believe this until you see it, but I'll tell you now, because we can't talk, not even whisper, once we get there. Remember that. They might notice you.

THE French Quarter is two centuries or more old, you know. There's a hundred blocks of it now but you only know half of it. "The rest of it's down there," he said, almost shouting, and pointing at his feet. "Only about fifty people know this, and you'll be surprised who they are.

"Yes, there's something down there, under these crumbling buildings and banquettes that have been here since white men were here. But it's been down there long before that, long before there was a Vieux Carre, and probably even before there were Indians. It's probably been there forever.

"You didn't think the old town was built here, in the middle of a God-forsaken swamp, for nothing, did you? Not when it's a lot better for a townsite a little farther up the river.

"We all go down there, once a year, the last night of carnival. Our fathers did, and their fathers before them, and theirs, and God knows who else before that. I don't know why we go down there now, really, but we do, and when you see who else goes down, maybe you'll think it's gotten us results. You'll see some pretty rough things, Paul, and I hope you won't give yourself away."

"For God's sake, man, what are you talking about?" I demanded, thoroughly disgusted now. "What's down there?"

"Catacombs," he croaked. "Miles of them. Nobody's been through them all, that we know of, and we don't know how far or how deep they go, but they seem to cover all the Quarter—underneath."

Well, Jim, this was the first concrete statement of the night, and you'll understand that it was enough to make me pull on the evil-smelling old robe and pull the cowl over my head, as Tessier did.

"It's nearly time now. We must go, and remember, whatever you do, don't say a word once we step out this door. Keep absolutely quiet and don't stare. If anybody notices you aren't one of us, God help me...and you."

WITH that, he doused the lights and opened a rear door. The blackness of the night made it seem nearly light within the store. Tessier looked up at me and in the dimness at the door his disgusting face was almost pitiful with a fearfulness that was beginning to pervade it. I think he was starting to wish he hadn't brought me, and I was about to offer to leave, when an overpowering stench of whiskey floated into my nostrils, gagging me, and I pushed him out the door.

We were in a small, rundown courtyard, piled around with boxes and crates and old packing and stuffing. Tessier tugged at the flowing sleeve of my cassock and I started after him through the blackness.

We passed out through the little courtyard and into a long, high-walled passageway. The din of the celebration burst afresh into my ears, and above the walls and the rooftops of the old town we were creeping through, the lights offered an eerie glow. Raucous, obscene and wildly incongruous music shrieked at us from the nearby Bourbon Street dives as we walked silently through the deserted, musty outdoor corridor. The walk led to an old wooden door and through that we went into another courtyard. It was pitch black at eye-level but I could hear the bubbling of a fountain nearby over the roar of the crowds in the streets outside.

Tessier opened a protesting door and we were on a side street, Conti, I think it was. It is the last place-memory I have of that night. Nobody took notice of us, with more strangely costumed figures to be seen anywhere during Mardi Gras, and we slipped across the street and into another doorway.

We didn't, I don't think, cross another street. But it seems that Tessier, growing surprisingly steadier in that oppressively hot, dank air, led me through an endless series of courtyards, passages, plank doors and private alleys until I was perfectly lost. I guess we must have crossed a street somewhere. I remember I never lost sight of the dim glow above the crumbling rooftops, and I could always hear the laughing, milling crowds in the streets.

It seemed we had been threading our way through those ancient galleried courtyards for more than half an hour when Tessier suddenly pushed open a door and only blackness looked out. We went in and he shut the door and for long moments I couldn't see a thing. Then, just as I was growing accustomed to the utter darkness, the door opened again and three more hooded and cowled figures slunk in.

As best I could tell, Jim, the place was an old slave-quarters; it had only one big room, and another small floor above; but we were there only long enough for Tessier to light a soaked rag on the end of a club-like piece of wood and he was bearing one of those torches so beloved of the pulp magazine artists.

Then he walked to the middle of the room and began tugging at a ring on the floor. One of the three strangers went to help him. I glanced around enough to see that the place was falling apart, the two windows boarded up.

THEN Tessier was tugging at my sleeve. The other three had already gone down the hole that their efforts had opened. Now Tessier was ready to descend into the square-shaped hole in the brick floor. There wasn't a ladder there. Rather, there were steps, hewn and placed into the immemorially soggy ground. Tessier went down and motioned for me to pull the door shut above me as I followed. And I was groping for the lid to the trap when I noticed that I could no longer hear the carnival revelers. Then I pulled the trap door shut above me and it clanged into place with a startling boom that was answered by an echo from the bowels of the earth.

I had never known it before, but apparently I suffer from claustrophobia. No doubt it was enhanced by the utter weirdness of everything I had been doing and everything I had seen for the past hour; but when the door shut over my head and I looked down at the fire-lit, endless steps running into the worm-riddled earth, an icy chill settled behind my forehead and I had to fight off the advance guard of panic.

The three persons that had descended before us were already out of sight, but I fancied I could hear footsteps echoing back through that terrible mouldy tunnel. The slightest noise produced unerringly somber results in that nether world.

Tessier was pulling at me again, and we began the descent. His torch cast shadows about us. I could see that the walls of the sharply declining hole were earthen; it was not shorn up in any manner that I could discern. The steps were of stone, worn unaccountably smooth at the edges, since Tessier told me this eerie pilgrimage was made only once a year, on the last day of carnival. I wondered how this seemingly small amount of stone could produce such perfect echoes.

Down and down we went, Jim, until my legs were about to give out. Tessier was clutching at the earth, and now we had gone so far down that it was fairly oozing with slime and wetness, and revolting green slime on the steps made the descent treacherous. Every so often we passed holes nearly a foot large in the walls, and they reminded me of the little worm passages in a spadeful of upturned earth.

The indescribably foul odor that seemed almost to ooze visibly from the black earthen walls was becoming unbearable and I feared I would fall on the slippery steps and retch when the steps suddenly halted and Tessier's torch flared out in a large, high ceilinged earth chamber.

THE chamber was like an overturned bowl, and must have been twenty feet high at its peak, and probably twenty feet across. It was like an eldritch fearsome vestibule, for six black openings had been cut into the circular walls. Tessier walked to the center of the earthen room and looked about, a puzzled expression on his fat features, while great drops of moisture oozed from the blackish-yellow ceiling and dripped on his mouldering cassock. Then he nodded to himself and started into one of the six openings, beckoning me to follow with a jerk of his flaming torch.

We entered the slightly round door and I found myself peering down an almost—as far as I could tell from Tessier's torch—illimitable catacomb. The old fool had been speaking the truth. The French Quarter was undermined with these sinister dank tunnels, although I have no idea how far below the gay carnival crowds we were.

Tessier, apparently sober now and growing increasingly agitated, waddled as briskly as he could down the slightly concave floor of the round catacomb. I found it hardly high enough to stand erect, and began walking with a stoop, but even so something wet and wholly loathsome seeped through the cowl into my hair and down my face occasionally.

The catacomb wasn't as long as I must have thought, for we hadn't walked long before some sort of noise seemed to float to our ears over the drum-like beats of our footsteps. The stone had stopped with the steps, and all about us was bloated earth now, but still those perfect reproductions of every sound struck our ears like mocking laughter. Strange growths tugged at my cowl and my head was soggy with clinging lumps of swollen dirt as we forged on; soon the cowl was pushed back and my hair was growing matted with that unnamable excretion of the earth that dripped on it.

All the time the buzzing grew louder, and soon I seemed to detect a glow of light far down the catacomb we were following, far beyond the feeble reach of Tessier's faggot. Still we kept on that soggy path in the tunnel, although at intervals of about twenty paces new catacombs yawned blackly at us from either side; it is a wonder we were not lost forever in that murky awfulness below New Orleans. Better perhaps for me that we had been.

The noise grew louder, and the glow brighter, and my fear, thrust back by ever-present conscious effort, surged back in a great wave when from a side catacomb belched a soggy thump as I passed; a thump almost inaudible, giving the impression of fathomless distance. I nearly cried out, but Tessier did not falter; apparently the growing growl from ahead had drowned that awful flopping sound from his ears.

I was staggering, nearly sick with a fear that I could hardly hold in my stomach, when the end of the catacomb appeared and I saw a milling crowd of the cowled figures. Thirty more paces to the blazingly lighted door and I almost fainted when I saw black hands bigger than a man reaching down for the hooded forms.

A PARALYZING, sickening horror gripped me when I saw those two great ebony hands cupping down as if to reach under the crowd of tan-robed men, but in another instant I realized that those gruesome claws were part of a terrible titan statue that hovered like a monstrous demon of death over the illimitable chamber and its occupants. As the terrible fright poured from me like an outgoing tide, leaving me weak and queasy, I gazed awestruck at that chamber, at the great black figure that dominated it—that was it, almost, and the sinister group gathered under the fearful shadow of the giant.

The chamber was so vast that the torches held on poles not far from the mouth of the catacomb in which we stood, and ranging far back until they were only little evil stars, seemed to illuminate only fractions of it. Jim, it seemed to me to cover more than a square mile; of course I can't be sure since I couldn't see the far reaches of the dome-shaped, although oblong, earthen grotto, and my mental state then was admittedly wretched.

In the center, under that breathtaking, all-encompassing figure, stood about fifty persons, dressed like Tessier and me. When I saw some of their faces, I could hardly believe it, just as Tessier had warned. The very contemporary fathers of the city of New Orleans stood there, looking rather ridiculous; their uncomfortably smiling faces peering from the shadows of their cowls.

I will not name the men I saw; great politicians, whose reputations were not of the highest but certainly spoke of nothing like this; financial and shipping barons; university heads—you'd really be shocked there, Jim—mingling with sinister-visaged, ill-reputed but vaguely affluent dwellers of the French Quarter, about whose lives a strange aura of mystery had been attached in that sane world somewhere above us.

They were talking among one another, somewhat self-consciously it seemed, and their faces bore rather embarrassed grins, as if they didn't want to be there, saw no reason for it, and felt silly. Apparently, Jim, they had no conception of what that eyeless thing was that stooped high above them.

The titan stone statue had its feet somewhere in the black recesses of the vast chamber, an egg-shaped auditorium about two hundred feet high at its apex, which was almost directly above us. There at the crown was that bloated head, yet the knee of that great black figure was dimly visible in the shadows, far, far away, slightly bent. The other knee was invisible in the blackness. Its arms were bowed and outstretched downward, bent at the elbows, and appeared about to scoop up us all. The whole great figure gave the impression of a vast black demon hunter, running in city-spanning strides, snatching up its victims in its black, slime-dripping paws.

There above us, Jim, bore down that head for which you have searched the world over; I recognized it from your talks, although neither your words nor mine could describe its blank awfulness. You hunted for years to no avail, but I—God help me—found it.

HIGH above us, yet it must have been a hundred yards across, was a head without a face; a great, ebony head with no features save long, pointed ears almost like wings.

Hurtling over us in his slime-dripping foulness was the Mighty Messenger, the Crawling Chaos from the blackness below the nighted pyramids. Forgotten for centuries upon centuries, buried with civilizations older than man, here he was below the heart of New Orleans, and these great men were vapid fools beneath him, they who would have fled screaming had they known what that magnificently wrought stone colossus represented.

It was set into the bowels of the earth, only a giant bas relief, and it seemed to nearly cover all of the great chamber's ceiling and part of its sides.

My eyes caught, over the heads of the milling crowd beneath the statue, stone steps rising out of the foul earth and leading to a slimy altar between the outstretched hands of the black god.

My senses still reel when I think of that sight—the flickering torches lighting the end of the vast egg-like chamber with its sloping walls hewn from the dirt, and that hideous black giant loping bestially out of the black reaches of the chamber, faceless, reaching impersonally out for us.

Tessier nudged me back to what remained of my senses. I looked down at him and he bore an abjectly fearful, pleading expression. His fat little face conveyed to me perfectly the idea that if it should be discovered that an outsider was in this great dank chamber of horrors, neither of us would ever see the daylight world again.

We joined the group of men moving about the wet stone altar, men who should have been leading the gay Mardi Gras revels somewhere above us instead of lurking furtively under flickering torches in this huge subterranean chamber.

AS far as the eye could follow the walls of the chamber, more catacombs opened, so many I could not begin to count them. In a moment of startling lucidity, I wondered whether I should ever feel safe again in the French Quarter, or all of New Orleans for that matter, knowing the vast emptiness that lay beneath its crust. The remembrance of this thought now makes me want to scream.

The voices of the crowd, gathered round the altar, seemed by the strange acoustics of that accursed nether world to come from everywhere, from even the very unseen feet of the thing that hovered above. Drops of moisture, falling as if from the sky, plopped with revolting little thuds upon us. I stood among the hooded visitors to the depths, and tried to make myself inconspicuous. They seemed to be waiting for something, and the babble swelled when a lone hooded figure came out of the entryway catacomb with a bulky package beneath his arm, wrapped in coarse brown paper.

The man was one of New Orleans' leading morticians. Apparently, whatever he had brought in the package was what had been awaited, for the voices died and perfect silence filled the chamber, except for the plops falling from the great ceiling above. Gathering his robes about him, he started up the wide slippery flight of stairs to the altar, and in the dancing light of the torches the fingers of the black thing seemed to twitch.

He placed the package on the altar and began a high, wailing sort of song-chant. I could make out nothing of what he said, and it seemed to be repeated almost simultaneously everywhere in the vast sunken room. I watched with a sick dread as his hands began to fumble with the knots in the shop cord that held the package together.

The paper fell open and as I strained morbidly to see what was between those titanic black hands, the horror descended upon me.

A muffled roar welled up from the far reaches of the blasted cavern, from the feet of the Mighty Messenger, and grew louder and louder like a vast bowling ball rumbling down a giant's alley toward cowering ten-pins. The faces of the crowd whitened and the last thing I saw was the mortician with his hands wildly outstretched; then a colossal blast of wind blew me from my feet and plunged the great cavern into the blackness of bottomless hell.

I seemed to fall into the very abyss of terror, terror so great that saliva choked me and I clutched myself into a quivering, mindless ball there on the foul dank floor. The coldness of death gripped my brain and I know not how long I lay there trembling and drooling like a stricken idiot.

WHEN thought returned to me the great cave was soundless. I dared not open my eyes for a wild fear of what might be before them. Slowly I relaxed my aching muscles and listened for some sound, something. But there was nothing— nothing at all where there had been fifty people. Even the incessant drip from the ceiling far above me was no more. Then panic came surging back—where was I? Was I still in the cavern? How long had abject terror held me senseless?

Timidly I made an effort to open my eyes. I couldn't at first—the very muscles seemed locked. But then, slowly, they seemed to part; it felt like an infinity. Then they must have been open, but I saw nothing. Only blackness.

My first thought was blindness. I moved my hand until it was before my face, but I could see nothing. I could see no more with my eyes open than I could with them closed.

The noise of rising from that miserable floor sounded like the clash of doom in the utter silence, but nothing touched me. I took a step. Nothing happened—only the sound of the footfall. It seemed like one step was taken everywhere in that great cave. I looked up where I had last seen that faceless evil, but here was only blackness, the blackness of the pit.

I began stepping forward into the blackness, gingerly; my hands in front of me like a blind man. Maybe I was blind. I had no matches, no way to make a light to try to see. But then my hands touched slimy stone and I knew at least that I was still in the great chamber, at the foot of the altar between the hands of the giant. I recoiled from that thing and remembrance of the package on the altar.

I turned, gropingly. I could not even think of what had happened to the others—to Tessier, who had brought a stranger into their midst. I began walking toward the wall upon which the entry catacomb opened—or toward where I thought it was. Then I remembered dismally that the catacomb to the slave quarters in the old town was only one of seemingly hundreds that opened into the chamber, and that I should probably die of hunger before I could even explore part of the first one I found.

But I kept walking, growing more bold in my steps as I grew used to utter blackness, keeping one hand before me. The hand gouged into the pulpy wall, and I sidled to my right, feeling all the while for an opening. Then my hand hit an empty spot—I felt gingerly around for the roof of the catacomb and jerked my hand away in disgust when I realized it was in one of those evil foot-wide holes.

I KEPT going, and the next pocket my hand found proved to be a catacomb. Whether it was the one to the surface, or whether there were others which also led to the surface I could not know. I entered.

After I had gone a few steps, I noticed that the sounds of my footsteps were more normal in the close confines of the tunnel than they had been in that time-eroded chamber. Then my head, the cowl fallen from it, slid into the roof of the catacomb and furrowed into that repulsive slimy mud. I began to walk with a slight stoop.

The catacomb seemed to take no curves, or at least they were very gradual ones, for only occasionally did I seem to stagger into the wall and recoil from its shocking pulpiness, I do not know how long I must have walked—all thoughts of time were far from my grasp—before it seemed that sight was dimly returning, faintly and blueishly.

A pale blue gas seemed to escape weakly from the moss-ridden walls of that infernal passageway, and I could see very dimly, not close at hand, but at a distance of many paces. The sight was limited to a faint recognition of the slightly tubular outlines of the benighted subterranean pathway.

On and on I went, and in the mouldy coolness I grew calmer, and it seemed that the drippings from the ceiling that plagued our entry were not to be found in this tunnel. But the abysmal stench of the first one, a smell of things eon-dead and decaying, like the river of time suddenly run dry, clung all about me, and breathing was a laborious thing.

As I walked, I seemed to become aware of a sense of tension, of cosmic apprehension, as though the catacombs were holding their breath. So strongly did this feeling grip me that I almost unconsciously began to hold my breath, even more than the foul odor made necessary. I held my breath as I walked, then expended it and drew a new lungfull like a child playing at hide-and-go-seek. And then I caught myself walking along with catlike steps, almost on my toes. I found myself listening with all my senses, joining the catacombs in their brooding alertness.

I tiptoed drunkenly down that ghastly tunnel, straining my ears as if I was trying to hear the expectancy of the walls. I jumped and rammed my head into the slimy soft roof when I trod on something that crunched under my foot. I didn't shout, but I started to run, and then the noise of my running frightened me worse than ever, so I gripped myself and resumed walking. I looked over my shoulder, timidly, apprehensively, into the blue light, now glimmering about where I had been when I walked on that thing that crunched. But all I could see was something small which reflected the blue light a fraction brighter than the floor.

AND as I walked, my heart pumping loudly, I could almost hear it too. I listened. I listened because the walls and the ceiling and the floor of that earthen catacomb were listening with a malign expectancy. They were waiting and listening for something; the very air about me seemed alive.

Then it came.

I felt it first. The earth was trembling around me—above me, at my side, but mainly under my feet. It was trembling like the skin of a slowly beaten drum. As I stood rooted with the now familiar sick fear caressing me, I expected the walls to begin crumbling. It began slightly, ever so slightly, but even then it seemed hideous because the very catacomb itself seemed to tense and draw up. The booming rhythmic vibrations increased, and increased, and then I heard it and screamed.

It sounded at first like the distant throbbing of a drum, but when it grew a little louder I knew what it was, and it was worse than what I had feared. A wave of cosmic terror shot through my body at the sound of those obscene loping footsteps, the footsteps of a hunting beast.

I fought the terror that was clutching at my brain and stiffened and felt the cool sucking mud at the top of my head.

The mud carried the vibrations of those awful padding footfalls that grew louder and the vibrations grew stronger.

I know only this, Jim, and I knew it as I stood there trembling with an ague of terror. No sane, living man ever saw the thing that was hurrying down that catacomb after me. There weren't two feet, there were four. And they didn't run in the greyhound gallop of two and two.

No, each of those unnameable paws came down in turn—one…two…three…four…one…two…three…four, and the space between the shock of the footsteps as they grew near was too damnably far apart. And as it came closer, that mind-blasting, space eating loping, like that of some fiend-wrought wolf of hell, the very catacomb around me bounced and trembled and squished, and the noise of that hunting creature's pads was like muffled cannon's roar. And then came the thought that sent me reeling, screaming like a stricken animal into a panicked flight.

What manner of thing, star-sent or earth-begotten, could make such dreadfully loud footsteps and cause the very earth to tremble, and still be small enough to course through a tunnel in which I could not stand erect?

I remember no more of that catacomb clearly. I remember only a wild, careening run, bouncing and staggering through that fiend-cursed catacomb, screaming in terror as the footsteps of my monstrous pursuer grew into my ears until I thought I was being buffeted by thunder; running, running forever, falling, crawling, staggering up, whimpering like a lost child and smelling a charnel smell of long sealed tombs freshly opened like a hot searing blast and then suddenly I fell, fell and sank into murky tepid water that blanketed my brain.

I RECOVERED in a waterfront doctor's office where my stomach was being pumped of the things I had swallowed. The doctor said I was otherwise fit and when he had finished wrenching my intestines, I staggered home.

I had been pulled out of the Mississippi River at the Barrack Street wharf at dawn, nearly drowned. Apparently I had fallen into some underground reach or pool of the mother of rivers, and had floated into the channel which sane men see. I tried to sleep when I got home, but I couldn't and still haven't. The thought of what lay beneath me was too awful.

The morning paper was at my door, and I fetched it when I realized sleep would not come, and may never come again. I opened the door and looked out at the sweaty dawn, at the last staggering remnants of the last night of carnival, at the streamers and confetti and torn masks and glass trinkets scattered over Chartres Street, the leftovers of revelry, and I seemed to feel better.

But then I glanced at the paper and choked with shock. There, on the front page, was a photograph of a high city official reviewing a Mardi Gras krewe parade, a parade held well after the time I had seen him gazing up at the gruesome altar somewhere below me now.

My loathing for the French Quarter became so great then that within a few hours I had packed my suitcase and had taken a room uptown in the Garden District, the staid, oak-lined old Garden District. It seemed to refresh me. But last night, the first night in that little room in the great old mansion, as I almost began to doze, it seemed that I felt the ground trembling below me with great shuddering footsteps…

I snapped to attention and the sensation was gone. My nerves were wrecked. It was then that I began to toy with the idea of visiting you.

I made up my mind in a flash an hour ago when the landlady came and told me she was sorry, but that I should have to move.

I asked her why, and she told me that her house was suddenly and unaccountably sinking into the earth.

THE END

BEHIND THE DOOR

By Jack Sharkey

A love of death, a love of darkness…that had been her whole thrill-seeking life…

THE party had long been growing dull for her when Miriam first saw him, in the curving shadow of the marble staircase in the entrance foyer, politely assisting Karen Allenby out of her ermine stole. Miriam had never particularly liked Karen—and was absolutely positive she had not invited her—but the greeting she extended, rushing open-armed toward the small, plumpish blonde, was effusive in the extreme. "*So* glad you could make it…! Thought you'd *never* arrive… Been waiting for *ages*…" until the other woman, her face a mingled mask of perplexity and pleased surprise, was babbling hasty introductions, and Miriam finally saw him face to face.

"But he's charming!" she was saying over her shoulder to Karen, keeping her hand snugly inside the polite clasp of his gloved fingers and her eyes boring deep into his own. "Where did you ever find him?!"

Karen, flustered at all the attention, murmured something about mutual friends, but Miriam was hardly listening as, with neat ambidexterity, she waved Karen on into the ballroom with one arm and commandeered Karen's escort with a swift motion of the other. Karen, momentarily miffed as she abruptly realized the reason behind the other's warm reception, still had the good grace and sense not to make an issue of it. Escorts were not hard to come by; invitations to Miriam Ivers' parties were.

With a barefaced lie—"I see Charles over there!"—and a careless prognostication—"I'll see you both in a moment."—Karen resigned herself to being manless for the few minutes it would take her to charm some other hapless female free of her own partner, and hurried off to join the guests, in the brightly lit ballroom of the Ivers' mansion.

MIRIAM, still standing in the foyer with her arm linked firmly through that of the man smiled up at him and asked, "Shall we join the others?" Something in her inflection made the phrase a genuine query rather than a polite suggestion.

"I think not," he said, a briefly discerning smile just touching the outer corners of his lips. "But where else can we go?" His glance about the foyer seemed to say that, large as Miriam's house was, she had more than enough guests in it to make prolonged privacy a grim unlikelihood. "Is there really a place where two people can have an uninterrupted conversation?"

Miriam, though trembling slightly in his presence, carried the game a step further. "Are you so certain I want to be alone with you?"

"If you don't," he said, "I can always rejoin Karen."

A bit annoyed at having to drop pretenses, but somehow pleased that he'd seen so quickly through them, Miriam took an even firmer grip upon his arm. "Just you try and get away," she said. Then, "There is a place we can go. And we won't be disturbed."

Moving across the foyer at right angles to the ballroom entrance, Miriam drew him down a short corridor and stopped before a thick, dark-stained oaken door. She reached inside the bosom of her dress and withdrew a stout iron key on the end of a strong silver chain. He raised an eyebrow at the heavy bulk of the key, but Miriam laughed off his amusement with a blithe shrug.

"I think a key is a reflection of the strength of its lock," she said, simply, turning the key in the slot beneath the door handle. "Something in platinum, perhaps, with a delicate filigree in its design, would be more feminine, I suppose. But then I'd always be concerned about the security of—" She stopped speaking as the key turned the bolt, and replaced it within her gown.

"Of?" he prompted, feeling that the question was expected of him.

"Come and see," she said, turning the handle and going through the doorway. It was dark inside the chamber, and only when he was once more beside her, and the door closed and fastened with a triple series of steel bolts, did she flick the lights on.

Her companion looked slowly around the room, seeing the room itself, first, not its contents. "There are no windows," he observed.

"I should hope not," said Miriam. "Other than myself, you are the first person to enter these premises."

"Not even the builders?" he said, mockingly.

"Them, of course," Miriam said, with brief irritation. "But at that time, these were only rooms. They had not yet been—filled."

"The contents must be strange."

"Come and see," she said, once again, and took his gloved hand to lead him forward. Then she lifted his hand before her face, and said, fighting the tremor in her voice, "Some of the things may be dusty. You'd—you'd better remove your gloves."

HE locked eyes with her, then, his gaze mocking and unwavering, he began to comply. Only when he was through could Miriam pull her gaze from his own and look at his strong, firm-fleshed bronze hands. She reached for them, tentatively, then impulsively clasped them with her own.

"They're cold," she said. "Cold as death."

"The night has not been a warm one," he replied.

"No," she said, turning away to hide her triumphant smile from his piercing gaze. "It hasn't. But come and see the exhibits." She started across the floor. "You might say that the story of my life was in these rooms, in the form of souvenirs."

In the first of the rooms, the things on display were of a relatively mild order. A loving cup, won by Miriam in a skydiving meet of parachutists at the age of nineteen. In a glass case, a headlight and part of a snapped steering wheel.

"When I was twenty, I tried auto-racing. These are the only pieces left untouched by the crash and fire that nearly cost me my life, and—" She touched another cup. "—this was the reward of my efforts."

He nodded silently, and she led him on through the room and its silent exhibits. A facemask and fins, in another case below the stuffed and mounted head of a Mako shark, told their own story. As did the rifles in their rack beside the magnificent head of a tiger, and the razor-edged knife mounted in juxtaposition to a photograph of Miriam, scratched, bleeding, muddy and exultant, standing in a bathing suit beside the body of a fifteen-foot crocodile.

Pointing to the photograph she said, "It was too large to have on exhibit here. I settled for the teeth and claws." She pulled open a drawer, removed a box covered and lined with red satin and opened it to give proof to her statement. Again her companion nodded silently. Then as she put the box away again, he spoke.

"You apparently live for danger, for new experience."

"This," she said, "is only the half of it." Suddenly dismissing the rest of the displays, similar in kind to those already seen, she led him through a draped archway into the next of the rooms. Here his eyes widened, and a flicker of real surprise moved across his erstwhile impassive features for a fraction of a moment. "You *have* been restless!" he said, with solemn appreciation.

Miriam watched his face, watched his eyes roaming over the exhibits as she spoke. "I find that even *these* activities palled upon me after a while. I've hunted heads with the Jivaro, I've tasted human flesh and found it good to eat, I've taken parts in pageants and rituals that would make pagan Rome turn away in terror and disgust. Are you surprised?"

For the first time since entering the second of the rooms, he looked directly at her. "No," he said. "I'm not. And I don't think you expected me to be."

Miriam smiled then, a smile of relief that was oddly tangled with an emotion of heart-pounding fear and anticipation, then gripped his icy fingers and led him through another draped archway into the third and final room.

YOU astonish me, Miss Ivers," he said, coming to a halt just within the other room.

"How so?" she asked, moving softly to his side, her footsteps muffled by the heavy oriental carpet.

"This room," he said, throwing out one arm in a sweeping gesture that ended with him facing her again. "The velvet hangings edged in gold, the crystal chandeliers, those bizarre bronze incense-burners— All quite exotically beautiful, yet... Anticlimactic, after the foregoing chambers."

"This room," she said, her heart pounding wildly, "has been designed to witness scenes beside which all the events reflected in those first two rooms would pale." A shrewd smile played upon her lips, then, and she did not repress it. She stepped to the small chrome-and-formica bar and began to fill a glass. She filled only one, and took a deep draught of it before facing him again. "I hope," she said, with a flare of courage, "that you don't absolutely *need* squalor? I'd hate to think your existence really depended upon dreary candlelit places, choked with the smell of mold, and noisy with scurrying rats with hot bloodshot eyes?" When he did not immediately reply, she added, "Surely Bram Stoker did not exaggerate?"

His bronzed hands rose and took her slim shoulders. They felt like soft curves of ice upon her flesh. Miriam suddenly lifted the glass and finished her drink, her body tense and trembling as she felt his eyes upon the alabaster curve of her throat. And still he did not speak.

"Well?" she said huskily. "Here I am. Alone with you in this room. The hangings would muffle any outcry I might make. I am completely at your mercy…" Her heart's steady pounding was becoming painful, and her breath was drawn by an effort through dry, parted lips.

He continued only to stare, however, and kept only his light grip upon her shoulders as he said, "Miss Ivers, I have the distinct feeling that *were* I to 'do' anything, you would not *make* that outcry."

"What do you think?" she said, matching his burning gaze with unwinking eyes. "Why don't you…try…?"

HE suddenly let his arms drop to his sides and yawned. "Perhaps it is your very compliance that puts me off," he said, dropping into a large armchair and dangling one leg casually over the side, swinging his foot almost lackadaisically. "Are you in any rush?"

"Please," she said, all the hauteur gone from her voice as she sank down beside him and insinuated herself into his reluctant embrace. "You can't refuse me. Not now! You don't know the effort, the agony it cost me to go up and take you from Karen, tonight. I knew what you were then—almost—and I wanted to go to you, but I was afraid... I—I still am afraid. But willing."

He studied her features emotionlessly, then said, "You seem to have overcome that siege of dread admirably."

She shivered in his arms. "I had. I really had, until—"

"Until?" he asked, with slow, lazy smile.

"Until I realized you were toying with me. All along, you've *known* what I wanted. And yet, you continually say and do things to tease me, to prolong my anticipation of what is to come."

"Are you *sure* it is to come?" he said, doing the very thing of which he was being accused.

"Oh, please stop!" she begged. "It took a terrible effort of will to bring you here. But when you mock me, I start to lose my nerve, to become afraid again."

"Then do you really think you should sit so close?"

"When one is afraid," Miriam said slowly, "one must cling to something. Even to the thing one fears most."

He considered this, then said, "Shall I tell you a part of the reason I am 'playing' in this manner?" She nodded, afraid to speak. "Because your conduct fascinates me. I have had to work long, hard hours to claim most of my victims. And yet, you practically jump into my lap—*literally* jump into my lap—with an almost direct demand that I sink my fangs into that slender throat. Why?"

Miriam spoke quietly, with returning calm. "Do you know what necrophilia is?"

"Love of death, darkness, horror," he said, nodding.

Miriam tilted her head slightly toward the preceding two chambers. "Long ago, the ordinary excitements of life palled on me. I sought escape into the extraordinary, into that seldom-heard-of world of crawling mists, incantations, and creatures who seemed like normal people but were not."

"And seeking, what did you find?" he asked, interested.

"Old wives' tales!" Miriam's smile was bitter. "Castles haunted by nothing but perilously crumbling stonework and far too many vermin. There was a hypnotist once—I thought I'd actually found my way beyond the Barrier, but—it was all trickery, illusion! But then, tonight, there *you* were..."

He stared at her, quizzically. "And you desire...?"

35

She spoke swiftly, fearful of the results of her own words. "To shun the sunlight, to be of the undead. To sleep by day, to walk by night, my only sustenance the blood of the living, while I go on eternally neither of the living nor the dead." She clutched at him, her hands finding the sides of his face and holding his gaze to meet her own, her eyes wide and apprehensive. "Tell me it can be done! Or is that all a lie, too? Do not they who die of the vampire's bite become vampires themselves? Oh, tell me it's true, please!"

HE smiled his reassurance. "It is quite true." She sighed and relaxed in his arms, her head against his chest, her hair a gleaming cascade across his white shirtfront. "But I must know something, before I do anything," he said earnestly.

She looked at him questioningly.

"Tonight," he said, "you looked at me, and you knew I was different. How? Where did I go wrong?"

She laughed almost airily, surprised at her own mirth. "There were certain signs. Nothing you need worry about, though. With years of looking for someone such as you, I've become a bit sensitized, I imagine."

"What signs?" he persisted intently.

"Well, of course, those *teeth* of yours!" she said, chidingly. "As you took Karen's wrap, you smiled. She didn't see; I did. Your canines extend at least half an inch lower than your other teeth. Like—" She found herself giving an inane giggle. "Like an unveiled portcullis!"

"What else?" he said, his eyes half-lidded and sleepy.

"Your eyes. They see too deeply into one's own. And there's a strangeness in them, an unearthly appetite that I immediately equated with feelings I've had, myself. But I wasn't sure, really sure, until I touched your hands. There is no warmth in them, none at all. Though I *was* a bit surprised at the healthy tone of your skin. For a creature that shuns daylight, you're magnificently bronzed."

"Heredity," he said, dismissing it with a shrug. "My lineal ancestors have always been dark skinned. The mere shift from normal life into the life I now lead does not remove all former physical traits." His voice was lulling, crooning. It made her head spin to listen to him. His words were reaching Miriam in a grey limbo through which she felt herself sinking, giddily.

"I didn't know," she murmured, her eyes nearly closed, "that people were so dark in the Balkans."

"I am not from the Balkans," he said softly. "My origin is further to the east, in Nepal."

The last word stirred some spark within Miriam, a spark that brought her to full awareness with a sharp pang of fright.

"Who— What are you?" she said, realizing even as she spoke that his arms were holding her rigidly prisoner.

"Haven't you guessed?" he said. "What other creature do you know that has fangs, cold blood—and toys and teases before striking?"

And in one terrible flash of memory, Miriam knew. Her mouth was opening to cry out, then the sound stopped in her lungs as she saw the sides of his throat bulge and distend like a hideous goiter, while his hollow fangs descended into her pulsing throat and released their burning venom.

"A cobra," her mind kept screaming at her, "he's a cobra!"

But Miriam had been correct in at least one thing. The velvet hangings of the room were more than sufficient to muffle her ultimate shriek of agony.

THE END

THE ROUND TOWER

By Stanton A. Coblentz

The ghostly voice pleaded for the stranger to come on; some counter voice, maybe an inward devil, warned him back.

OF ALL the shocking and macabre experiences of my life, the one that I shall longest remember occurred a few years ago in Paris.

Like hundreds of other young Americans, I was then an art student in the French metropolis. Having been there several years, I had acquired a fair speaking knowledge of the language, as well as an acquaintance with many odd nooks and corners of the city, which I used to visit for my own amusement. I did not foresee that one of my strolls of discovery through the winding ancient streets was to involve me in a dread adventure.

One rather hot and sultry August evening, just as twilight was softening the hard stone outlines of the buildings, I was making a random pilgrimage through an old part of the city. I did not know just where I was; but suddenly I found myself in a district I did not remember ever having seen before. Emerging from the defile of a crazy twisted alley, I found myself in a large stone court opposite a grim but imposing edifice.

Four or five stories high, it looked like the typical medieval fortress. Each of its four corners was featured by a round tower which, with its mere slits of windows and its pointed spear-sharp peak, might have come straight from the Middle Ages. The central structure also rose to a sharp spire, surmounting all the others; its meager windows, not quite so narrow as those of the towers, were crossed by iron bars on the two lower floors. But what most surprised me were the three successive rows of stone ramparts, each higher than the one before it, which separated me from the castle; and the musket-bearing sentries that stood in front.

"Strange," I thought, "I've never run across this place before, nor even heard it mentioned."

But curiosity is one of my dominant traits; I wouldn't have been true to my own nature if I had not started toward the castle. I will admit that I did have a creepy sensation as I approached; something within me seemed to pull me back, as if a voice were crying, "Keep away! Keep away!" But a counter-voice—probably some devil inside me—was urging me forward.

I fully expected to be stopped by the guards; but they stood sleepily at their posts, and appeared not even to notice me. So stiff and motionless they seemed that a fleeting doubt came over me as to whether they were live men or dummies. Besides, there was something peculiar about their uniforms; in the gathering twilight, it was hard to observe details, but their clothes seemed rather like museum pieces—almost what you would have expected of guards a hundred years ago.

Not being challenged, I kept on. I knew that it was reckless of me; but I passed through a first gate, a second, and a third, and not a hand or a voice was lifted to stop me. By the time I was in the castle itself, and saw its gray stone walls enclosing me in a sort of heavy dusk, a chill was stealing along my spine despite the heat. A musty smell, as if from bygone centuries, was in my nostrils; and a cold sweat burst out on my brows and the palms of my hands as I turned to leave.

It was then that I first heard the voice from above. It was a plaintive voice, in a woman's melodious tones. *"Monsieur! Monsieur!"*

"Qu'est que c'est que ça? Qu'est que c'est que ça?" I called back, almost automatically ("What is it? What is it?").

But the chill along my spine deepened. More of that clammy sweat came out on my brow. I am sorry to own it, but I had no wish except to dash out through the three gates, past the stone ramparts, and on to the known, safe streets.

Yet within me some resisting voice cried out, "Jim, you crazy fool! What are you scared of?" And so, though shuddering, I held my ground.

"Will you come up, *monsieur?*" the voice invited, in the same soft feminine tones, which yet had an urgency that I could not miss. Frankness compels me to admit that there was nothing I desired less than to ascend those winding old stone stairs in the semi-darkness. But here was a challenge to my manliness. If I dashed away like a trembling rabbit, I'd never again be able to look myself in the face. Besides, mightn't someone really be needing my help?

WHILE my mind traveled romantically between hopes of rescuing maiden innocence and fears of being trapped into some monstrous den, I took my way slowly up the spiral stairs. Through foot-deep slits in the rock-walls, barely enough light was admitted to enable me to stumble up in a shadowy sort of way. Nevertheless, something within me still seemed to be pressing my reluctant feet forward, at the same time as a counter-force screamed that I was the world's prize fool, and would race away if I valued my skin.

That climb up the old stairway seemed never-ending, although actually I could not have mounted more than two or three flights. Once or twice, owing to some irregularity in the stone, I stumbled and almost fell. "Here, Mister, here!" the woman's voice kept encouraging. And if it hadn't been for that repeated summons, surely my courage would have given out. Even so, I noted something a little strange about the voice, the tones not quite those of the Parisian French I had learned to speak; the speaker apparently had a slight foreign accent.

At last, puffing a little, I found myself in a tower room—a small chamber whose round stone walls were slitted with just windows enough to make the outlines of objects mistily visible. The place was without furniture, except for a bare table and several chairs near the further wall; but what drew my attention, what held me galvanized, were the human occupants.

So as to see them more clearly, I flashed on my cigarette lighter—at which they drew back in a wide-mouthed startled sort of way, as if they had never seen such a device before. But in that glimpse of a few seconds, before I let the flame die out, I clearly saw the faces; the fat, stolid-looking man, with double chins and a beefy complexion; the alert, bright-eyed boy of seven or eight, and a girl of fourteen or fifteen; and the two women, the younger of a rather commonplace appearance, but the elder of a striking aspect, almost regal in the proud tilt of the shapely head, the lovely contours of the cheeks and lips, and the imperious flash of eyes that seemed made to command.

"Oh, *monsieur,*" she exclaimed. "Thank you, sir, thank you very much."

All at once it struck me that there was something unutterably sad about the tones; something unspeakably sad, too, in the looks of the two women and the man, something bleak that seemed to pervade the atmosphere like a dissolved essence, until I caught its contagion and felt as if a whole world's sorrow were pressing down upon my head.

Now, as never before, I wanted to flee. But something held me rooted to the spot. I was like a man in a dread dream, who knows he is dreaming and yet cannot awaken; repelled and at the same time fascinated, I watched the elder woman approach with outflung arms.

THERE was, let me not deny it, a seductive charm about her glowing femininity. Although she was no longer young I took her to be somewhere in the nether years just beyond thirty-five—there was something extraordinarily appealing and sweet in the smile which she flashed upon me, a plaintive smile as of one who looks at you from depths of unbearable suffering. At the same time, there was something that drew me to her; held me spellbound with a magnetic compulsion. I could have imagined men easily and willingly enslaved to that woman.

"*Monsieur,*" she pleaded—and for the sake of convenience I give the English equivalent of her words—"*monsieur,* they have ringed us around. What are we to do? In the name of the good Lord, what are we to do?"

"They permit us not even a newspaper, *monsieur,*" rumbled the heavy voice of the man, as his portly form slouched forward.

"They stand over us all the time. We have no privacy except in our beds," put in the younger woman, with a despairing gesture of one bony hand.

"They inspect all our food—every bit of bread and meat, suspecting it may contain secret papers," the elder woman lamented. "Worse still—our doors are all locked from outside. We can hardly move a step without being trailed by a guard. We cannot read, we can hardly think without being inspected. Oh, was ever anyone tormented with such vile persecution?"

"Was anyone ever tormented with such vile persecution?" the second lady took up the cry, in a thin wailing voice that sent the shudders again coursing down my spine.

As if by instinct, I was backing toward the door. I wondered if I was not the victim of some frightful hallucination.

"But what do you want me to do?" I blurted out, as with one hand I groped behind me for the doorknob.

"Do? What do we want you to do, *monsieur?*" groaned the elder woman. "Speak with *them!* Plead with *them!* Beg them to treat us like human beings—not like beasts in cages!"

"But *who* am I to speak to? Who are they? What do you mean, Madam?"

"Who but our persecutors—our oppressors?"

"Who but our persecutors—our oppressors?" echoed the other woman, with a ghostly repetition of the words.

By this time it was so dark that the five persons made but shadows indistinctly seen against the dungeon-like gloom. There was no arguing now with my fear; it was taking command of me; the next instant, had the man not surmised my thoughts by some clairvoyant perception, I would have left the dolorous strangers to their fate and dashed pell-mell down the tower stairs.

"Hold, *monsieur,*" his voice detained me. "It is growing late—we need a light."

And then, with startled eyes, I witnessed one of the eeriest, one of the most inexplicable incidents of all. Suddenly, though I had seen no lantern, there was a light in the room! It was a sort of gray-white phosphorescence, midway between the hue of a light fog and that of pewter; and it seemed to come from nowhere in particular, but filled the room with a fluctuating radiance, at times bright enough to reveal every object, at times permitting everything to sink back almost into invisibility. By this illumination all things—even the man's beefy face—took on a ghastly pallor; my own hand, outstretched in a gesture of spontaneous horror, startled me with its pale, spectral quality.

"Do not be afraid, *monsieur,*" one of the women spoke reassuringly. *"They* will not find you. The guards were sleeping; else you could not have come up. You were heaven-sent to help us in our need."

My knees quivering beneath me, I did not feel heaven-sent to help anyone. In that uncanny wavering light, which struck my disordered imagination as almost sepulchral, I was more frightened than in the darkness. I was just a little relieved, however, to see how the small boy, curled up near the wall with some straw for a pillow, was sleeping an apparently normal childhood sleep.

Nevertheless, I had found the doorknob, and was drawing it toward me. A blast of chilly air, contrasting weirdly with the heat of the summer evening, swept up the tower stairs.

A second more, and I would have been gone. But the elder woman, crossing the room like a flash of light, had placed herself next to me; between me and the door. I could see her big sad eyes, not a foot from mine, glowing as if from immense hollow depths; I could see her long, pale proud face alternately brightening and darkening by the flickers of the changeable unearthly light. And once more she exercised that strange, that magical compulsion upon me. My limbs were frozen. I could merely stare—and wonder.

"It is not for our own sakes, *monsieur,*" she resumed, in a voice that shook and wavered even more than did the light. "It is not for our own sakes that I beg your aid, but for our poor, innocent children. For their sakes, in the name of heaven's mercy, go out and plead with our oppressors, *monsieur*. Rush forth—rush forth and summon help, before it is too late!"

"Before it is too late!" came a low sobbing echo.

"But you—who are you?" I demanded, growing more mystified from minute to minute.

"We? Who are we? Is there anyone in all Paris that does not know?"

"Is there anyone in all Paris that does not know?" there sounded a sobbing refrain.

But they seemed not to hear, or at least not to believe my denials.

"Look at me! Do you not recognize me?" the man demanded, thrusting his face within inches of mine. "Who in all the land could help recognizing me?"

Observing the round, commonplace features, the paunchy cheeks, the sensual lips and dull eyes, I failed to recognize anyone I had ever known.

"Ah, *monsieur*, you must be a stranger in the land."

"I—I—yes, I am a stranger—from California," I managed to grasp at a straw.

"From where do you say, *monsieur?*" he asked, as if he had never heard of my native state. And then dismally he went on, half to himself, "Am I then so changed by my hardships that I cannot be recognized? Ah, no doubt I had a different look in the old times, when I went forth daily in the hunt. Yes, that was a sport worthy of a king—chasing the antlered stag. A sport worthy of a king!"

"And I," bewailed the elder woman, her eyes downcast, her whole form seeming indistinctly to sag, "perhaps I also am changed—oh, how changed from the days when I led in gay revels and frolics, and banquets and masked halls, and was merry the whole day long—and the whole night long, too! Little did I suspect, in those old happy times, what a bitter blow was in store for me."

"Little did I suspect," moaned the second woman. "Little did we all suspect!"

Had I chanced upon a band of lunatics? Was this old tower the hospital where these poor deranged wretches were kept? This seemed to me, all in all, the most plausible solution. Nevertheless, it did not explain the weird light, which still pervaded the grim round tower room from some unseen source. Nor did it account for various other incidents, which I report even now with a tingling sensation along the spine and a numbing clutch at the heart.

IT MAY have been only the wind; but the door, which I had opened slightly, suddenly closed with a dull thudding jar. Yet how could it have been the wind, since the door opened inward, and hence a breeze from below would have pushed the door wider open? And from inside the closed room, how could an air current originate? But I was sure that no hand, and least of all mine, had touched the door.

Even as I struggled to regain my composure, I reached again for the door handle, more determined than ever to leave. But, as I did so, my shaken nerves were shattered by another shock. With a series of high-pitched yipping barks, a small creature ran out as if from nowhere and began cavorting about my knees. Where had the little dog come from? I was certain it had not been in the room before. I was equally convinced that there was no way for it to enter. By the flickering grayish-white light, it had a sort of half-solid appearance as I reached down to pet it; and somehow I was not quite able to place a hand upon it. Eluding my touch, it ran over to the elder woman, who bent down and caressed it. And then, as suddenly as it had come, it was gone. But from someone's throat—the adolescent girl's, I believe—there burst a spasm of uncanny hollow laughter.

Then, as I pulled at the doorknob, the elder woman was again at my side, her lovely sad eyes fixing me with a stare of such terrible intensity that I was gripped powerless in my place.

My hand dropped from the doorknob; for the first time, I knew myself to be a prisoner.

"What is to happen to us, *monsieur?*" she lamented, not hysterically, but with an air of dignified restraint beneath which I could feel the hot passion smoldering. "What is to happen to us all? Time after time we hear the tocsin sounding below us on the streets. We hear the crowds shouting. But we can only guess what it all means. Can you not tell us, *monsieur,* what it means?"

"Can you not tell us, *monsieur?*" echoed the younger woman.

I shook my head, helplessly.

"Ah, *monsieur,* you are like them all," the first speaker sighed. "Like the guards—like that monster who has charge of us. You know, yet you will tell us nothing."

"You know, yet you will tell us nothing," came the unfailing repetition.

"I feel it in my bones, a worse fate is in store for us," the woman moaned. One pale hand moved significantly across her neck. "My sainted mother, who was far wiser than I, foresaw it all long ago; but then I was too young and giddy to listen. Now that she is in her grave—*monsieur,* sometimes at night I can see her before me, warning, warning, warning—"

"Warning, warning, warning—" took up the other woman.

"Come, come now. Things are not always so bad, are they?" the rumbling voice of the man broke out in incongruous, soothing contrast. "We have no complaints about many things—least of all, about the food, now have we? At noon we have three soups, two entrees, two roasts, fruit, cheese, claret, and champagne—it is not all we have known in our better days, *monsieur,* but it is not bad. It is not bad. Then the boy and I, on fine days, are allowed to walk in the court below—"

"*You* can walk there, but not I!" broke out the elder woman, who was evidently his wife. "You can submit yourself to the staring insolence of those beasts of guards—not I! You can console yourself with your fine meals—not I, not I! I—I think of the fate that is in store for us all. I—I think of the future of our poor children!"

"I—think of the future of our poor children!" came the inevitable echo.

The boy, slumbering against the wall, chose this particular moment to turn over in his sleep and moan.

I FOR my part would have left then and there—had this been possible. But even if I had not already been riveted to the spot, I would have been held by the woman's anguished cry.

"Think of our friends—our poor friends—the ones who did not escape, or came back out of loyalty to us—those tigers in human form have cut their heads from their bodies—torn them limb from limb!"

"Have cut their heads from their bodies—torn them limb from limb!"

"Come, come, my dear," interposed the man, still in a placating voice, "we cannot always think of these horrible things. Come, come, play for me at the clavecin, as of old—sing to me, my dear."

As if from nowhere, an old-fashioned musical instrument—a clavecin, or harpsichord—appeared before us. It could not have been there before without being seen, for it was a huge thing on legs, nearly as large as a modern piano. Yet there it was, clearly visible in the wavering grayish light; with a stool before it, at which the elder woman seated herself.

As my lips opened in a half-uttered cry of horror, the player began plucking at the strings—and the strangest melodies I had ever heard began coming forth, while she accompanied them in a quivering sad voice of a subdued loveliness. The music was low, almost ghostly faint; and was charged with such a deep, throbbing sorrow that, at the first note, the tears began coursing down my cheeks. As the woman went on and on with her song, its melancholy increased, though it still had the same eerily distant quality; it seemed that I was listening to a plaint from across countless years and remotest places. Now everyone in the room appeared to have forgotten my presence; the younger woman, the man and the girl gathered about the player, as if to drink in every note; even the small boy arose and joined the group; and as they did so the light, as if condensed by some unseen reflector, suddenly concentrated upon them, leaving the rest of the room in shadow. And then the illumination, wavering and flickering more than ever, began to dwindle...until suddenly, without warning, it went out and I found myself in blackness.

But still, from amid the coaly gloom, that phantom-thin music continued to sound, the voice of the singer blended with the notes of the instrument, unspeakably sad, immensely distant, fading like the wind-borne tones of receding minstrels.

Only then did all my concentrated dread and horror find expression in one tremendous scream. Fumbling and groping, somehow I found the door; somehow I forced my limbs free of the spell that had gripped them, and started down the twisted stairs. And then all at once everything went blank.

WHEN I came to myself, still listening to that sad, faint music, I was lying on a Paris street. The glow of late twilight was in the air; a small crowd had gathered about me.

"Does *monsieur* need help?" a man's voice sympathetically asked. "He stumbled and fell, and has been many minutes coming to. No doubt it was only the heat."

"No doubt—it was the heat," I agreed, as I struggled to my feet. But in my ears that phantom music still made a dismal refrain.

Next day I reported my experience to my friend Jacques Chervier, a student at the Sorbonne, whose specialty was Parisian history.

He looked at me sharply as I finished. "Just where did you say this happened?"

I mentioned the exact street location, of which I had taken note after the adventure.

"So?" he answered, significantly. "So? Well, this *is* strange. Do you know you were walking on the exact site of the old Temple?"

"What in thunder was the Temple?"

"It was the old castle of the Knights Templars, which was torn down in 1811, at the age of almost six hundred years."

"Torn down in 1811?" I repeated, dully.

"It's famous as the scene of many historic episodes," Jacques warmed to his theme, "not the least notable being the imprisonment of a king and queen of France, along with their two children, and Madame Elizabeth, the king's sister. That was back in 1792. You know, of course, what king and queen I refer to."

I could only mumble something incoherent.

"Louis the Sixteenth and Marie Antoinette were both lodged there before being sent to the guillotine. The old castle, from all I can make out, was exactly as you have described it, even to the small dog that kept the prisoners company."

"But that doesn't explain why I, of all persons, and at this particular time—"

"Don't you recall the date?"

"Let's see. Today's the fourteenth, isn't it?"

"And yesterday was the thirteenth. It was on August thirteenth, just at about sunset, that Louis the Sixteenth and Marie Antoinette were imprisoned in the Temple. Perhaps every year, on the anniversary of that event—"

But I did not hear the remainder of Jacques' speech. I was not interested in his explanations. In my ears a thin, sorrowful music seemed to be playing; I was back in a tower room, in a wavering fog-gray light, where five shadowy figures were gathered, among them a woman whose deep pleading tragic eyes seemed to call and call across an immeasurable gulf.

THE END

HATCHERY OF DREAMS

By Fritz Leiber

*Giles Wardwell was a man not easily given to following the directions of
a blue lizard. However, his wife was missing, the other witc—er, girls
were cursed, and all in all there was no hope for it.*

WHEN Giles Wardwell woke up Saturday morning and Joan
wasn't beside him in bed or anywhere in the house and there
was no message on the slate in the kitchen or any response
when he banged on the door of her lab, and when a glance
showed their blue car sitting on the drive, his first impulse was
to report the matter to CAMZ at once.

Grim old Mr. Copps himself had warned the whole CAMZ
staff that all their lives and those of their loved ones were in
slight but definite danger from America's enemies now that
Copps, Arbuthnot, Mather, and Zim were doing public relations
work for the Secondman Missiles Project. Mr. Zim, looking
almost equally a dour Puritan father despite his Turkish
background, had filled them in with some excruciating first-
hand details on Russian espionage methods.

Just before they'd gone to sleep last night Joan had asked
Giles, "Do the Russians have hypnosis beams? I have the
feeling someone's trying to get control of my mind." And he
had replied in a joking way that made him sick to remember,
"Only in science-fiction magazines," to her first remark and
"Probably your mother-in-law, God help us," to her second.

Giles decided to put on his glasses and have a closer look
around before calling CAMZ. He didn't find the red nightgown
Joan had been wearing, but he did find the little penned note on
the bedside table.

"Dear Giles (it read), I'm taking a vacation from our
marriage, maybe for a month, maybe forever. In case it's the
latter I'll let you know. You know I don't fit in. Anyhow, I

can't stick your stodgy conformity—or your mother's!—any longer. Maybe being with other humans will give me perspective. You can be respectable to the hilt and tell people I'm visiting Mable in Wisconsin, but that's not where I'm going. Good luck. Joan."

When Giles Wardwell had read that, Russia was a name in the geography books, CAMZ were eccentric wheels, and an old fear of his had become an active torment: the knowledge that he was fifteen years older than Joan and a proper Bostonian, and that being bald as an egg from thirty-five on was not at all the same thing as being romantically shaven-headed like Yul Brynner.

HE'D been afraid once or twice before that Joan was unhappy, though that was by no means his deepest fear about her. He'd known she couldn't stand his mother, though they only saw the old lady two or three times a week. He'd thought Joan was restless lately, in spite of her bridge and cosmetics hobbies. And certainly she didn't exactly fit in—she had no real friends he knew of in the Boston area except for the three amusing but socially off-trail women who made up her bridge foursome.

He wondered where she could have gone. Mr. and Mrs. Bishop—Joan's parents—were both dead and there were no uncles, aunts, or close cousins. Mable was just a college roommate, rarely mentioned. Joan did have a little money in an account of her own.

While he was thinking these things, Giles' feet had been carrying him, still in his dull olive pullover pajamas, on another circuit of the house and now brought him up short at the door to Joan's lab. He hesitated—he'd always sensed (though Joan had never told him in so many words) that she didn't like him to barge into her perfume distillery and he had made a point of never offending, and besides the place was associated in his mind with his deepest fear about her.

Then he opened the door and went in.

His first impression was of gloom—the shades were tightly drawn—and an unnatural heat.

The small flasks and jars, the electric mixer for cold cream, and the elaborate distilling setups all seemed to be in their usual places.

He switched on the overhead light.

Then he saw it: a silver-sided platform with heavy cables leading from it and resting on it on its side a huge white egg almost exactly the size of his own head—in fact, his instant fantastic thought was that it was a horrid tableau set up to ridicule his baldness.

He went up to it. The heat was coming from the platform, all right—the humpy soft reddish fabric on which the egg rested was almost too hot to touch. And there seemed to be a faint vibration in the stuff, barely perceptible to the fingertips.

The egg looked astonishingly genuine. Minute pores dimpled its surface.

But it was far too large for an ostrich egg or any other Giles could conceive. And it was being kept at a far higher temperature, he was quite sure, than that used for any normal hatching. He started to turn the heat down, then wondered if he could figure out how, then decided not to try. He put his ear near the shell but couldn't hear anything moving inside.

Beside the platform was a deep cardboard box big enough to have held the egg. It was silvered on the outside, half full of cotton wool, and silver ribbons were strewn around.

Giles recognized the box. Joan had brought it back from her last Bridge Wednesday, explaining it contained a china atrocity she'd won but never wanted to look at again and which she intended to give Giles' mother for her birthday.

Vastly confused, Giles clamped onto one valid-seeming train of thought with just two cars: one—no woman with a fabulous egg hatching in her laboratory would willingly go away for a day, let alone a month or forever, no matter how much she loathed her husband; two—if anyone knew anything about Joan or the egg, it would be one or more of her three bridge partners: Mary

Nurse, Margo Cory, and Alice Something-or-other—Greene? No, Redd!

THIRTY minutes later Giles had hurriedly dressed, sketchily shaved, swallowed a cup of coffee with a tablespoon of the powdered in it, and was piloting the blue, sedately chromeless car from the Wardwell home "back of Back Bay," as he liked to describe it, to Margo Cory's improbable address on Prince Street in Boston's crooked, crowded North End.

None of the three women had been in the phone books and Joan didn't keep an address book Giles could find. Margo Cory's address had only turned up on an empty envelope that had slipped down behind Joan's desk.

Giles never liked visiting the North End and he didn't want to think about the egg because it was, to put it mildly, impossible. He spent the drive totting up how stodgily conformist he could be accused of being. He was at least par for the Boston course, he decided. For instance, he had recently given up chess and concentrated on bird-watching because Mr. Mather had pointed out that too many Slavic and Baltic types played chess. "Semites too, of course," Mather had finished primly. "I think we must look on it as purely a Russian game."

Could his Sunday bird-watching have anything to do with the egg? More fantastic ridicule? Giles doubted if he had ever trained his binoculars on a bird that had an egg much bigger than a gumdrop.

Margo Cory's address turned out to be a brand-new narrow tall glass-walled apartment building. As he went up to the twelfth floor in the newfangled glass-backed elevator, the Old North Church became visible across the roofs and then the green square of Copps Hill Burying Ground over toward the Inner Harbor.

Margo Cory's apartment was furnished in pale Swedish modern that went oddly with the dark tone in the glass. Margo herself wore bare feet, a gray linen robe and her short hair was tousled like a boy's. It gave Giles a pang to see how young she was, remembering Joan was no older. He must seem an old fogey to them all, he told himself.

He thought she was carrying, hugged to her chest, a motionless pale tan kitten, then he saw it had overbuilt shoulders, canine teeth like great daggers, and forepaws that suggested hands.

Margo noted his gaze and giggled. "Kitty's just a Steiff toy, made of plush," she said. "Did you know teddy bears were Steiff toys named after Teddy Roosevelt? This one's a kind of saber-tooth tiger. Here, look."

She thrust it briefly toward him. With the same movement the top of her robe fell apart, showing she was not at all boyish in that area and dressed solely for showering. She seemed unconscious of the exposure.

"No, I haven't seen Joan since Wednesday," she told Giles. She swung nervously toward the view-wall with a flash of legs. "Why don't you come over here beside me," she said with an odd chuckle, "and enjoy my view?"

Another time Giles might have been tempted, proper Bostonian or no, now he said, "Miss Cory, I *am* looking for my wife."

She faced him. "You really are worried about Joan, aren't you?"

"Of course!" He grimaced at her and rapidly waved his fingers together at chest level. She scowled back at him and at last pulled her robe tight around her.

"I'm an exhibitionist, Mr. Wardwell, *and* a nymphomaniac," she announced defiantly. "It's a very rare combination."

"Really, Miss Cory, you don't have to tell me these things," he countered.

"I certainly do," she retorted. "If I tell them I don't have to do them. Think what I'm sparing you. But if I can't do them I have to tell them."

He might have reacted stuffily to this frankness. Instead he felt something open inside himself that he had kept carefully closed all day in spite of the egg and other shocks.

"Miss Cory," he said, "do you think my wife dabbles in witchcraft?"

"*Dabbles?*" the girl yelled. "Why, what a weird question. There's no such thing as witchcraft."

"I know," Giles said, pouring it off his chest, "but she has this lab where she concocts things, and I've heard her mutter gibberish that might be incantations and spells, and she has a lonely bitter attitude toward life, and then she could be descended from the first witch hanged at Salem in 1692—even if Bridget Bishop isn't known to have had children. And then we've got the tradition of witchcraft all around us here in New England and Boston and especially right here in the North End." He gestured at the smoky window. "Why right over there in Copps Hill the Mathers are buried who did so much to fight it and—"

"Excuse me, Mr. Wardwell, but I can't listen to you any longer," the girl interrupted. "I'm a bit psychotic, as I've told you, some days more than others, and today is one of the real bad ones—I'd fall apart if it weren't for Kitty here." She clutched the plush saber-tooth to her. "I'll give you Alice Redd's address—maybe she can tell you something about Joan."

She called brightly after him down the corridor, incidentally letting her robe fall open again, "Remember, Mr. Wardwell, there's no such thing as witchcraft!"

ALICE REDD lived in a dignified old apartment on Louisburg Square back across the Common and she seemed in other ways the antithesis of Margo. Cory—a china-delicate young woman with pale reddish hair and wearing a robe of thick brocaded white silk that was conspicuously buttoned from neck to hem.

She spoiled the effect somewhat by moaning immediately, "Come in quickly, Mr. Wardwell, so I can collapse again. Ooh, what a fuzzy black head I've got inside, this morning. I know I shouldn't mix barbiturates with alcohol, but there must be more to it than that."

She pointed vaguely at a chair and let herself down onto a spindle-legged couch, to the head of which was hanging by one paw a small dark brown stiff monkey made of what Giles decided must be the finest basket weave—the texture suggested tiny scales.

Alice Redd reached out feebly and put a finger in the other paw. "Pongo's such a help on mornings like this," she told Giles. "I don't know what I'd do without him. He keeps off the black megrims and things. He's supposed to come from Hong Kong or maybe Malaya.

"Yes, Mr. Wardwell, I do so much enjoy the bridge with Joan and the other girls. Do you know, we're hoping eventually to get together three tables, so there'd be twelve of us, and have duplicate tournaments. Then we'd need a man to be tournament director, a woman would be much too flighty. Has Joan said anything to you—? Ooh, my head!

"No, I haven't seen Joan since Wednesday. Mary Nurse might be able to tell you something. I'll give you her address, though she's been laid up with 'flu the last two days. There seems to be something wrong with all of us, doesn't there? Oooh!

"No, I don't think Joan was unhappy, Mr. Wardwell. I'll tell you one thing, though—she didn't like those CAMZ people you work for, she thought they were too restrictive and inquiring and dictatorial. Certainly we have to worry about the Russians, but Joan says those CAMZ people enjoy worrying, they must bathe in black megrims. I know they're fine old Boston men, most of them, but didn't Mr. Arbuthnot work for Senator McCarthy and isn't Mr. Mather descended from the witch-hunting Mathers—Cotton, Increase, and— Oooh! Pongo, come here, comfort Mother."

"Speaking of witches, Miss Redd," Giles said on impulse, "I've just had an amusing thought. You know how each witch is supposed to have a familiar?—a little animal given her by Satan to protect her and help her work magic? Well, if old

Cotton Mather could have been with me this morning and seen Mary Cory with Kitty and you with Pongo—"

"Ha-ha-ha, very funny. And Mary Nurse with Pounce. He'd have called them poppets, because they aren't alive, but he'd have claimed they came alive when people's backs were turned—Oooh! Pongo, make it stop!

"But Mr. Wardwell, if you were seriously thinking about witchcraft, surely you'd have asked Joan herself— No, I can see you're the Boston type who never asks crucial questions until it's much too late or something— Oooh!"

"I wonder," Giles said softly, "in what *form* Satan would give familiars to witches? Not in a brown paper bag, surely, or just hand them over by the scruff of the neck—you'd think there'd be a little more ceremony to it."

"Ha-ha-ha— Oooh! Mr. Wardwell, I'm sorry, but Pongo and I are going to have to curl up and go to sleep, it's the only way we'll ever get through this. But first I'll write you Mary Nurse's address."

GILES didn't look at it until he was outside, standing beside the black iron pickets fencing the private park that occupied Louisburg Square. It turned out to be on Salem Street and he shrank from going back into the North End, so he drove home, relieved to find the house wasn't burning down, and sat watching the egg and thinking a great variety of mad disturbing thoughts.

He reread Joan's note several times. As far as he could tell, it was her handwriting or a good imitation, but he noticed now that there were three expressions in it which she detested: "In case," "Anyhow," and "humans" for "human beings." If someone had wanted to convince him that Joan had run away and keep him from making inquiries, they might have concocted a note like this.

Once he got a tack hammer and poised it above the egg…and after a few seconds carried the hammer back to the kitchen.

And once he thought he heard something stir inside the egg. He bent his ear to it until his cheek was burning hot, but heard nothing more.

After three hours of that he drove back to the North End. He passed the CAMZ headquarters in the new building in Sewall Court, recalling that it was named for Judge Sam Sewall, who had presided over the Salem witch trials. He passed the Paul Revere house with its strange nail-studded door exactly like that in the house of the hanged Salem witch Rebecca Nurse.

Nurse.

Salem Street was noisy with pushcarts and the evening air seemed to carry as much Italian as English.

Mary Nurse's address was a dreary walk-up over a fish store with windows smeary-tracked by live snails and tiny climbing squid. He remembered Joan telling him Mary Nurse was an artist keen on local color.

But she'd made some changes. Her door at the end of the corridor wasn't like the others, but unpainted oak studded with rows of nail-heads.

In answer to his knock a deep voice called to him to come in.

The room was stuffy and crowded, easels elbowing chairs and bookcases—studio and living room combined.

And bedroom. The light of two thick candles showed Mary Nurse lying on a wide studio couch under a quilt of diamond patches. She was a big girl—five foot ten, he'd judged—but now she lay like a log, looking really sick, pale, her thick blonde hair streaming across the pillow.

But her deep voice was steady enough. "I've been expecting you, Giles Wardwell. Margo Cory dropped in this afternoon."

"I'm sorry about your 'flu," Giles said.

"This isn't 'flu," Mary Nurse said with a deep unhumorous chuckle. "Someone's put a curse on me. On all of us, I'd say. What are you looking around for?"

"Pounce," Giles admitted.

Again the big blonde chuckled. She beckoned to Giles and lifted the quilt a little. Giles looked—and almost jumped out of the room.

Crouched on the sheet beside her, just under her arm, was a jet-black spider with a body big as a flattened grapefruit and furry black legs that would have spanned a platter. Around the body were wedges of bright green, while two ruby-red eyes glared up at him.

It couldn't be real, Giles told himself. It must be—

"Black velvet." For a third time Mary Nurse chuckled. She dropped the quilt. "Just the same, I'd probably be dead without Pounce. You've surely noticed by now how neurotically dependent we are on our little…toys. That's why Joan's in trouble—she doesn't have one…yet."

Giles was staring at the top of a bookcase back in the shadows. It seemed to have an egg on it as big as that in Joan's lab.

"Surely you've noticed other things about us too," Mary Nurse was saying.

"Your door, your name," Giles said, edging between an easel and a chair toward the bookcase.

"All our names are witch names. Even your name, Giles Wardwell. Samuel Wardwell was one of the five wizards hung in Salem. Giles Cory was pressed to death with rocks on his chest for refusing to testify."

Giles saw that the egg was an empty shell, cracked across and with a huge hole in one side. "What's that?" he asked sharply.

"That's the shell of a spider—I mean, dinosaur…" Mary Nurse broke off and looked at him burningly. "I don't think we need to fence any longer, Giles Wardwell. You've found Joan's egg? Unbroken?"

"Yes. Yes."

"Then if you love your wife, be there when it hatches. I think there's time. I'd go but I'm too cursed to move, I'd send the Black Man, but we haven't one, Joan's only hope and safety are in the egg. Follow the signs. Call it Grizzle. Don't ask questions. Hurry!"

"I will."

"The Horned God go with you, Giles Wardwell."

THE lab seemed hotter than before when Giles got back to it, but that may have been because he was sweating. At first the egg seemed intact, then he saw there was a tiny triple crack radiating from a point near the top. As he watched, one of the branches lengthened abruptly by the width of a finger. There was a faint scratching and rustling inside.

He settled down to watch, gripping his knees with shaking hands. The heat alone was making him feel faint. He stripped off his coat and shirt, noting without much surprise that he was still wearing his pajama top under the latter.

The cracks lengthened. Others appeared. Suddenly bits of shell flew and a tiny blue arm with a jagged crest on it like a lizard's shot out, groped around wildly, and then jerked in.

Trembling, Giles moved around the egg, trying to peer in but staying at arm's length.

Two tiny blue hands were methodically breaking away small fragments of shell, enlarging the hole. He couldn't see more of the creature, it was too dark inside.

The room began to swim, Giles dragged at the collar of his pajamas, then staggered to the window and heaved it up, sucked in three breaths of cool air. The room steadied. He saw that the hole in the egg was now big as a spread hand.

He was halfway back to it when something blue shot out, scurried in a circle across the floor three times, too fast to be seen definitely, and dove out the open window.

Giles grabbed up his coat and went out the front door and looked around in the dark. He couldn't see anything on the lawn or drive. He walked around the front of his car and froze.

A stocky jewel-blue lizard was crouched down on the hood of his car exactly as if it were a moderately ornate radiator ornament. It seemed to grip into the blue-painted metal with its hind claws and left forepaw or arm. The right arm, extended beside its hideously crested face, was pointed straight ahead.

"Grizzle!" Giles ejaculated.

The blue creature shivered and stretched its arm still further forward.

Giles climbed in and started the car, his eyes on Grizzle. As he neared the street, the foreward-pointing arm swung abruptly to the right. Giles obeyed, his heart pounding.

Follow the signs!

THEY were near the Common when Giles began to guess where they were going. As they neared Sewall Court, Grizzle raised its foreward-pointing arm as if to say, "Go slow," and then suddenly pointed downward as if for "Stop."

Fred, the CAMZ garage man, came up to the window. He was looking at the hood. Then, "Take her for you, Mr. Wardwell?" They traded places. As Giles was walking away, "Mr. Wardwell!" Fred called excitedly. Giles turned back. "I'd have sworn," Fred said from behind the wheel, "that you'd put a blue radiator ornament on your car, a sort of wild dinosaur. But now it's gone."

Giles said, a bit stuffily, "Blue? Wild? Now, Fred, would anyone be apt to do a thing like that to his car, in Boston?"

Inside the lobby Grizzle was playing unseen around the feet of George, the night guard and elevator-man. Giles kept his eyes away from the familiar.

"Fifth floor, Mr. Wardwell?" George volunteered. "All our big ones are up there." He stared at Giles' pajama top under his coat. "They sure pulled you out of bed in a hurry, Mr. Wardwell. Must be some real emergency, though I haven't taken up any army men."

Giles maintained a dignified mysterious silence.

On the fifth floor the drapes were drawn tight behind the heavy glass wall of the main office. A little light shone through the drapes toward one end, not much. As the elevator door closed, Giles headed down the hall toward the office he shared, but there was a tug at his trouser leg, Grizzle led him to Mr. Arbuthnot's office, which was next to the end of the main office away from the light.

Arbuthnot's office was empty and dark, but the door from it to the main office was open. Giles walked to it and stopped.

Mr. Copps, Mr. Arbuthnot, Mr. Mather, and Mr. Zim were all standing toward the other end of the main office, looking very serious and dignified and businesslike in their dark suits, except that Mr. Zim was holding a small golden wand and wearing a tall conical black hat covered with golden stars and moons, and Mr. Arbuthnot was cradling in his arms a sub-machinegun.

And Joan was there, facing Giles' end of the office, the single light glaring full in her face. She was sitting up straight and defiant-faced on a stool with her arms stretched out straight to either side of her by thin white ropes anchored to filing cabinets.

She was wearing her red nightgown. A bit of Giles' mind jumped back to 1692 Salem, where Bridget Bishop had worn "a red paragon bodice" before her grim sober judges.

JOAN flirted her black hair away from her eyes with a shake of her head and said loudly, "But this is ridiculous, I keep telling you. My husband has never told me a word about the Second Missiles Project. I have no Communist connections. Presumably I was cleared by the F.B.I. at the same time Giles was. The rest is nonsense—or insanity."

"Must I take you over that ground again?" Mr. Mather said in his soft voice that was so clear and far-carrying. "Mrs. Wardwell, America has older and more formidable enemies than Communism. Unfortunately, the F.B.I. does not clear for witchcraft. But CAMZ, which embodies the finest traditions of Old New England, does. And somehow advertising is more sensitive to the occult than is the military." He tapped a sheaf of papers in his hand. "Confess yourself a witch, Joan Wardwell, tell where and how you bound yourself to Satan, detail for us your spells and magics, above all name the other witches of your coven—or you will force us to prove these facts upon your body! Mr. Copps, is the needle ready?"

"You can't make me testify against myself," Joan countered. "I plead the Fifth Amendment!"

"*Our* Massachusetts never ratified it," Mr. Mather told her. "Remember what happened to Giles Cory, Mr. Copps?"

Giles surged forward, then stopped. Four men and a sub-machinegun! His hands turned icy cold. Then something hot stroked his cheek, his face turned as cold as if a mask of ice had been slipped over it, and he almost shrieked.

Grizzle had climbed the front of his suit, was clinging to his left lapel as a sailor might to a sail, and had just finished licking his cheek with his long black tongue.

Mr. Arbuthnot turned and stared straight at the door of his office, leveling the gun, Giles froze, hoping the gloom would hide him though afraid his white hands and face were bound to stand out. But after a searching glance, Arbuthnot turned back toward Joan.

Mr. Mather was saying, "Joan Bishop Wardwell, consider well the helplessness of your situation. Your poor foolish husband, deceived by the note you wrote at our hypnotic dictation when we summoned you, believes you have deserted him. Your sister witches, who and wherever they may be, are held in check by Mr. Zim's helpful little spells. Confess yourself, redeem your wickedness, salvage what you can of the good American girl who yielded to the blandishments of Satan."

"I won't!" Joan cried ringingly. "Compared to your brand of Americanism, witchcraft is the soul of decency."

"The needle!"

Grizzle, still clinging to Giles with hind claws and one forepaw, tweaked Giles' arm painfully with the other, then pointed commandingly at Arbuthnot.

Follow the signs!

GOING behind Joan, Mr. Copps ripped her nightgown down the back and poised something that was glittering, long, and terribly slim.

Giles walked out into the main office, raising his right hand and pointing straight at Mr. Arbuthnot—though he almost dropped it when he saw that his hand was no longer flesh-colored but dead black.

Arbuthnot froze in mid-whirl. His flesh turned a faint gray. The sub-machinegun thudded on the thick-piled carpet.

The finger with which Giles had pointed at him was flesh-colored again and the rest of his hand was no longer dead black but charcoal gray.

Successively, copying Grizzle's gestures, Giles pointed his second finger, ring finger, and thumb at Mr. Zim, Mr. Copps, and Mr. Mather.

With each pointing, the man indicated froze and faintly grayed, while Giles' flesh lightened by stages until at the end he was no darker than they were.

For once in his life Giles Wardwell was seething with anger.

"You persecuting, smug, self-satisfied, hypocritical fiends!" he shouted. "You're worse than the Russians with your brainwashing. Now listen to me—you're going to forget this witch hunting obsession forever, I command it! *Silentium, silentium, mutus, mutus, mutus.* I'm letting you off easy—if you'd actually injured my wife, I'd make you really suffer. But believe me, after this you're never going to browbeat me, any of you. And I'm going to start playing chess again and seeing my mother as often as I please!"

He stopped because Joan was laughing delightedly.

"Darling, they can't hear you," she called to him happily. "The Black Man's spell works a lot faster than barbiturates. For hours at least they'll be dead asleep. Now cut me loose and let's get out of here. I think your charm's certain to work, but to make sure we'll take Mr. Mather's papers and Mr. Zim's wand and cap and Mr. Arbuthnot's sub-machinegun and drop them in the Charles. You've got your little finger to put the night guard asleep and your left hand for emergencies. Is that Grizzle? He's a dear!"

A HALF-hour later they were driving slowly home through Back Bay, Joan sat close to Giles, her head resting on his shoulder. Grizzle was curled on Joan's shoulder, holding her ripped red nightgown together with his hind claws. The car's heater flooded them with pleasant warmth.

"Giles," Joan said sleepily, "there's one more question I want to ask you. When you visited Margo, and Alice and Mary today, did you find them...attractive?"

"Rather," he admitted. "I must say they're very weird women, but then it looks as if I'm going to have to get used to a great many strange things. Pounce, for instance. Yes, to tell the truth I found all three girls quite attractive."

Joan nodded without opening her eyes. "I was afraid of that," she said. "You see, as Black Man of our little coven you will have certain duties and privileges. Oh well, I suppose I'll simply have to accept it."

Then, with a sleepy chuckle, she added, "But don't you forget, Giles Wardwell, now and forever, that I'm your First Witch."

THE END

Drive-Thru

By Gregory Luce

Editor's note: The inspiration for this little morsel is an old drive-in restaurant in Walla Walla, Washington called The Ice Berg, which is still there after all these years and serves the best vanilla milkshakes known to mankind.

–Greg Luce,
Editor-in-Chief,
Armchair Fiction

Charlie Bunson hated old Mister Sagunsky.

Sagunsky was one of the richest geezers in Walla Walla, although you'd never know it judging by his scrubby appearance: old, ragged clothes, worn-out shoes, and that same crumpled, ancient-looking felt hat that always sat atop his balding head. He lived in a squalid-looking old bungalow on the south side of town and drove a pollution-belching '68 Galaxy 500. He was the local patriarch of ultra-cheapness.

"Money's no good unless you got it," he always proclaimed defensively whenever asked about his spendthrift ways.

Sagunsky was also a widower and hated cooking, but he adamantly refused to cater to the spendier, "classier" restaurants around town. It was always cheap, greasy fast food, and "Bunson's Burner" was one of his regular haunts.

And Charlie Bunson loathed him for it.

Nearly every evening around six o'clock Sagunsky would come sputtering up to Charlie's drive-thru, always ordering the same thing: one bacon-cheese, a medium fry, and a large chocolate malt—$2.90. It was an easy order to fill for any other customer, but not old man Sagunsky. He was the world's most hypercritical fuddy-duddy, the prototype for mean-spirited, self-indulgent over-particularity; and to make matters worse, Sagunsky didn't care much for Charlie. In fact, he despised him, not in a hateful way, but in a mocking, intimidating manner that always sent Charlie to the furthest edge of his self-control.

Things like, "Be sure to hold the damn tomatoes you stupid SOB," would often come blaring over the intercom while Charlie rushed to cook the old man's order.

Sometimes Sagunsky was more to the point: "I want that burger well-done...cook the hell out of it. If the insides' red I'm gonna come in there and kick your fat ass."

Before pulling away, Sagunsky would always take a long hit off his malt to "test" it. "This is too damn thick you incompetent beef-burner. Whadya' want me to do...suck my brains out?"

Any other customer to address Charlie in this type of degrading manner would normally be given an immediate heave-ho—*sayanara*! But Sagunsky was the great uncle of Bunson's landlord, and when Charlie signed a five-year lease on the property, one of the stipulations was that he serve the aged relative on a nightly basis—with a fifty percent discount to boot!

A knot tightened in Charlie's stomach every time he thought of it.

"How could I have been so incredibly stupid," he muttered every time the old man came driving up. Bunson hadn't given it too much consideration at the time—a fringe benefit for his landlord, something to appease the dietary whims of an elderly eccentric—but now he hated himself for having agreed, in writing no less, to anything so torturous.

"Try to ignore him," his landlord would say. "He's just a crotchety old man. Take his order, give him his food, and get him the hell out of there. He won't bother you...too much." But the nightly routine of verbal tongue-bashing had become nearly unbearable—a festering boil, ready to explode. However, the one thing that really put Charlie over the edge wasn't the abuse...

It was that measly 10-cent tip the old man always left him.

"Keep the change, sonny," Sagunsky would always say in a raspy, sarcastic voice as he laid three one-dollar bills on the window counter. Not that Bunson minded getting an extra dime for his troubles, or even that he expected to *get* tips from his customers; but after enduring five minutes of unexpurgated rudeness every night, this was too much—insult to injury, pure and simple. The fact that the grizzled old tightwad was swollen with wealth only made it all the more intolerable.

"That stinking lowdown son-of-a—" Charlie would grumble, always catching himself before letting any profanity slip out. It wasn't in Bunson's nature to curse, no matter how many four-letter rim-shots Sagunsky bounced off him. Charlie's conservative baby-boomer breeding was deep-rooted in verbal etiquette—no swearing, period. The worst he could do was an occasional, "Aw fudge," muttered through gritted teeth as the old man's car rumbled away from the drive-thru.

So he bit his lip and lived with the situation.

Then came the great day.

At about 2:30 p.m. one July afternoon, Charlie's assistant, Paula, came running back from her lunch break. She threw open the backdoor and burst into the kitchen. A folded newspaper was in her hand.

"Charlie...look at this!"

She shoved the newspaper in his face. Charlie's eyes zeroed in on the story; a moment later his jaw hit the floor.

Sagunsky was dead.

"Holy sweet mother of—" Charlie cried out, almost choking on the words.

And what a death. It hadn't been a quick-acting massive stroke, or even an agony-wracked heart attack—nothing that merciful. The old man was cremated in a major smash-up on Interstate 84 early that morning. Charlie's eyes widened as he read the grisly account. Sagunsky's car had slammed into the rear end of a slow-moving vehicle that had fueled up just minutes before the accident. The occupants of both vehicles were incinerated.

Charlie read the account over and over for the next several minutes, standing behind the grill with a glazed look on his face. His mind whirled with disbelief.

Pinch me I must be dreaming.

Over the next hour or so the glazed expression on Bunson's face eventually turned into a somber look of satisfaction. A short while later, Paula peered through the kitchen portal and thought she detected a slight grin just wrinkling the outer edges of Charlie's mouth. By late afternoon it was definite, Charlie had a big smile on his face.

"Well...I haven't seen your 'happy face' in a long time," Paula commented.

Charlie ignored the remark. He was too deep in pleasant thoughts: no more insults, no more 10-cent tips, *no more Sagunsky!*

The smile on his face got even bigger.

By 6:00 p.m. Charlie was actually whistling while flipping burgers. Paula leaned in through the portal just in time to see him talking to himself.

"Keep the change, sonny," Charlie muttered softly then laughed out loud.

Paula raised an eyebrow disapprovingly. "C'mon, Charlie, I know you hated the old tightwad, but you don't have to act so happy. I mean, the man *is* dead, you know."

Bunson barely acknowledged what she had said. He shrugged it off and started smiling again. There was no room in his heart for guilt. Why should there be? Sagunsky had put him through a seemingly endless year-and-a-half of verbal abuse. Charlie pressed his spatula down hard on a frying burger patty and imagined it was Sagunsky's burning flesh, popping and sizzling against the scorching asphalt of the accident scene.

"He always liked his meat well done," he chuckled gleefully.

The sound of a car pulling up to the drive-thru finally broke through his exhilaration. Charlie reached over and pressed down on the intercom button.

"Good evening. Can I take your order please?"

A second later the intercom speaker roared to life. A friendly-sounding adult male voice crackled over the system. *"Yeah...I've got a pretty big order for you,"*

Charlie's face winced. "How big."

"Colossal," the static voice responded, *"Got a little league team waiting over at Pioneer Park. End of the season party...you know."*

A massive order right in the middle of the evening rush—it was the kind of end-of-the-day annoyance Bunson detested.

"All right," Charlie said as he grabbed a pencil, "what'll it be?"

He scribbled frantically on his order pad: nine burgers, six hot dogs, four corndogs, eight fries, seven onion rings, eight sodas, six shakes, and five malts. It took Charlie's stubby fingers a couple of minutes to total everything up on the calculator.

"All right, your total's gonna be $99.90 at the window.

"Okay."

Charlie set about to his task and began working feverishly on the hot food while Paula scrambled back and forth up front working on the drinks. A couple of minutes went by when the intercom suddenly came to life again.

"Listen…I forgot to mention…five of those burgers need cheese on 'em."

Charlie's eyebrows wrinkled with a slight look of irritation. He moved over and pressed the intercom button down.

"Got it."

Just as he got back to the grill, the intercom crackled again.

"Move your fat ass."

Bunson straightened up immediately; his eyes widened with a big look of surprise. Had he heard right? He saw Paula move by the kitchen portal and called out to her.

"Did you hear that?"

Paula leaned in. "About the cheese?"

"No…after that."

Paula shook her head. "Just cheese." She glanced out her side window. "Got some other cars comin' in. We better get moving."

Charlie stared at the intercom for a moment with an odd expression of puzzlement on his face then he went back to his grill, a little confused. Less than a minute went by before the intercom blared out again.

"Listen…I forgot to mention…hold the tomatoes on three of those cheeseburgers."

Charlie frowned with irritation. He whisked over to the intercom and pressed the button.

"Got it."

He was almost back to the grill, when suddenly…

"Get your fat ass moving or I'll come in there and kick it."

Bunson whirled around. His eyes zeroed in on the intercom. It sat there, cold and lifeless, staring back at him.

"Paula, did you copy that?" he called out, his gaze still fixed on the intercom.

"Three cheese, no tomatoes…right?" she shouted from up front.

"After that, after that."

She leaned in through the portal again. "Nope…nothin' else. What's goin' on?"

"Nothing, nothing."

She looked over at the grill. "Better get on it, Charlie. More cars comin' in."

Charlie bent back over the grill, working frantically to keep up. By this time there were half a dozen cars in line. Some of the drivers started sounding their horns. Charlie was just bagging the hot dogs when the intercom sounded yet again.

"Listen…I forgot to mention…three of the hot dogs are mustard only. Put mustard and relish on the other three with onions on one of those."

Charlie turned toward the intercom, noticeably perturbed. He walked over and slammed down the button.

"Got it. Is there anything else?" he asked testily. Charlie waited a moment. There was no response.

"Sir…are you there?"

There was still no response. Charlie moved back toward the grill.

"Yeah. Take one of those dogs and shove it up your fat ass."

Bunson spun around, almost tripping over his own feet, and did a double take at the intercom. He couldn't believe what he was hearing. There was something else, too.

The voice seemed to have changed.

It wasn't the chummy-sounding little league parent that had placed the order a few minutes earlier—not anymore. This was somebody else, someone with a decidedly malicious sense of humor. But there was something even more unnerving than that.

The voice now had a familiar ring to it.

Alarms were going off in Charlie's brain. "No, no, no…can't be, can't be," he whispered anxiously to himself. Paula *must* have heard it this time. She had to. He glanced hopefully to the front. *C'mon, Paula…act surprised, act indignant…say* something *about it, will ya?* Charlie moved over to the portal and peered through. Paula was scurrying about filling sodas with no apparent reaction to the static-laced slur that had burned Charlie's ears just moments before.

"What on earth's going on here?" Charlie muttered under his breath. He stepped briskly over to the intercom and slammed down the button.

"Sir, did you say something else?"

There was no response.

"Sir?"

No response.

"Sir, can you hear me?"

Still no response.

Bunson stood silent for a few moments, staring hypnotically at the intercom. He must be imagining things, he thought, that had to be it; but a feeling of dread was welling up in the pit of his stomach. He knew whom the voice sounded like, but it just couldn't be.

It couldn't be.

The sound of car horns wailing in unison finally snapped him out of it. He shuffled quickly back to the grill and continued his frantic efforts to finish the order. Charlie was falling hopelessly behind. Four of the burgers had been burned in the confusion and had to be re-cooked, after that a couple of orders of fries went flying through the air as he carried them over to the counter for bagging, a greasy spot by the fryer causing him to fall on his rear. Charlie almost cursed in frustration.

"Aw fudge," he growled through clinched teeth.

A moment later Paula stuck her head through the portal. "He still hasn't pulled up to the window, yet. Tell him to move forward, there's six or seven cars behind him waiting to order."

Charlie waddled quickly over to the intercom and pressed the button down.

"Sir. I need you to pull up. We've got other cars waiting to order."

There was no response, then Charlie noticed the intercom button seemed to be broken. He punched it hard several times in exasperation.

"Son-of-a…" Charlie caught himself again before any profanity slipped out. In frustration he turned the intercom off and yanked the plug out of the wall, then he shouted up to Paula, "The intercom's busted. Lean out the window and wave him forward."

"Why don't you get your fat ass up there and do it yourself."

Charlie froze. He turned slowly and stared at the intercom in trembling disbelief. The power switch was still turned to "off," and the plug lay motionless on the floor.

"This is not happening," he murmured in a low, frightened tone, "this is *not* happening."

Fear drove Charlie into denial at this point; he mechanically returned to the grill and worked feverishly on the rest of the order. He tried to pretend he hadn't heard the familiar, mean-spirited voice that had just echoed through his kitchen. The horns of the other cars in line were blasting away now in collective frustration. Charlie was close to his wits' end as he struggled to complete his task.

"Get your fat ass moving Charlie…before it's too late."

"It's not him…he's dead," Charlie whispered

"Move your fat ass."

"It can't be him…I know he's dead."

"Move that lard-butt fat ass!"

"Shut up, will ya. You're dead! YOU'RE DEAD!"

"MOVE THAT BIG, FAT, STINKING LARD-BUTT FAT ASS!"

Charlie was shaking with terror and near-exhaustion. He was perilously close to cracking up and he felt like he was going to vomit. Perspiration dripped off his forehead in showers, some of it falling onto the hot grill, sizzling as it hit. His heart pounded wildly and he panted for each breath of grease-stenched oxygen.

Paula leaned in through the portal. "What the hell's going on, Charlie? We're gonna have a riot out there in a minute if you don't get that food up here. The drinks are all done."

Somehow, Charlie managed to get everything bagged up and ready to go, but he was almost to the point of collapsing—his hands were shaking, his chest was heaving, and his clothes were nearly drenched in his own sweat. He called Paula back into the kitchen; she helped him bring everything up to the front window. It was then Bunson noticed the car was still nowhere in sight.

"Where is he?"

"I don't know what's going on." Paula answered. "I waved him up two or three times, but he just keeps sitting back there by the speaker."

Charlie leaned out the pickup window and frantically waved the vehicle forward. After a few seconds it started to slowly glide toward the window.

Charlie and Paula were busy organizing the bags on the front counter as the car pulled to a stop next to the pickup window. Suddenly they heard the sound of an electric window going down. Paula looked to her left and screamed in Bunson's ear, almost shattering his eardrum. A second later she hit the floor in a dead faint, her body collapsing at the foot of the Sweden Soft Serve ice cream machine. Charlie let out a gasp and staggered back.

Extending over his window counter was a charred skeletal hand protruding out of the sleeve of a Sunday-best dress-jacket. In its bony grip were two pieces of folding money.

As his head began to swim with sudden, total shock, Charlie Bunson managed to mutter softly...

"Oh shit."

The skeletal hand dropped two fifty-dollar bills lightly on the counter as Bunson keeled over backwards. His plummeting carcass slammed onto the hard, greasy floor. *Smack!* An artery in Charlie's brain burst and his heart muscles began to convulse violently. As his consciousness faded, he could hear the chuckling of a raspy graveyard voice...

"Heh, heh, heh...keep the change, Sonny."

THE END

HORN O' PLENTY

By Richard Casey

Musical car horns are all right—in their place. But when one takes a man's job away from him, it's time for action!

"HOT-LIPS" JOHNSON walked lazily out of Casey's Dance Palace, his trumpet dangling from his right hand, perspiration standing out on his black forehead. The parking lot was dusty and hot under a July Harlem moon. Hot-Lips stared around him, trying to find company for the few minutes he planned to rest. Inside, the boys were "grooving it on down" with the *Two-o'clock Jump*. Hot-Lips snapped his fingers in rhythm with the music, and wandered toward the street.

"That you, Johnson?"

Hot-Lips stopped in his tracks, swayed around with the music and stared behind him. His eyes twinkled.

"How come I didn' see you when I stepped out?"

Charlie Washington, a little out of bounds in his tight trousers and sweatshirt, grinned from ear to ear.

"Guess I and my old horn was listenin' to the jive hounds in there," he admitted. "Ol' horn kinda likes jive."

Hot-Lips looked puzzled.

"What you talking 'bout, tall, dark and handsome? What horn you talking 'bout?"

Charlie Washington backed toward his Ford that was parked under the window.

"My bugle-horn, of course," he said. "Me, I got one of them bugle-horns on the car. Shore does like music."

Hot-Lips was a little worried about Charlie's condition.

"Ain't no horn can listen to music," he said. "You're crazy as a skeeterbug."

Charlie Washington frowned.

"Ain't neither," he protested. "This ol' bugle-horn just listens to music and plays it all by itself."

75

In spite of himself, Hot-Lips was growing interested. He followed Charlie Washington, and together they lifted the hood on the Ford. Underneath was the shining horn. It had four trumpets.

"This here horn used to play just one tune," Charlie Washington said dolefully. "Just the first few notes of *Bugle Call Rag*. Shore got tiresome."

"Go on," Hot-Lips said. "You ain't telling me it can play *more* than that now?"

Charlie Washington nodded.

"Been playing right along with you all evening," he claimed seriously. "Can't quite decide which one of you is hottest."

That was a personal slam against the best trumpet man in Harlem. Hot-Lips backed away slowly, his fingers itching for competition.

"How long dis horn been playing like me?"

Charlie Washington looked thoughtful.

"First time was at the carnival," he said. "Ol' horn just ripped off some notes from the merry-go-round, then stopped. Tell you, I was some surprised."

"I should think," Hot-Lips agreed. "How 'bout a little jam session just so's I can make sure?"

Charlie Washington looked pleased.

"Sho' would be somethin'!" he agreed. "Now, I'd like to hear you two take off on the *Two-o'clock Jump!*"

Hot-Lips Johnson was grinning. He polished his beloved trumpet on his sleeve, lifted it in the air and placed his lips to the mouthpiece.

"Give!" Charlie Washington begged.

Hot-Lips gave!

IN ALL Harlem there was no other playing like that. At his lips, the trumpet became something fit for Gabriel to rave about. When he ran up and down the scale, every curly-headed baby in the district climbed out of its cradle and got ready to cut a rug.

The first bell-like notes escaped Hot-Lips trumpet. Inside Casey's dance hall the band stopped playing. A hush fell over everyone. Johnson was doing a solitary jam session. Man, *that* was something to stop the world for!

But what was the other sound? There couldn't be anyone in Harlem who had the nerve to stand up to Hot-Lips...

As the crowd drifted to the doors and windows, staring out at the dusky figures in the parking lot *two* trumpets started to work together.

At first, the second one was a little fuzzy. Then it caught up with Hot-Lips and started to put in the licks that Johnson missed.

In five minutes the crowd at Casey's was swaying, punch-drunk. In ten minutes a first class contest was going on, and Hot-Lips was sweating to keep up. In a half-hour the story was all over town.

Charlie Washington had bought a bugle-horn that could keep pace with the best rhythm-man in town.

From then on, the story grew like the immortal beanstalk. Charlie Washington, worth two bits and not a cent more, had become famous. Every boy in the neighborhood bought a horn and tried to work it out on the trumpet of Hot-Lips Johnson. *That* rhythm man fell in love with Charlie's car and offered him twice what it was worth just so he'd have the horn around when he felt a spell coming on.

IT NEVER occurred to anyone that the horn might someday out-play Hot-Lips himself. Johnson played his best, and he played often. The horn seemed to listen and learn. Once in a while it knocked off a tune or two when Johnson wasn't around.

Then Hot-Lips went to Albany for a week, to play with Jan Strutter's Hot Numbers, and Charlie's Ford got a contract at Casey's Dance Palace.

They say there was never anything funnier in Harlem than the sight of Charlie Washington's old Ford, its hood pushed up, squatting there in the brass section. They say that nothing Hot-Lips Johnson ever produced could equal the quality and tone that the bugle-horn turned out.

Harlem came and saw and paid homage. The cats were wild for more. Major Bowes made an offer and Charlie turned it down. He was happy at Casey's.

Then Hot-Lips came back from his week, ready to accept the cheers of the crowd he expected at the station. He wandered around to Casey's that night with an almost pale expression on his face. His pep was gone. His job was gone. Casey's Rhythm Cats didn't need him any more. He had been replaced by the machine age. Canned music, played by a bugle-horn, and contained in the rattling body of a decrepit Ford.

If Johnson had been a better man, he might have stuck it out. Instead, it drove him to cheap dance halls, and increased his yen for raw whiskey. He got a little short of cash and joined up with Spike Howard's gang of hoodlums.

Spike was plenty smart. He sent Johnson out on a couple of small safecracking jobs, just to get the feel of things. Then, one night, he sent for Johnson and met him behind the gambling room at Casey's Dance Palace.

Spike had been in every crooked deal he could find since his Mammy first tossed him into the street. He had a scar on his cheek from an old razor fight and he'd been collecting on that scar ever since.

"Look here, Johnson," Spike said, as soon as they could talk alone. "You been working fo' me about two months now. Ain't it time you caught up on yo' *own* homework?"

Johnson scowled.

"What you talking 'bout?"

Spike grinned and it made the scar glow as though it were bleeding.

"This Charlie Washington boy," Spike prompted. "You ain't gonna let him get *away* with what he done, is you?"

Hot-Lips scowled a little harder.

"Ain't nothin' *I* can do, is there?"

"Ain't no reason why you can't *steal* that four-wheeled jukebox?"

Johnson looked startled.

"Never thought of it like that."

Spike pushed a wad of greenbacks across the table.

"I can peddle that jumpin' jive-hound to a guy in Chicago," he said. "You can count one hundred bucks in the hunk of dough. You deliver that four-wheeled trumpet to the freight siding down near my place and the *money is yo's.*"

Johnson brightened.

"You can also get your ol' job back with Casey," Spike said, adding the clinching touch.

Johnson stood up slowly, and when he went out, the money was clenched tightly in his big hand.

IT MIGHT have worked, too. He might have succeeded in stealing Charlie Washington's Ford if he had disconnected the horn before he drove it out of Casey's Dance Palace.

But the horn objected.

Casey's was deserted at four o'clock. Hot-Lips Johnson managed to back the Ford out the rear door and get as far as the street.

What happened after that is history in Harlem.

The trumpet horns started to bleat the minute they reached the street. It was terrible.

First came the *Bugle Call Rag.*

"You can't get 'em up,
You can't get 'em up,
You can't get 'em up this morning."

High and shrill came the warning in Harlem's deserted streets.

Windows flew open and lights went on. Heads poked out the windows and started a cry of protest.

Johnson, driving as fast as the car would go, felt sweat pop cut on his forehead.

The horn was silent for only an instant after finishing the last notes of the *Rag.* Then, evidently becoming playful, it imitated a police siren for five blocks and worked from that right into a heartbreaking rendition of *It's Murder, He Says.*

By this time, Johnson had gone completely wild. He cut across lots between a couple of apartment buildings.

As he emerged on the street again, holding fiercely to the wheel, the horns broke into the sad, mournful strains of *In The Hush Of Evening.*

That was too much.

Hot-Lips Johnson cleared the door and fell headlong into the street. By this time a crowd had collected on the sidewalk. The Ford didn't stop rolling. It rounded the next corner and sped down between the lines of men and women who filled the sidewalks.

There are those who will swear that as it neared the building excavation on the next corner, those trumpets were dolefully swinging out with *My Last Goodbye*.

It was a fact that the deep excavation was half filled with water. The Ford didn't hesitate, but plunged straight through the fence and tipped end over end into ten feet of muddy water.

A howl of sadness arose and swelled until it reached the outskirts of Harlem.

The last tune that Charlie Washington's bugle-horn ever played, was beating shrilly against the night as the Ford plunged toward the water.

"And so help me," Charlie Washington said afterward, with tears in his eyes, "that ol' Ford was tooting *Taps* just as it went under."

SOMEHOW, when it was all over, no one had the heart to punish Hot-Lips Johnson. He hung around Casey's for a long time, pleading with Charlie Washington for forgiveness. Perhaps Charlie felt that he hadn't been entirely fair with Hot-Lips. Anyway, after a few weeks, Hot-Lips was back in the band. His trumpet was sweeter than ever, but he never played again within hearing distance of a bugle-horn.

THE END

AT THE END OF THE CORRIDOR

By Evangeline Walton

A story of the Greek undead—if dead men could walk because they had reason for revenge, a lot of them would have done it these last few years.

WHENEVER Philip Martin felt like being funny he would say that he was a professional grave robber. If people looked properly shocked he would add, "I began with a king's grave," and then grin. A mild joke, not in the best of taste perhaps, but then everything about Philip was mild; his nearsighted brown eyes, his tall, shambling frame, his face that never had been quite young. Even his shy way of showing off, of hoping, a little wistfully, that he could shock people or make them laugh.

As a matter of fact, His Majesty the King had been dead about 3,000 years when Philip and his father, the late and distinguished James K. Martin, Ph.D., had dug him up. It is generally considered respectable to rob a man's grave if he has been dead long enough. The Martins, father and son, had always made a most correct and respectable thing of grave robbing, just as they had of everything else they turned their well-kept, somewhat dry Bostonian hands to. That anything could ever change this (or indeed his own prim, proper personal life) Philip never dreamed when he set out for Greece to carry on the work of the late Dr. Kimon Dragoumis. He was contemptuously amused when, at a farewell dinner, a slightly tipsy Parisian savant said to him:

"Some day you may rob one grave too many, my friend."

Philip grinned. "You mean curses? That old tripe about ancient tombs having invisible guardians?"

M. de Lesseps smiled. "You think me a foolish old man, *hein?* Not all ancient things are toothless. Yet you may be wise, my young friend. Perhaps it is safer to rob the tombs of the ancient dead, of those who have had time to forget their wrongs. When I was young I too went to Greece, to Maina where the old blood is purest, to write a book. But I saw what I dared not write. There are dead there who need no curses—they can *act!*" He shuddered and crossed himself.

Philip said indulgently, "If dead men could walk because they had reason for revenge, a lot of them would have done it these last few years. The men who died in concentration camps, for instance."

The savant said seriously, "That depends on the man, my friend. On what he studied while he was alive, what he knew and believed. On what his background was. Among simple yet ancient peoples, who are still near the source of things, there are survivals—" He rambled on, learnedly yet drunkenly, about primeval man, about vision and gifts that his modern descendants had lost. Until Philip got very bored, and took too many drinks.

He had a headache next morning, when he boarded the plane for Athens. But it was only the beginning of his headaches. For when he reached the little seaside village that had been the site of Dragoumis' work he found—nothing. Only the few *tholoi* that the great Greek had first found and explored were still visible. The bulk of that underground collection of mysterious Mycenean tomb-chambers had vanished as if the hills out of whose sides they had been carved had swallowed them up again.

It seemed strange, in spite of the disaster that had come upon Dr. Dragoumis and his co-workers; the guerrilla warfare that had raged for years afterward through this grim land of sea and mountains, and was still uncomfortably near. So near, in fact, that it had taken Philip years to get his own permit to dig.

A landslide had covered the excavations; that was all he could learn. Though some of the villagers must have known the approximate location of the buried sites they would tell him nothing. They acted either sullen or blandly ignorant—too ignorant. He had a queer and unreasonable feeling that they were afraid.

Sophoulis, the local school-teacher, advised him to go to Mme. Dragoumis, "She may still have some of her husband's papers, kyrie."

"You mean she still lives here?" Philip asked in surprise. He had heard of Mme. Dragoumis as one of the famous beauties of the Balkans, a very gay and fashionable woman, much younger than her husband. "In that island villa of theirs?"

"She will not leave it, kyrie. Not for an hour. Not once since that night the doctor died has she set foot on the mainland. She says that her husband is still alive—that she must be there to greet him if he returns."

"She dares not leave it," Mrs. Sophoulis said with a hard little smile. "Her family has been worried about her, and once they even sent doctors to take her away, but she locked herself in her room and said she would kill herself if they broke the doors down—that it would be better to die that way than to go ashore."

Philip felt a little apprehensive. The lady might not be sane enough to be of any help to him.

"I thought the Nazis shot Dr. Dragoumis," he said.

"So it is said. None knows," Sophoulis said heavily. "They suspected him of hiding arms, arms smuggled in from British submarines; and perhaps he was. Or perhaps he had found tombs in which there were precious things—treasures that he feared the Nazis might carry off to Germany. Certainly he was doing something that he wished to keep secret. He was a giant who could outdig any of his men, and toward the last he dug oftenest by moonlight—and alone."

"It must have been the tombs themselves that he wished to protect," Philip said stiffly. "No true scientist would risk such monuments of the past by storing arms in them."

"Who knows, kyrie? A true patriot will risk anything. At least there was talk. Too much talk. Perhaps even someone who wished to talk too much. So the Nazis waited for him, that night at the villa. Kyria Dragoumis says that they shot him as he was escaping through the French windows, but that so great was his strength that he ran on, with their bullets in him. And later, when they searched the *tholoi* where they thought he might be hiding, the mountain itself slid forward and covered them—yes, the very mountains seemed angry that the invaders should dare go poking about among their bowels. It took them two days to dig out the bodies of their Gestapo men, kyrie."

MRS. SOPHOULIS cut in excitedly, her dark eyes bright, "But they never found the doctor, kyrie! And some of our people say that they have seen him since, by moonlight, pacing the cliffs above the sea, and looking out toward his home across the waters."

Her husband laughed a little uneasily. "Our peasants hereabouts are still very superstitious, kyrie. They can see anything."

"So it seems," said Philip dryly. "You think that Mme. Dragoumis might be able to help me then?"

"She would not!" Mrs. Sophoulis snorted. "She never knew anything about it; she took no interest in it. Or in anything but parties and young men. She stays on the island now only because she is afraid—not for love of her dear dead husband, poof! Keep away from her, kyrie; she is bad luck, that one."

Sophoulis' fist pounded the table. "Be still, woman! None has any right to speak against Kyria Dragoumis; I have told you that I will have no idiotic women's gossip in my house."

There was evidently some local feeling against Mme. Dragoumis, Philip thought as he left. Possibly only among the women; Sophoulis was clearly either too fair-minded or too cautious to lend himself to it. Yet what fear could they possible think kept Mme. Dragoumis on the island—surely government guards could have kept her safe from any guerrilla ambush? The whole business was a puzzle. Why should Dragoumis have been fool enough, that night, to attempt escape? He could not have hidden anything incriminating in the tombs. "Attempted escape" was an age-old, trite pretext to cover murder; but why should anybody have wanted to murder Dragoumis, a scientist who had surely had too much sense to take any interest in anything but his work?

Well, it was none of his business. What concerned him was to find a way into those lost Mycenean vaults without blasting holes in their sides while he was at it. He took a boat and had himself rowed out to the island. To the little landing-stage from which broad steps led up to a white villa above the sea; a villa set like a pearl upon a terrace made green and silver by the foliage of orange and olive trees.

Or so he thought until he saw Anthi Dragoumis and knew the difference between pearl and setting. Between life and mere existence.

She was a beauty. She was delight, and wonder, and youth—the youth that Philip had never had. She set fire to the dry man as flame fires tinder.

And she was gracious to him, she was kind. Yes, she still had some of her husband's papers, she would show them to him, and search for more. He could help her search if he liked. He did. He went again and again to that villa on the island. He filled his eyes and ears with her; with the soft music of her voice, with the curves of her body that made softer music whenever she moved. With the warm red of her lips, and the depths of her shining eyes.

And then one day she let him fill his arms...

He tried, after that, to get her to marry him and go away with him. "Your husband is dead, Anthi. He has been dead these five years. It cannot hurt you to accept that now. You do not love him any more."

But she shook her head. "He was not too badly hurt that night; he rowed himself back to the mainland. He was a peasant, born in a hut in Maina—not civilized, like you and me, for all his learning. He was very strong, Philip; strong like the men of an earlier world. It would be hard for him to die."

JEALOUSY leapt in him. So that was it—Dragoumis' brute strength had dazzled her, his hard peasant heritage! That was

85

what she liked in a man. He said roughly, "If he's alive, why hasn't he come back to you? What could he have been afraid of, after the Nazis left? Afraid enough to make him stay away from a wife like you?" He kissed her, hard and savagely. He strained her close, trying to hurt her, to prove that he too was strong.

She laughed up into his face and stroked his cheek. "You would not stay away from me, would you, my Philip? Don't worry; I love you more than I ever loved him. You are much younger than he was. Though he loved me very much; as much as you could ever do."

"Then why would he stay away from you?" Philip muttered.

She looked up at him very seriously then, her eyes gone grave. "Because, that last night, he accused me of betraying him to the Nazis. Because the officer who came to arrest him was a young and very handsome man I had danced with several times in Athens." She shivered. "But he was not handsome when they dug him out from under the mountain, after he had tried to follow my husband into the ancient tombs."

Philip stared at her in horror. "You don't mean that Dragoumis did have explosives in there and deliberately set them off—that he'd have destroyed *tholoi* just to kill a few men?"

She laughed. "Not a few men, no. One man—the man he thought had taken me from him. You would not do that, would you, my archaeologist, my ruin-lover? After all, it was Kimon, my poor, aging Kimon, who loved me best."

Suspicion stabbed him suddenly, like a knife twisting in his flesh. He shook her. "Did you love the German then, Anthi? He was younger than your husband, too—and so handsome!"

But that insulted her. She stormed at him, she raged and wept until he practically had to go down on his knees and apologize to her. Until suspicion faded, became a shameful outrage that he dared not even remember.

When she was quiet again he tried once more to persuade her that her husband must be dead. "No living man could have

stayed away from you so long. Whatever he was fool or mad
enough to believe for the moment he could not—you are so
beautiful, Anthi!" But she only wept again and shivered.

"You did not know Kimon, my Philip. I did." She peered
nervously over her shoulder, at the shadows that seemed to have
grown, blacker, over the bed. "He was so strong, Philip. He
was like the giant who could not die so long as he could touch
his mother, the earth. Nothing could ever kill him completely,
here in his own hills. I think that he is still waiting somewhere,
inside the mountain, in his *tholoi*—waiting, watching for me.
That is why I never dare set foot on the mainland. Why I never
can unless he is found—and laid."

Philip stared at her blankly. "But even if he were there,
Anthi—a madman, in hiding, getting food somehow—he'd have
stolen a boat and come out here long ago. You must see that."

She looked very straight at him then. Her eyes were pits of
blackness, blacker than the shadows. Her voice was hushed,
almost a whisper: *"There are those who cannot cross water."*

For a minute he did not understand. Then his face went
whiter than hers. With an incredulous, yet comprehending
horror. For now at last he knew. Evil things could not cross
water—the unalive yet undead could not, the terrible *vrykolakes*
of Greek belief.

All these years she had been lying, all these years she had
believed her husband dead! A man no longer, but a thing of
supernatural evil, an avenger who was seeking her.

Why? *About what else had she lied?*

But she had risen, she was coming toward him. Her eyes
held his. Their warm brightness was all around him, and her
arms were round his neck.

"You will do that for me, my Philip? You will find him and
lay him, so that we can go away together and be married? So
that we can forget him and love each other, always?" She
pressed her cheek against his. "You will set me free from fear.
You will do that for your Anthi, Philip? For me?" Her lips
moved along his cheek softly, touched his ear.

He stood quite still in her arms. He said hoarsely, "How could I find him, even if he were there?"

She said softly, almost crooning, "You will find him. You will lay him. For your Anthi. For me."

He did not answer. He stood there horrified, trying to think. In England and in Poland they used to bury the unquiet dead with stakes through their hearts. To keep them down, to keep them from walking. What had been done to such dead men in Greece? He could not remember. Something not so simple as a stake, he thought—something horrible—

She pressed herself closer against him. She whispered, "It will not be so hard. I can tell you where to find the last tomb he found—the greatest, the royal *tholos,* the one he said he kept secret for fear the Nazis would loot it."

"You think he would have gone there, knowing that you knew the place?" Philip laughed harshly.

"He would have, to save what he could. He loved it more than anything, even me. Night after night he used to tell me of it, to describe his precious day's work when I wanted to sleep. But now at last that will be useful. It will help you to find him, and then you will cut off his arms and legs—so that he will have no feet to follow us, no hands to strike us!"

Philip said bitterly, "Do you want to tie them under his armpits, as murderers used to do in Solon's time? Are you mad, Anthi? I am, to listen to you."

She flung back her head, her eyes hard with suspicion. "No, I do not want them tied under his armpits. I want them brought here to me, tonight! There are signs by which I shall know them—do not think that you can deceive me. If I do not get them I will never marry you—you shall never touch me again!"

NIGHT found Philip on the mountainside; high above the lights of the village. He had one man with him, a big fellow with the brawn of an ox and almost as few brains. He came from another village, and if by any unlucky chance he should see Dr. Dragoumis' body he would not recognize it. He had said nothing, only looked scared and crossed himself when Philip had explained the need for this secret digging by night.

"There may be treasures in this tomb, Costa, golden things that it would be risky to let the guerrillas hear of. Though there is probably nothing but pottery and old stones. And perhaps fragments of some old king's body—if it is not well-preserved I may bring them up."

Costa would not be surprised, now, if he saw pieces of a corpse. Philip gagged at the thought. It would hardly look human now, after so many years in the musty dark. Or would it? Philip did not know. He shuddered. How could Anthi be afraid of such a thing, lying there helpless, horrible in its rottenness and decay; pitiful because of the very hideousness that cancelled its onetime humanity?

She was waiting for him now, below, in a boat about a hundred yards offshore. She had to come so far to show him which particular crag covered the buried entrance to the *dromos*, to that great passageway leading into the mountain's heart. He had expected her to go back after that, but she was still there, her boat a tiny dark speck upon the moonlit waters. Waiting vulture-like, eager for her prey.

She was grimly thorough, he thought. Ancient murderers were supposed to have been satisfied with cutting off their victims' hands and feet, but she could imagine the corpse running after her fleetly on the stumps of footless legs, catching and crushing her in handless arms, in an embrace that would break the bones—

He shuddered again, mopped his forehead. Easy for a man to have fancies here, amid all this bleak wilderness of rock.

"What is it? Are you tired, kyrie?" asked Costa hopefully. "We have been digging almost four hours now. You could go down to the boat, to the lady. Did she bring wine for us, kyrie?"

Philip hesitated. He was tired, and the light was very bad. He had expected the moon to be bright tonight, to make the mountain almost as light as day. But instead, though it shone clear and bright upon the sea, some trick of cloud-shadows cut it off from the slopes, shrouded them in pitch. He and Costa had to work by lantern-light, and they kept the lantern muffled, for fear it might be seen from the village below. The shadows all around them were dancing, dancing, like immense black cats playing with two trapped mice.

What if he was to assert himself, to go down to Anthi and tell her that he would do her work another night, when the light was better—?

But then she would laugh at his weakness. And she would be right. Was it not weakness?

He answered Costa's proposition shortly: "No." He set his teeth and plunged his spade into the earth. Hard, with renewed vigor. And suddenly the spade struck hollowness; sank into the earth as if hands had reached up from below and seized it. A dislodged pebble went rattling on down inside the hole, down, down, into gulf-like space.

Costa crossed himself again and gasped, "May the Panagia— may the Virgin and all the blessed saints preserve us!"

Earth and massive stones fell together with a great thud. A pit opened, almost beneath their feet. The Greek cried out and jumped back. But Philip laughed. His eyes were shining. He forgot Anthi; he forgot Dragoumis. This was what he had come to Greece to find; the discovery he had dreamed for years of making; this was triumph and fulfillment!

He dug feverishly; he urged Costa on with both praise and curses. Until the hole lay like a wide-open mouth at their feet, a mouth blacker, more thickly solid, than the blackness of the night.

Philip tied a rope to the lantern. He lowered it into the pit and leaned over, watching course after course of great stone blocks appear and disappear as its golden eye sank deeper, farther into the dark. At last it came to rest upon a rock floor many feet below, making a tiny brilliant island there.

Philip took an axe, a flashlight, and some cloths, set another rope around his waist and prepared to follow the lantern.

"Wait here, Costa. When I jerk the rope raise me."

He wondered fleetingly why he had said that. Surely it would have been simpler to say that he would shout up from the depths? Then he forgot it as he swung downward into space.

HE LOOKED about him eagerly as he landed. To his right, within a few feet of his descent, the passageway was blocked by rough masses of earth and rock. Probably these covered the real entrance to the *dromos,* that which had been hidden for tens of centuries until Dragoumis pierced its age-old seals; on that fatal night it must have been crushed by the landslide that had buried his pursuers. But to the left the passage stretched on, seemingly endless, into the mountain's heart. For a little way only the lantern's light pierced it, breaking the darkness into pieces, into dancing shadows.

Did one of those shadows dart back as he looked, one a little thicker, a little blacker, than its fellows?

He did not heed it. His heart felt light, exultant, as he leveled his flashlight and walked on, toward the blackness that looked solid as a wall. He no longer even felt horror of the axe beneath his arm. If Dragoumis could have chosen, surely he would have had his dead body dismembered a thousand times rather than let his great discovery be lost again, hidden from mankind, perhaps for more centuries. For on no other terms would Anthi ever have disclosed the secret. Poor girl! Later, when her hysterical, superstitious obsession was over, she would regret this, she would be kind and gentle and fastidious again, as a woman should be. Now he must do whatever was necessary to bring her peace.

He went on into the shadows, and they retreated before him slowly, steadily. He followed them down that stone corridor that led through the earth's bowels.

Once or twice it seemed to him that he heard a faint curious rustling among those dark, wavering shapes that recoiled before his flashlight. As if someone were walking ahead of him, stealthily. He decided that it must be some trick of echoes, reverberating oddly in that subterranean place. It could not be bats, for there was never anything where the light came; throw his flashlight where he would, its beams found only great, bare blocks of stone.

Then he came at last to the black rectangle of the inner portal, the opening into that great, circular chamber Anthi had told him of. There Dragoumis had found golden vessels and golden filigree-work, and images of gods that no man had worshipped for ages. There he had found bones, and there, perhaps, he had left his own.

And there, at last, fear took Philip. It closed round his throat like an icy hand. In his inner ears a far-off voice seemed to cry: *"Do not disturb the dead! Do not disturb the dead!"*

He shrugged. That voice came out of his childhood, out of superstitions and conventional moralities engraved upon the young mind as a phonograph record is engraved upon wax. He thought, "I am being foolish as Anthi. I have handled many mummies, I have felt their dry, withered flesh slough off my hands. What difference is there, what real difference? A man can be as dead in three minutes as he will be in three thousand years."

He swung the flashlight forward, toward the inner chamber.

He saw the gleam of gold, he saw strange, grotesque shapes of stone. He saw carved stone *larnaki,* and, in the far corner, a table of red marble. Its legs gleamed under the light, like blood.

Was there something on top of the table, among the shadows? Something long and dark and still, like the outstretched form of a man?

Once again fear took him. He could not bear to throw the flashlight upon the tabletop, to see. He edged slowly into the chamber, moving cautiously, laboriously, as if through invisible barriers. There were no more echoes. In the deathly silence he heard nothing but the fierce, hard pounding of his heart.

Suddenly he stopped. He could not bear to go farther, to come within touching distance of that thing that might be lying there.

He set his teeth and his will. Slowly, as if it were a rock too heavy for him to move, the flashlight came up. Its beams touched something; something upon the tabletop.

A man's hand that lay, lax and brown and leathery, upon red marble. A large hand, larger than most men's. Firm and sleek as leather it looked; and yet, in some curious and subtle way, as lifeless. None could have mistaken it for the hand of a living man. Philip's brain reeled; through it ran dizzily words he had heard among the Greek peasants and never heeded; the bodies of the walking dead—of those whom the earth had not loosed—were incorruptible; undecaying!

And as he looked the hand changed. The fingers tensed, the long tendons on the back of it rose and stiffened, as if that dark recumbent form were bracing itself to rise!

With a strangled cry of horror Philip hurled himself forward, the axe gleaming above his head.

COSTA shivered. The night wind was cold, and once a cry had seemed to drift up from the depths below. He had listened closely after that, but he had not been able to tell whether the cry was repeated, whether a faint horrible screaming, muffled by distance, had come up from the earth.

The rope at his feet jerked suddenly, convulsively, like a great snake. He cried out and jumped back, then remembered and gasped with relief.

The signal!

Gladly he hauled his master up. "The saints be thanked, kyrie! You are safe! I thought I heard something—"

The tall man did not answer. He turned and strode off down the mountainside, with long, swift strides. "He goes very fast," Costa thought, "as if there were something before—or behind him—for which he could not bear to wait. He does not even stop to give me any of the bundles he carries." He followed with the lantern, looking curiously at those bundles. They were long and narrow, they looked like human arms and legs. When he saw a limp hand dangling from one of them he crossed himself.

"The old king must have come all to pieces. Who would have thought he would still have looked so human?"

He gained a little on his master. The lantern rays fell on those packages, and Costa's eyes grew large and round. After that he walked more slowly, and let the distance widen between himself and the tall figure ahead. For through the cloth wrappings something dank was seeping, something that stained the white linen.

He dropped farther behind, when they came within sight of the shore and his master spurted suddenly, running out with demonic speed onto the white sands. The clouds had left the moon; the beach was almost as bright as day.

A cry came from the boat. The waiting woman tugged at the oars and swung it in, closer. She leaped out upon the sands. Her voice pealed out, a song of gladness:

"You have them, Philip! You have them—"

She ran forward, her arms outstretched, her face bright with triumph. The man waited for her. He had stopped and stood very still; he made no move, either to meet or welcome her. And when she reached him she did not even look at him. She only clutched, with hands as terribly eager as her eyes, at those packages he carried.

Silently, he let her take them. Silently, he stood over her as she unwrapped them. As their ugly, stained contents fell from her paralyzed hands to the earth—

And then she screamed. Terribly and horribly she screamed. For the first time she looked up into his face, and saw it. He took off his hat, Philip Martin's hat, and moved toward her, and in that clear moonlight, for all the distance, Costa saw that his head was not Philip Martin's head.

After that Costa's eyes closed and he knelt and prayed. He did not see what made the lady scream again. Her cries kept on for quite a long time, but at last the beach was silent. There was no sound on it, even the sound of a retreating footstep. And then, and only then, did Costa find the strength to run away.

Later, the Athenian newspapers carried feature headlines: FRESH GUERRILLA OUTRAGES! MUTILATED BODY OF AMERICAN ARCHAEOLOGIST FOUND IN MYCENEAN TOMB! On a nearby beach had been found the bodies of Kyria Anthi Dragoumis and of a man who must have been one of the guerrilla murderers. A giant of a man, whose body, unaccountably, crumbled and fell apart when it was touched.

THE END

REBELS' REST

By Seabury Quinn

"If you're a natural man, God save ye; but if you're a Thing o' the Darkness..."

EILEEN walked faster as she neared the cemetery. It was not like an Irish graveyard, this little Pennsylvania burying ground, not like the little acres planted to God's harvest which she had known at home. There was no church to send the music of its bells across the low green billows of its mounded graves, no yews and holly-trees in which the kind winds whispered slumber-songs, no lich gate at its entrance underneath whose gable the tired living and the peaceful dead might pause a moment in eternity ere they went diverse ways. Like most things in this strange new land it seemed to be entirely functional. Just as no one ever thought of dropping into the cool, whisper-haunted shadows of the church for rest and prayer and meditation on a summer's afternoon, so no one ever thought of going to the cemetery save when friends or relatives were buried. No one ever thought of stopping there to kneel beside the grave of some loved one and whisper, "God give you rest and caring, dear soul!"

They seemed to dread the dead in America. At home it had been different. Kinfolk and friends and neighbors did not change essentially when they moved from their cottages to the churchyard. But...

She drew her hooded cape more closely round her and walked faster as she reached the cemetery wall. Perhaps the dead were unfriendly in America. So many of the living were.

It was in 1918 that Chris Huncke met Sheilah Maclintock. He was a Pennsylvania Dutchman, big, blond, rather stolid, unimaginative, and very handsome in his American uniform. Sheilah was his opposite, small, black-haired, blue-eyed, as typically Irish as a sprig of shamrock. She was a member of the Women's Motor Corps, and piloted an antique Daimler with the expertness of a racing driver, making mock of London fogs, policemen, two-star generals and even second lieutenants with sharp-witted Hibernian impartiality. Christian fell in love with her at first sight, Sheilah needed several looks before she gave her heart and unswerving devotion to the big, inarticulate American.

He brought her back in 1919, rushed her round New York in a deliriously ecstatic honeymoon, then took her to his farm near Chambersburg, where he shed his uniform and the never-quite-convincing air of gay insouciance he had worn with it, and reverted to type.

His father and his father's great-grand father had been farmers, sturdy folk who held their land by grant from Governor Penn and later stubbornly against both redskins and redcoats. Their ways were right and all their judgments true.

Sheilah stood it for as long as she could, which was not quite a year. The atmosphere of the old house, the seldom-opened "best room" with its horsehair furniture, waxed flowers and shell ornaments spread like a miasma over the entire place, stifling her. Who could sing songs of the mountainy men of Donegal or the leprechaun or the *gean canach,* the love-talker, with a picture of *Grosvater* Huneke, dressed in broadcloth and starched linen and bearded like a billygoat, scowling disapprovingly down at her? Who could stand the dour, uncompromising religiosity of the neighbors?

She loved the out of doors, did Sheilah Maclintock, the soft; sweet rain, the limpid sunshine, the springiness of fresh green turf. One day as she walked home from the village the urge to feel the caress of the roadside grass against her feet was more than she could withstand, and so she dropped down on a wayside boulder to peel off shoes and stockings when who should drive by in his Stutz Bearcat but Emil Herbst, son of Max Herbst, the president of the savings bank.

Prohibition had not yet come to America, but foregleamings of its high morality had reached the county, which had voted dry at the last election. Consequently nearly every second shop in the village was a speakeasy, and when Emil gathered with other village *jeunes dorés* behind Gus Schwing's pool parlor that evening he had provocative things to say concerning Sheilah's pretty feet and legs and Sheilah's deportment on the public highway. The story of her escapade spread with fissionable swiftness through the village and surrounding country, and next morning Mrs. Friedrich Eichelburg was early on the telephone.

As she took up the receiver Sheilah heard the sequenced clickings of a dozen others being lifted. Everyone on the line was indulging in a little morning's eavesdropping.

"Good morning, Mrs. Huncke," her self-appointed mentor greeted. "I feel it is my Christian duty to tell you—" then for the next half-hour she discoursed upon the differences between American morality and the loose-reined mores of decadent Europe.

"Ochone!" exploded Sheilah when she could wedge a word in. "Your Christian duty is it, ye *sthronsuch?* Faith, 'tis meself that's after thinkin' ye'd be servin' both your God and neighbors better if ye kept your sharp nose out o' other people's business!"

THE ladies of the congregation didn't quite draw their skirts aside as she passed after that, but she was not invited to their *kaffee klatches,* nor to help with the church suppers, nor serve on their committees. Perhaps it would not be quite accurate to say that they sent her to Coventry, but certainly they consigned her to Birmingham.

And so, before a year had passed she packed her scanty wardrobe, for she'd take nothing Christian's money bought, and set out for the home she'd left six years before when she went off to do her bit in the Great War.

She hitchhiked as far as Harrisburg, and there she found employment as a waitress and saved every spare penny till she had enough to pay her steerage passage back to Galway. She left no note of farewell, and if Christian made an effort to find her it was not apparent. The ostracism, which the neighbors had visited on his wife, had extended to him; he was a gregarious soul, and life had not been pleasant on the farm since Sheilah came. When the days stretched into weeks, and the weeks to months, and still no word of her, he gradually accepted the verdict that she was "no better than she should be," and found contentment if not happiness in a second marriage.

Sheilah shared a cottage with her aged Uncle Brian, cooked his meals and washed his clothes and worked his patch of garden, for he was infirm with rheumatism, and also something of a *sleiveen,* which is to say he was a man who'd rather take his ease than not, and didn't worry overmuch if the weeds grew waist-high. It was a bleak, bare spot on which the cottage stood, all day and night they heard the angry surges of the Atlantic, in summer there was salt spray in the air, in winter there were bitter winds and storms. Before she'd been home two months Sheilah gave birth to Christian's child, a daughter whom she named Eileen.

She had small traffic with the country folk, and they in turn were reticent, respecting her privacy. If on occasion neighbor women speculated over a pleasant scandal-flavored dish of tea that she was neither wife nor widow, they kept their speculations to themselves and caused her no embarrassment.

Each night when Sheilah knelt to pray she begged, "God keep and prosper him," and when she rose from her knees it was with that sick, awful feeling of emptiness which one who has not lost the thing that she most loves cannot know. *"Ullagone, avourneen,"* she would whisper, "we loved, each other so! Where did all the beautiful, sweet love go? Why did you ever let 'em; take you from me—and me from you?"

Then one night when she had reached thirty-eight and looked at least fifteen years older, Sheilah heard the Woman of the Shee sing underneath her window, and knew her time was come. "I'm goin', pulse o' me heart," she told Eileen, "and it's precious little I can leave ye. In the ginger jar fornenst the clock's a hoard o' twenty pounds. 'Twill care for my buryin' and pay your passage to your father in America, and for the love he bore me when we two were wed he'll take ye in and look after ye. Bid him a kindly greetin', child, and tell him that I loved him to the last."

It seemed to Christian time flowed backward for him when Eileen arrived. She had blue-black Irish hair and intensely blue eyes; her skin was like damask, glowing, warm; even the dimple in her pointed chin and the soft-lipped, tender smile of her were reminiscent of her mother. He felt as if Sheilah had come back to him, and the old love woke and stirred the spiced embalmings in its tomb. She was his daughter, yes, but she was something more, she was the reincarnation of the first and only real love of his life.

And because he loved her he was harsh with her. Her every little fault was magnified because it seemed to detract from the ideal of perfection he imagined her to be, and he was heavy-tongued in his scoldings.

But if Christian lashed his daughter with scourges his wife Beulah scourged her with scorpions. If Beulah Huncke had once been pretty nothing in her makeup testified to it. Everything about her was sharp with cutting sharpness. Her thin shoulders, her small, bright, vindictive eyes, her narrow profile, her thin, long hands and feet revealed her as a woman of edges, not curves. She wore her hair in a small knot at the back of her head, and drew it back so tightly that it seemed to make her eyeballs pop; her voice rasped like a file on steel, as if there were a grit of malice in her throat. Heaven had denied her offspring, and this frustration added gall and wormwood to the acid of her nature. In Eileen she found someone on whom she could vent her spite against life.

That afternoon she had been more than usually unbearable. "I s'pose you figger on settin' 'round and waiting for your pap to die and leave the farm to you?" she asked Eileen. "Well, leave me tell you, Missie, you'll never get an inch o' *this* land. I'll see to it that he cuts you out o' his will. And meantime there'll be no idle hands around here. I need some things at Eberhardt's. Go get 'em for me. Right away, not next week." She handed Eileen a small shopping list—thread, needles, pins, little, unconsidered trifles that could be packed in a pocket—and, "Now, off you go," she ordered, "and see that you get back by supper time. No traipsing off with men, the way your mother—

"Leave my mother out o' this, ye *collich*," Eileen broke in with a wrathful sob. "'Tis a thing you're not fit to soil her name with your foul tongue!"

THEY said that ghosts walked in the little cemetery after sunset. Ghosts of the men who lay in Rebels' Rest.

Eileen had heard a dozen different versions of the story, yet all were substantially the same. How John McCausland's men had ridden into Chambersburg that morning in July of '64, levied a tribute of a hundred thousand dollars on the town, then burnt it to the ground and rode away with shouts of laughter. By God, their cause might be a lost one, but they, at least, had singed old Grant's whiskers! And then the tale went on to tell how the militia and the enraged farmers poured a spilth of lead on them as they rode pell-mell to rejoin Jubal Early, how saddle after saddle had been emptied, so that where six hundred laughing, roistering bully boys had ridden into Chambersburg that morning a scant five hundred reached McConnellsburg.

Death had wiped out animosities, so when the rebels had retreated the farmers gathered up their dead and laid them side by side with demurely folded hands on their breasts and caps pulled down upon their faces, and when a plot had been marked off for them in the graveyard old Pastor Brubaker had read his office over them.

They had been buried properly, those wild Virginia lads, with prayer and Scripture reading, aye, and a word of forgiveness from the pastor, but still men said they could not rest. Some said they found the cold earth of this northern country a hard bed; some— and these were the majority—declared they hungered for revenge.

The whispering night wind chased the clouds that clawed with ghostly fingers at the newly risen moon as Eileen reached the cemetery gate, and for an instant everything was almost bright as noon, then a black cloud wrack slid over the moon's disc, and shadows obscured everything.

She felt everything inside her coming loose, and had no notion what to do about it as the cloud-curtain moved away and she saw a form by the grilled gate of the graveyard.

It was a man—or shaped like one—a slim and neatly built young man with sunburned cheeks and a thin line of dark mustache across his upper lip. He wore a gray suit and long boots, a yellow kerchief looped about his neck, and a little yellow cap with a black leather visor was set jauntily upon his curling hair.

"*Ovoch!*" Eileen felt the hot breath churn in her throat. "If you're a natural man, God save ye, sir; but if you're a Thing o' the Darkness, Christ's agony between us!"

"Faith, 'tis a long time I've been waitin' for a civil word!" The young man smiled and raised a hand to his cap in semi-military salute. "Thank ye kindly for your courtesy, me dear. I could not spake till I was spoken to, an' though I've waited more nor eighty year before this selfsame gate the only greetin' I've received until jist now has been a frightening squeal."

"God save us all," Eileen quavered, "you're Irish!"

"As Irish as they come, me jewel. I'm Teig McCarthy—Teig O'Shane McCarthy, late—too late, God knows!—o' th' parish o' Clondevaddock in th' County o' Galway."

Fear slipped from Eileen as a wave slides off the beach: "And whatever are ye doin' here, poor creature?" she asked.

"Ochone, 'tis a long story, so it is, yet not so long as I could wish for," answered he with an infectious grin. "'Teig, *avick',* me father—may th' turf lie lightly on him!—says to me, 'there's naught but mortgages to be raised on th' ould place, an' precious few o' them. Ye'd best be goin' to Ameriky to seek your fortune, as your Cousin Dion did.'

"So off I goes like any silly goose o' Westmeath, an' prisently I comes to rest on Misther Dabney Fortesque's plantation in Virginny. There's war abrewin' in th' States, an' prisently they're callin' ivery able-bodied man to th' colors. You know how 'tis, pulse o' me heart; a fight's a fight to an Irishman, an' divil a bit cared I which side I fought on, so long as they were givin' me a horse to ride an' three meals ivery day an' now an' then a spot o' pay.

"Then off we rides, an' prisently we comes to Chambersburg where we scares th' Yankees out o' siven years fine growth before we sets th' town ablaze about their ears. But as we rides away one of 'em gets me in th' chist wid his bullet and drops me deader nor a herring! Ah, well, I don't know as I should complain. 'Twas war, an' if he hadn't shot me 'tis altogether likely I'd ha' shot him. At any rate, they gave me dacent buryin', an' here I've been for more nor eighty year—"

"But why is it you're walkin' now?" Eileen demanded. "Is it that ye have a debt unpaid, or sins upon your soul—"

"Whist, dear one, don't be talkin'!" he broke in. "We're a queer lot, an' a lonesome lot, we dead folk from th' *Innis Fodhla.* Were you yersilf in some strange land for eighty year an' more, an' niver able to go back, there'd be a hunger on your soul for news o' home. Isn't it so?"

"It is!" Eileen agreed fervently. "And ghost or man, 'tis glad I am I've found ye, Teig McCarthy, for 'tis meself that comes from County Galway, with the heart o' me a-breakin' to go home."

IMPULSIVELY she put her hands out to him. *"Och*, Teig McCarthy, can't you see me heart is hollow with homesickness?"

"Hold hard, Eileen *alannah!*" he warned. "I'm yearnin' for ye like a drunkard for his draught, but if ye put your lips to mine ye join me. Mind ye, girl, th' quick an' dead can't mingle, an' th' dead may not come back!"

"No matter, Teig *avourneen,*" she breathed softly. "No— matter—" Her voice sank to a muted whisper and her eyes closed as she leant toward him with parted lips. "Ah, Teig, Teig McCarthy, ye jewel o' the world!"

Slowly, deliberately, he drew her to him, put his arms about her, kissed her on the mouth. He kissed her slowly, bending her head back against his arm till she felt weak and helpless, and glad to be that way at last. A cloud-veil crept across the moon like a blind being drawn, and darkness spread over the landscape. All about them was the scent of pine trees and the stillness of the night.

Suppertime came at the Huneke farm, but no Eileen. Night passed and morning dawned, cool, clear and lovely, with limpid, bright pellucid air and sunlight sparkling over everything. But no sign of Eileen.

With dogs borrowed from the sheriff's office they traced her from the village to the cemetery, and at the gate the hounds gave little frightened whimpers and cringed against the deputy.

There was a susurrus of gossip at the next meeting of the Ladies' Sewing Circle. "The cemetery, eh?" Mrs. Thea Hauptmann shook her head like one who fears—and hopes for— the worst. "The cemetery. H'mm. A nice, secluded, woodsy place. Like mother like daughter, I always say. You listen to me once. That girl went off with someone!"

Which was unquestionably so.

THE END

DEATH HAS GREEN EYES

By John W. Jakes

*Because red is usually the danger signal. Henry Brundage walked
straight into trouble when the green lights began to beckon...*

BEHIND him, Mrs. Pietro was shrieking. Behind him too,
in the dingy apartment, lay his wife; his nagging, irritable and
now very dead wife. Henry Brundage ran wildly down the
twilight-washed street. His gray hair flapped, and the gun was
still in his left hand.

People turned to peer at him, and then stopped to stare. The
gun joggled as he ran on, his mind whirled and burned by the
thought of his crime, and the more horrible thought that he
must run, for he had been discovered.

For years he had struggled with his fear of the forces of
justice; a fear that had kept his wife alive. Long months ago he
had bought a gun. Several times he had almost worked himself
into a violent rage, in which he would have killed her. But her
voice always stopped him. She would look at him and seem to
see what he planned, and her great green eyes would bulge wide
with mirth as she laughed. "You'll never do it, Henry. Because
you know they'll catch you. They always catch killers. You
know if you ever killed me there would be no way out. You
would be caught. Every road in the world leads back to one
point. The police." And then she had laughed hilariously,
jeering at his fright.

But now it was done. She had been weak with a cold and a
fever. She hadn't been able to talk to him, except in frantic
whispers. He had overcome the fear of the law and shot her to
death. Only Mrs. Pietro, the landlady, had come running into
the room, and seen him with the gun in his hand.

So he was running, without thought of anything but escape.
Escape that led back to the police, who even now might be

answering a call from Mrs. Pietro to the station house a few blocks away.

His breath drove sharp jabs of pain through his body. Stumbling, he leaned on an iron railing. He raised his eyes and saw the gloomy frame of an el station towering against the sky.

Elevated train, he thought. Train. Move. Escape. *Escape!*

He took a step toward the first stair and clawed at the rail. The world around him tilted and fell away. Darkness seeped in about the edges of his vision, like ink on a blotter. He felt himself pulled down.

Brundage struggled to rise, fighting back the dark. His breathing, which he had not been able to hear for a moment, sounded again. He pulled himself upright. His body felt remote, as if it were slipping away in another direction, and his consciousness was the only thing to be preserved.

Sobbing with loud jagged gasps, he raced up the shadowy stairs. He could hear Mrs. Pietro down the block, jabbering to the neighbors. And there were other voices. Mumbling, curious voices. Voices that would bring the law.

As he staggered to the landing, he was vaguely aware that he should remember something about the el station. He almost felt that he shouldn't be there, but the notion vanished in the stress of the moment.

For here was sanctuary; moving wheels that would roll far from his apartment; and beyond, buses or trains into the great dark night of the whole wide world. They would never find him.

HE RUSHED past the ticket window, not even glancing to see if the cashier was there. A single car waited on the platform, yellow light spilling from it. Hastily he pocketed the gun.

The conductor on the train platform was an indistinct blur. Brundage couldn't make out even the semblance of a face or figure. But the lights of the train were comforting. He gasped and hurried inside, huddling down on a cream wicker seat. With a ghostly sigh, the wheels began to turn.

After a few moments of calm relief, Brundage examined his situation. The car was empty, and the conductor was a dark blob on the platform, motionless. A clackety-clackety echoed within Brundage's thoughts. *Killed her dead,* it repeated, *killed her dead.* The tone was one of extreme pleasure.

He wiped one veined hand across his forehead and brushed back a lock of gray hair dangling before his eyes. The fear was slowly vanishing. What an easy thing after all. The police would never trace him. And his disgusting wife would no longer mock him because he was a rather pathetic failure as a human being. Her immense green eyes were closed. Forever.

He noticed that the train was curving around a bend. That wasn't correct. Not correct at all. He knew, as most citizens of the city knew, the direction in which the elevated ran. That direction was straight.

Rising, with the secure weight of the gun pressing his side, he moved to the platform. The conductor remained formless darkness.

"Pardon me," Brundage said with a false calm, "where does this train stop?"

"We make one stop," was the answer, and Brundage realized that he should recognize the voice.

"What is the stop?"

"We make one stop," came the reply again, hollow and dismal.

Brundage felt a small shiver go dancing up his back with pattering feet. He also felt an urgent need to reassure himself of the security of the train.

"I wish you wouldn't stand out there," he said.

"Very well," answered the shapeless conductor. He walked forward into the car, and yellow light dripped down and washed away the black like vanishing dirt.

"Where is the one stop?" Brundage began.

He gagged and grasped for his gun, fumbling, *fumbling...*

For the conductor was not a conductor at all. He…or *it*…was a grotesque caricature of his wife, and from its face two monstrous green eyes bulged and burned.

"This train," wheezed the thing, "goes only one way, like all the other trains and all the other roads. To the police."

Brundage cried out brokenly. The gun was caught in the lining of his jacket. The green eyes were over him, pressing down.

As his gun came free, the yellow lights of the train vanished entirely. The old fear of being trapped fountained up in him, pouring through every nerve and fiber. With tremendous effort he tried to squeeze the trigger, but he could not. The eyes were two green suns, closer and closer. Over them he heard a mocking whine of speech, and it was his *wife's* voice. "The fear, Henry. The fear that always leads back…to the police…"

He saw the green eyes and they were all around him. They reached inside his skull and scorched his brain.

And then, for all time, there was nothing.

"IS THAT the whole story?" the sergeant said tiredly, fiddling with his pencil, weary of the long session of sobs and moans.

Mrs. Pietro leaned against the high desk, nodding and crying more loudly than ever.

"Shoquist," said the sergeant to another policeman standing by the woman, "when you got to the apartment, what did you find?"

Shoquist waved one hand aimlessly. "Found the woman, dead. The husband had gone."

"Did anybody on the street see him go?"

"Yeah. They said he ran about a block, and stopped a minute at the old el station. Then he started on again, down the street, just like he wasn't thinking. Bumping into things. Falling. By the time I took up the trail, he was gone completely."

"Well he sure as hell wouldn't have gone into the el station," the sergeant snorted. "There haven't been any trains running for eight months at least."

"I know that," Shoquist replied, "but I checked anyway. He wasn't there. And there's no way he could have gotten down beside the one stairway."

"Maybe he…" the sergeant was saying. There was a loud shouting. Another officer gestured wildly. Shoquist and the sergeant strode rapidly to where the policeman stood pointing at the sidewalk beyond the window glass.

"He came walking down the street," the man mumbled, "like he couldn't think, and something was dragging him to this place. He walked right up in front of the door, and looked at it, and all of a sudden, it was like…like his mind was *pulled back* from somewhere…" His face quivered as he breathed, "Christ, it was terrible."

Shoquist and the sergeant were already outside, kneeling beside the figure. "This is him all right," Shoquist asserted. "I saw a picture of him."

Henry Brundage lay on his back, arms and legs spread wide apart. The gun was still clutched in one hand. He was dead, but his mouth gaped and his face was twisted in a frightening expression.

In spite of death, his eyes were wide open. They seemed to be staring sightlessly in unearthly horror. They seemed to be watching the two light globes on either side of the station door.

The globes were like two great eyes of green brilliance, flaring in the night.

THE END

THE HAND OF SAINT URY

By Gordon MacCreagh

An old theory has it that a thought of hate can be a powerful enough force to persist after the death of its originator.

YOUNG Jimmy Doak presented his advertisement at the office of the *London Times:*

WANTED—Research worker, experienced in genealogy.
J. Doak, Hotel Cecil.

The girl behind the help-wanted desk smiled. Jimmy was immediately belligerent.

"And it does *not* stand for Joe."

The girl looked hurt. Being English, she had no idea that Joe Doak was an American collective cognomen assigned to ridicule. Her smile had been an unconscious recognition of Jimmy's handsome head with its wavy dark hair and serious eyes. Even the just now angry mouth was no detriment to a strong sort of attractiveness.

"And I suppose the ad is funny too?" Jimmy self-consciously challenged.

"Oh, by no means," the girl said quickly. "Thousands of Americans come to trace their family history. They're hoping always to find an old title—or at least a family ghost."

"Gosh, are there that many of them?" Jimmy went out grumbling. "Chasing antique families. I'd rather chase antiques."

Which is just what he went and did. It was in a little lost end of an alley off Marrowbone Road that he found a little lost Old Curiosity Shop that might have survived right out of Dickens, with a battered overhead sign and diamond pane windows and cobwebs all complete.

"Huh! Probably artificial." Jimmy had seen how spider webbing was made for American movies. "But good browsing, I expect."

That was just what the proprietor expected, too. He looked over the edge of his spectacles and invited crustily, "Just call me if you see anything as interests you." He went on picking at and polishing a trayful of the assorted rubbish that collects in a shop of that kind. A scuffling on a broad overhead shelf bothered him. He looked angrily through his eyebrows. "Blarsted nuisances! They don't usually get up there." But he did no more about it than go on with his work.

Jimmy presently brought a small jar to the counter. "What would you want for this majolica piece?"

The old man was irritable but honest.

"Well now, sir, I wouldn't delude you on that there. 'S a matterafact I don't believe it is genuine. You see—" The scuffling and scrabbling overhead distracted him. "If I 'ad a 'undred bloomin' traps I couldn't keep the bloody pests down. I thought I 'ad 'em rid; but never 'eard 'em so bold as now." He was turning the jar over in his hands when forcefully shoved objects clinked overhead and a grizzly object fell with a dry plop onto the counter. Jimmy started back from it, grimacing sickly. The thing was a human hand! Old and desiccate, the fingers gruesomely half hooked as though in some last spasm. A thin tracery of spider webs spanned the contorted fingertips. A particular horror was a ring that rattled on the withered first joint of the index finger, held in place by the thicker bent joint. It might have been a signet or something set with two little red stones, almost like snake eyes.

As Jimmy recoiled, the proprietor poked at it gingerly himself. "Cawn't say as I like it myself, sir. A beastly sort of a piece, what?"

"What the hell is it?" Jimmy asked. "I mean, where—" The shop was mustily stuffy. Jimmy took off his overcoat and dropped it on the counter. "Where did you ever get a thing like that?"

"It's supposed to be the 'and of Saint Ury, sir; though I 'ave no idea 'oo 'e ever was. That 'ole through the middle is said to be stigmata—what made 'im a saint, you know. Though if you awsk me," the man evinced all the disillusionment of an antiquarian, "—I'd say somebody bloody well drove a nail through it."

Jimmy shuddered away. He left the jar there and went to examine things at the far end of the shop. But that horrid relic persisted in his vision. Almost as though some involuntary war activity—shrapnel or something—had caused such a maiming that he had never known about it but for which he might indirectly blame. He could imagine the broken thing, hating the world, and wanting to get back at him. He could find no pleasure in browsing.

"Think I'll be going," he said. "Some other time perhaps—"

The proprietor was stuffing his rubbish amongst the other clutter of his shelves. "It's orl right, sir. Glad to 'ave you look around, sir."

JIMMY took up his coat and went. He was barely round the corner when he heard footsteps pattering after him; and there was the proprietor, panting and furious.

"You give me back that there 'and, young man," he spluttered. "Or I'll 'ave to call the police."

Jimmy recoiled. "What d'you mean, the hand? D'you think I'd touch the filthy thing."

"You certainly did, young feller. I've seen the likes o' you before. There it was a'lyin' one minute, and the next thing you was gone and it, too. You with them big pockets." He dived at Jimmy and thrust his hands into the overcoat pockets—and there, out of one of them, he fished the horrid object.

Jimmy's stomach heaved. His mouth opened in protest; but he had to shut it again quickly to swallow his nausea.

"There we are!" The proprietor triumphed. "You bloody Yanks'll swipe hanythink for a souvenir. Now just you pay me a pound, young man, and I'll say nothink about this."

"It's a racket!" Jimmy knew then. A damned panel joint game. Slip something into the chump's pocket and then yelp about shoplifting.

"One pound." The proprietor held out an open hand. "Or I ups and whistles for them."

So what could Jimmy do but pay? He was here on business; he couldn't waste time in a court over a shameful charge of shoplifting. He went to his hotel more disgruntled than ever about this whole silly business. He spent a night dreaming about dried hands that crawled like hairy spiders all over his bed.

OVER a fantastic breakfast of bloaters on toast and porridge he was discreetly paged—not piercingly shouted for by any brass-buttoned midget. A desk clerk bent over his table.

"A lady to see you, sir."

"A lady? I—I don't think I know any ladies in London."

"In response to an advertisement of yours, sir."

Jimmy went rather uncertainly to the lobby. In his mind had been an idea that it was professional men who did this sort of thing. He was quite glad that he had been wrong. A delightful picture awaited him; a girl, neatly dressed in something that showed a figure, with alert eyes in a fresh round face and a cute turned-up nose and full lips.

"I came in a hurry to be the first," she smiled at him ingenuously. "Because, frankly, I need the job, and the competition for this sort of thing is ferocious."

"Oh?" said Jimmy. "Are you—I mean, d'you know how to go about all this unpleasant business of digging up dead relatives?"

"Certainly, Mr. Doak. I have a certificate from the College of Heraldry." She fished papers out of a bag. "We are trained in all the various avenues of research. You wish, I presume, to trace your ancestry. Somewhere back from British stock, is it?"

Jimmy felt silly again. "It's just my dad. This name, you know. Like in a comic book. Well, Dad doesn't believe any human being was ever deliberately named Doak. He thinks there must be some mix-up somewhere along the line. He's heard so many wisecracks about it, it's got to be a complex."

"Surely. We understand about that. Thousands of corruptions crept into names during the illiterate Middle Ages. There were probably officials or other people who wrote down names in some sort of official capacity who didn't themselves really know how to spell—probably even often-illiterate pronunciations— We have old books and records about all those things."

"You do seem to know all about it. Then you'll take on the chore?"

The girl smiled confidently. "That's what I came for." And then diffidently, "Er, we usually work on a day and expense basis."

Jimmy was feeling more at ease since he knew there were other people who wished they could be called something else. "Oh, of course. You need a retaining fee or something."

The girl had two distinct dimples. "I could use it. And I shall go straight to the museum and have some information for you by tomorrow morning. You might, in the meantime, call up the paper and cancel your advertisement. Right? Cheerio."

JIMMY got a *Times* to look up the telephone number—and there the horrid story stared him in the face:
"American Accused of Shoplifting"

The rewrite man was able to see what seemed to Jimmy to be a far-fetched British humor in his shameful experience; and it was worse even than he knew. The story went on: "So badly did this queer fellow want the relic that he apparently returned that night and broke into the shop to get it. A mystery note, however, comes in, for the police report that only a single small pane of glass was broken; and the extraordinary part of it all was that the glass was pushed out from the *inside!* Almost as though the thing had loved him at first sight, and had jumped out to him of its own volition. Saintly hands, of course, have been known to accomplish miracles more astounding than that."

What a foul thought! That a thing like that should want to be friends! Jimmy had a creep all over to think of putting his hand into his pocket and finding the horny thing clasping his fingers. His next immediate reaction, naturally, was that he was a fugitive from lynx-eyed Scotland Yard. But the paper had given no description of him. He breathed easier, reflecting that the thing, after all, had no great value. It had remained, as its spider webs attested, on that top shelf for who knew how many years before it jumped down to— Jimmy, too, jumped from his chair with a hunted look. It had not been rats! If it had not jumped down of its own volition, how had the foul thing crawled into his pocket? Could it be really true that there were haunts in this old country of ancient traditions?

With a mad impulse Jimmy raced to his room to hunt through his coat pockets again. No. Thank God! Jimmy grinned sheepishly to himself. What a foolishness! But the beastly thing had made such a horrid impression on him. Why wouldn't it, getting into his pocket that way? Then Jimmy's eyes widened and he made a dash for his suitcase. Perhaps it— That damned reporter's loathsome suggestion that it had fallen in love with him—! He stood off to survey each tumbled article on the bed. His breath blew from him in a vast relief. He lit a comforting pipe and sat down to consider a reasonable theory for himself. The most reasonable one was that the proprietor, obviously a vile-tempered old crank, had flown into an insane rage and hurled the miserable thing through his own window pane. And then, repenting, he had gone out to retrieve the implement of his cunning racket, to find that some stray cat or something had run off with it, and he had been ashamed, then, to admit his silly rage.

"Bloody fool!" Jimmy expressed his quickly learned Anglicism. "And me too. This business of digging into dead men's pasts gets a guy morbid. But, phe-ew, what an experience!"

MORNING brought the girl, full of news and triumphant. "You never even asked my name," she blamed him and herself in the one breath. "And I was so staggered with the amount of money you advanced that I just ran. I'm Eula Bogue." She dimpled. "It used to be Boggs—that's how I got into this research work. And I have lots of news. Let's sit down and look at it."

In businesslike manner she spread sheaves of notes over the little desk. "For just now let's never mind all the false starts. Let's look first at what seems to be a definite lead. It goes a long, fascinatingly way back. There seems to have been a very old Anglo-Saxon name, Dork, or Dawk, or Dock, spelled half a dozen ways. Mostly north of England."

Jimmy whistled. "Whe-ee! As far back as that? Dad would sure be tickled. And it could be, I suppose, that it was twisted to Doak?"

"Oh, very possibly indeed. With the illiterate Puritan emigration from here, you know. And there's something even more exciting. Up in Cumberlandshire there's a little place called Dockbridge, apparently the family hometown, and there's one of those fearfully old manor houses that's been built over and rebuilt and remodeled and its' full of rats and rattly windows and a mouldy library and a housekeeper and—it's vacant!" She finished all of that in one breath.

Jimmy was thrilling in response to her enthusiasm. "You mean, we could go there and dig in the library?"

"If," she said uncertainly, "you could—I mean, all you Americans are rich, aren't you—if you could afford to rent the place for a week or so."

"Gee!" said Jimmy. "A post-grad in ancient history! I'll cable Dad we've got a hot lead. So let's go."

DOCKBRIDGE manor house was not quite as Eula had described it. The more modern part was not full of rats and even had a bathroom. It was built on a knoll and apparently at one time there had been a moat, now a sunken garden of unkempt cannas and iris and weeds. There were crumbly walls and moss-grown mounds of masonry, some of which had been rock gardened and then left. Clearly, with the current austerity, it was too expensive to keep up and now stood hopefully for rent.

The housekeeper, a gaunt lady dressed in ghostly gray, had lived so long with the older conventions that she turned a sternly disapproving eye on so modern an intrusion as a young man and a girl.

"I'm Mrs. Medford," she introduced herself. "And I'm as good a chaperone as any. So, if the young gentleman will carry the bags, I'll show you to your rooms."

She showed them to rooms discreetly separated at the two ends of a musty right-angled corridor. She had quite clearly moved her own things into a room right at the corner.

"So that, if you need 'elp, Miss, I'll 'ear your call."

"Why, the idea!" Eula flamed scarlet all round to the back of her neck.

"Oh, I down't mean from 'im, Miss. Though I wouldn't put it past 'im. We saw all about them good-lookin' Yanks during their invasion. It's just that old Sir 'arry's ghost miauws around moonless nights; 'im that was Prince Charlie's Marster of 'Orse when the old manor stood, what's foundations this is on."

Eula laughed gaily. "All my frowzy browsing"—as though she'd spent twenty years at it—"and I've never had a ghost yet."

The housekeeper's disapproval sank several notches lower. "It's you moderns as ain't no reverence. But *I* sees 'em!"

Jimmy stared at her. He was developing a habit of staring at these sudden surprises. Mrs. Medford seemed to be accustomed to surprising people. She added to this one, "You, sir, will not be 'earing the miaulin's and prowlin's on your side. You're over the old chapel. So your windows 'as the bars.

Jimmy looked his question at Eula, as though she ought to know all the conventions of old manors. The housekeeper offered the logical answer.

"Because them as don't say prayers regular goes balmy and jumps. I'll serve dinner before dark, sir and ma'am. We don't dress nowadays." She went sternly about her affairs.

"Is it an act?" Jimmy all unconsciously whispered it.

Eula giggled. "I think the poor soul has gone a little balmy herself, living alone in this mouldy old place. The library ought to yield pure gold. We'll dig tomorrow."

EVEN tomorrow's sun couldn't make a cheerful breakfast, because the morning paper had another item by the same rewrite man who dealt in humor.

NORTH LONDON DRUNKS HAVE
A NEW HEEBIE-JEEBIE

It's not pink elephants any more for a party of late home-stragglers from the Coach and Horn pub on the Lincoln Road. It's a five-legged spider the size of a saucer that runs along the dark gutters with the speed of a greyhound.

Well, of course, there was nothing so much to that. But Jimmy stared at the paper with a reluctant horror. For the item went on:

Curious verification comes from two boys—models of rectitude, their parents insist—who say they saw it by dawn's gray light, scuttling along a country lane ten miles farther North in Middlesex. Only, to their juvenile imaginations, not so far removed from fairy lore—

This was the part that held Jimmy's eyes in their wide stare.

—it looked more like a hand running on its fingertips.

"What's the matter?" Eula was alarmed at Jimmy's pallor.

He pushed the paper to her, waited while she read the item, and to her answering stare said, "Did you see the one about the Yank shoplifting a dead hand, and then the broken window?" And, as she nodded, he silently pointed his finger to his own chest.

"You? Good heavens! But you didn't, of course."

"No, I wouldn't touch the filthy thing. But—you know more about these antique incubi. What does it all mean? Why is it following me north?"

Eula was, for the first time, serious. "Why do you say 'incubi'? As though this one were hung onto you. Of course, we do have a lot of spooky legends in an old country like this; some of them accepted as authentic by professors of psychic lore; such as the Glastonbury crypt and the Monster of Glamis Castle. But a dried hand—" She closed her eyes in tight thought. "Wait a minute. Let me think. What is it about, somewhere, a 'hand of glory'—? But no. That's just black magic."

"Just black magic." Jimmy repeated it. "That's all. So what is this? A pure white symbol of grace?"

Eula made herself laugh again. "Oh, it's all rubbish! Some drunks have a D.T. and some boys read about it and let their imaginations run. This is our usual summer hysteria—to fill up space in the paper when there's no crime. You'll see."

AND within a couple of days they did see. A *Times* reader correspondent, and amateur entomologist, wrote a solemn article decrying hysteria and offered his theory that a tarantula (a large Central American spider, he injected his educational note) might very easily have been imported with a bunch of bananas and that, like all the arachnida, was capable of running with a considerable speed that to people under the influence of liquor—etc., etc.

"There! You see?" said Eula. "Now perhaps you can help me with some of this mouldy reading."

The reading proved to be exciting. The library, although a muddle of volumes saved up from, it seemed, the beginning of printing, but never indexed, contained ancient tomes of incunabula, and even manuscript.

"Priceless!" Eula mooned over the mess. "I mean, even in money. And to think that the owner never comes here, nor, I suppose, has ever opened a book."

The housekeeper stood at the door. She had an uncanny memory for having, once upon a time, dusted some volume and, if any of the old family names had appeared, remembering them.

"'E don't come," she stated like a Hecuba, "because this 'ouse gives 'im the 'errors."

"I think," said Jimmy, "some of these books all about battle and murder and sudden death would give me the horrors if I should read them all."

"That's out of the prayer book," Mrs. Medford accused him. "Which, if you doesn't say it reverent, the Lord says the blasphemers shall perish. And if you'd a but told me you was a'unting for old family names, I'd a told the young lady, pore thing, to look in that there book with the brown binding ate by roaches."

"Why poor thing?" Eula grimaced.

"Ah!" said Mrs. Medford.

Only that, "Aa-ah!" and she drifted grayly out.

But the book proved to be some of the gold mine Eula had expected.

"Look! Oh, looky! Here's 'Ye Hystorie of ye Familye of ye Noble Sieur Armand D'Auk wyth his Battailles and his Honneurs.'"

"They sure thought up long titles in those days," Jimmy obtusely said.

"Yes, but don't you see, Silly? There's your name! D'Auk!— Dork, Dock, Doak, and I suppose dozens of other spellings. Norman origin, not Anglo-Saxon. I expect we'll be finding your dad to be one of our oldest families."

"Golly!" said Jimmy. "Damn if I don't think it may be. Can you read that olde Englyshe stuff?"

"Of course. What the roaches haven't eaten. And—it seems there ought to be three more volumes of it. Perhaps Mrs. Medford knows where to find—we must get a ton of paper and you take the notes while I puzzle it all out."

THE excitement of this find was such that they didn't read the morning paper until the afternoon. And then both looked at each other, questioning what each thought. For a sober scientist had written his screed to the *Times*, attacking with all the virulence of scientists the "insufficiently informed" opinion of a layman who dared to shoot off his mouth.

A tarantula, he maintained, while capable of moving with considerable speed when attacking its food, was a creature as sedentary as a wolf spider or a common household daddy-long-legs; that all of them spent their life span within a circumscribed radius of perhaps no more than fifty feet; that the distance of ten miles was ridiculous to the point of impossibility; and that this thing that the boys had seen in upper Middlesex, whatever else it might be, was certainly not a tarantula; and furthermore, a tarantula was not a nocturnal hunter nor could it withstand the night temperatures of the English countryside; and, if it could, it would be in a lethargic and dormant condition.

His thorough disposal of that matter left Jimmy's dark question:

"Then what was it? If not my—" his inadvertent slip brought a shiver. "If not that damned hand?"

Eula reassured him. "Oh, what does it matter what it was? A something. A scurrying rat, a rabbit, an anything. We've got much more exciting things here to speculate about. Look. This D'Auks whole name was The Sieur Armand D'Auk D'Auberge and—" She suddenly clapped her hands. "Why, there it is! D'Auk D'Auberge— From which, following Grimm's law of colloquial sublimation, we get Dockbridge. This very village and the manor. Now for some of his 'battailles' and his 'honneurs', and there ought to be his 'offsprynges' somewhere."

THE research, while fascinating, was jarred to a standstill more than once by the morning paper that both of them avidly scanned for any follow-up on the tarantula that couldn't be a tarantula. The rewrite man was not laughing any more. He was calling it now, "The Spider Horror." There was the item about a lady, a stern and very well-balanced social worker, who was going home late from her church meeting and had been attacked by the Horror!

"I saw it in the moonlight," she related to her interviewer. "Scurrying along like a—well, like something I, for one, had never seen before. So I struck at it with my umbrella and—now I cannot truthfully say that it snarled at me; but I could see its wicked little red eyes; and then it leaped at me! At least three or four feet, the distance must have been from my umbrella end. And it caught me by the ankle and threw me down; and then I suppose—no, I have never fainted. I should say not. But then I don't know what happened. When I came to—I mean, when I could see again, it was gone."

"Did you notice," Jimmy pointed out, "*where* that happened? In Leicestershire."

"Well, so what?"

"Still coming *north!* Following!"

Eula shrank away, envisioning a dead, mummified hand's relentless coming. "But, Jimmy, it *can't* be! She saw its red eyes, she said."

"The ring!"

Eula's hand covered her lips. "D'you really think the thing is after you for some weird reason? Like a voodoo or something?"

"How should I know? I don't know anything about voodoo."

"But, coming from America, isn't that sort of in your back yard? Your Negroes, you know; and Haiti. Don't they kill chickens with their teeth and project occult 'sendings'? Little dolls and snakes and things to go and carry curses and—?"

"Helluva idea you've got of America," Jimmy growled.

"Well, I've read it somewhere. And you're the one who insists it's following you. Jimmy, I'm afraid."

"*You're* afraid?"

"Yes, because—I mean, if it's as real as that; not just summer hysteria; and if it can jump at a strong-minded lady who hits it with an umbrella and can catch her by the leg and throw her down, it could—" She shivered close to him.

It was Jimmy's role to comfort her. "Well, at least it didn't bite her when her strong mind went out like a weak light. After all, what can it do, wandering about the country like a homeless ghost—" He wished immediately he had not said that. "What I mean, what gave me the willies was just looking at the beastly thing. Come on, let's lunch."

Mrs. Medford supplied a skimpy lunch. "Seein' as 'ow the hiceman didn't come, the cold chicken went bad, so I gave it to Lady Jane."

Lady Jane was her woolly poodle that yapped at flies and assiduously hunted cockroaches in baseboard corners. The skimpiness of the lunch didn't matter because Mrs. Medford banished all appetite, remarking out of nowhere:

"It's a'comin' 'ome!"

Both Jimmy and Eula sat suddenly stiff in their chairs. Mrs. Medford answered their stares with, "I've read it in the paper, same's you 'ave." To which she added the shock, "And me bein' a seventh daughter, I *seen it!*"

"Good Lord!" Jimmy had until now been willing to accept Eula's comforting theory that he had received a gruesomely strong impression and was attaching it to similarly gruesome accounts in the newspaper. "What d'you mean, it's coming home and you've 'seen' it?"

"I don't know, sir, just what it means. All I can say is, I was a'setting with me old friend, Mrs. Shaughnessy, she being psychic (physic, she pronounced it) and all a suddent I seen it in the dark before my mind's eye. A yuman 'and it was and it was nailed to a board! And Mrs. Shaughnessy she says, 'If you seen it, that means it must belong in your 'ouse, else why wouldn't I seen it too?'"

Jimmy, sanely unaccustomed to the jargons and hallucinations of psychics, flouted the phantasmagoria. "You've been reading the horror story in the paper and so you sat wishing for spooks and you dreamed the picture up in your imagination." And he repeated his self encouragement. "After all, what could a thing like that do?"

"Ah!" said Mrs. Medford. "Aa-ah!"

The paper showed what it could do.

"A Mister Bill Dibbs," it reported, "of Kirkby-Sheperd in Westmoreland, a gentleman who has had his difficulties with Lord Gravely's gamekeeper, was strolling home with two dogs and a gun—harmlessly enjoying the moonlit night, he insists— when his dogs flushed the 'Spider Horror' out of a ditch. The thing raced, he reports, along the edge of the road with incredible speed. He just happened, he says, to have had a cartridge in his gun and he would have shot the whatever it was, but for the dogs that were too close after it. They chased it into a copse and there he heard all the frenzied barking and scuffling of what might have been a rabbit hunt. Until suddenly one of the dogs let out a piercing yelp and came cringing back to him in apparent terror, as though it might have found a bear, and the other dog was ominously silent. His gun ready for emergency, he entered the shadows of the copse to investigate, and there, to his consternation, found his dog dead. Strangled! Choked, Mr. Dibbs said, as though by some strong man. The gamekeeper reports having found nothing more menacing than rabbits in all the surrounding woods. The local police opinion is that it is funny that all these untoward happenings always occur at night and always to unreliable people."

Jimmy's only question to all this was, "Where's Westmoreland?"

"The shire just south of Cumberland where we are." Eula clung to his arm. "Jimmy, it can't be true, is it?"

"Comin' 'ome!" Jimmy quoted. "What do you in England do about getting a gun? And who is there who can tell us about the aims and motivations of this sort of thing? The whole works, I mean. All these stories added up, it can't be anything other than that brutal hand thing I saw in the store. The 'Hand of Saint Ury', he said; and not holy stigmata, but a nail hole. And our gray ghost woman threw her fit and saw it nailed to a board. So, very well, who can tell us what turned it loose. How? Why it's crawling home at night? Why pick on this place—on *me*—all the way up from London. If it gets here, what's it good for—or bad for? Who can tell us all about the rules and regulations of the haunt union?"

Eula frowned out of the window.

"There's a whole lot of psychic investigators. I think the best would be possibly Dr. Eugene Harries. He's one of the W. T. Stead Foundation and a member of the Psychic Research Society. They go about shooting holes into the ghost stories that crop up every now and then and they publish a bulletin about their findings. What I don't like is that every now and then, too, they find some horrid thing that they can't laugh off."

"Let's invite him in and throw the whole thing into his lap," said Jimmy promptly. "So we can put in a little time on our own work on ye olde Brityshe Familyes. The deeper we dig into the tomes, the better Dad will be pleased. Heck, make us Doaks respectable old-timers, and I'll hold him up to pay for our honeymoon."

"Wha-a-at?" Eula sprang away from him and put the great old carved desk between them, her eyes wider than at any time over Mrs. Medford's revelations.

"Well, we Doakses have to be respectable; and it would be the only way to quell Mrs. Medford's disapproving eye."

"Good-heavens!" The shock was burning Eula all the way up to her hair, rising like a red flame. "You Americans are certainly sudden. Is that the way you always propose?"

"Sometimes they do it in an automobile or some such romantic spot; but I figure you Englishers, with all your haunts and such, would have to be different."

Eula was recovering some of her composure. "Here we almost never marry our boss. We have too much work to do."

"Work to do *together*," Jimmy said. "Come on and dig. We've been neglecting the gold mine."

IT TURNED out to be, as Jimmy unknowingly said, a dynamite mine. Though, when they first found it, they were thrilled.

"Ooh, look! The Sieur D'Auk was 'Lord of ye High Justice and ye Middle and ye Low' and a 'ryghte valliante Carryer of ye Crosse.'"

"Does that mean a preacher? Another Saint?"

"No, silly. A crusader. He went to slaughter paynims."

"That makes us Doakses a whole lot respectable."

"And here's your—this is jolly exciting—here's Saint Ury!"

"I don't see him."

"You're not looking at the book. He isn't in my hair. Here—Benoit De La Ceinture. Benoit of the Belt. He wasn't a saint at all. He was seneschal of ye keepe—that means post commander while ye doughtie crusader was away. And then, as understanding of Norman French died out, our old colloquial adaptation law turned Ceinture into Saint Ury."

FURTHER investigation made him very far from a saint, and the two investigators sat looking at each other with gray faces.

The doughty crusader had come back, as crusaders did in those pre-telegraphic days, without notice and he found, as other warriors have, that his ladye faire whom he left to languish through his long absence had been more friendly than was thought proper, even in those days, with the captain of the home guard. Having the rights of the High Justice and the Middle and the Low, he flew into a right noble rage and struck off the seneschal's offending right hand and spiked it to the great oaken door of the keep for all to see how the penalties of philandering were paid, naming at the same time the child—the second of his house—"a bastarde by fulle acknowledgemente and herebye sundered from alle inheritance."

Jimmy put his own right hand over Eula's cold one. "So that's the Hand of Saint Ury. And it's coming home!" He essayed a lame joke. "Perhaps that leaves us Doaks not so awfully respectable."

"Don't joke about it," Eula shuddered. "Your line could have come from the earlier child and you'd be a descendant of D'Auk."

Jimmy did not perceive the dire import of this until Doctor Eugene Harries arrived. The doctor elaborated his theories of the case with professional obscurity.

"Interesting. Most interesting! From what you tell me, we must indubitably accept this scuttling creature of the dark as the hand of which you have traced the history. Quite clearly one of our more authentic cases."

"So all right," said Jimmy. "So it's a dead hand that was once nailed to the front door here, and it existed around somewhere and finally gathered cobwebs in an antique store. What I want to know is, what suddenly wakes it up? How? Why is it scuttling the night roads back to here? Who's it after?"

"Ah!" said the doctor, much as Mrs. Medford might. "These things are not very easy to explain. There is an old occult theory, now being almost reaccepted, that thoughts are *physical* forces; that a thought of hate can be a powerful enough force to persist after the death of its originator." He held up his hand. "A moment, please. I say the theory of thought force is being reaccepted in these modern days because you have the experiments of your own Dr. Rhine in America, who seems to have established that a concentrated thought can control so material a function as the roll of dice. In your big University of Ohio, isn't it?"

"Yes," Jimmy was closely following. "But that's a *live* thought."

"Ah!" the doctor said again. "But let us explore that liveness. A thought, an admittedly tangible force, has been created and projected into the, shall we say, surrounding ether? Where, then, is it, and for how long may it persist? To explain which very evanescent query let us consider the modern analogy of radio. A tangible impulse is projected. Where is it? It is everywhere. It can affect a properly tuned receiver at a great distance. It has been shown to circulate the earth with a certain perceptible time lapse and a diminished power that, however, can still affect a sufficiently delicately attuned receiver. Very well then; if once, we may logically assume the possibility of twice, or more, ad infinitum. Given, then, a sufficiently sensitive receiver, where, we may ask, is the point of extinction? The what you call *dead* hand is in this case the receiver, exactly attuned to the wave length of the powerfully projected thought of hate because it was a part of the original projector."

"SOUNDS hideously reasonable. But that's drawing it pretty thin, isn't it?"

"Admittedly so. But, the possibility accepted, the point is not one of tenuity but of capability to affect the receiver. In the case of radio, to make it talk; which means, first, to affect *physically* a receiving element and make it move! To revitalize it! To make it repeat the impulse that was originally projected!"

Jimmy and Eula were both hanging on the doctor's words with a growing unease. "You mean, this hate force could affect a damned thing like that hand and make it move? Well, then, why didn't it hit it long ago? I mean, any time after it whatever way got loose off the board where it couldn't run. What suddenly tuned it in now?"

The doctor beamed benignly upon his class of two. "We have considered, so far, the analogy of diminishing, though persisting, wave lengths or impulses. Let us now consider another ancient theory of magic that has been accepted by modern science—that of transmutation. We have derided the middle-age mystics for their belief in the transmutation of baser metals into gold. But our quite latest experiments have shown that the very atomic structure of so dead a substance as a metallic ore, when bombarded by certain electronic impulses, can be transmuted to another arrangement of its nuclei; that what we have called dead matter can be vitalized to become something so devastating as a bomb."

"That one," said Jimmy, "seems to be drifting far afield."

"By no means. The principle established, who, in these days, will be bold enough to set a limit upon material or transmuting agent? The analogy is that within *you*, the descendant of this Sieur D'Auk persist the genes that create a, let us no longer say, *psychic* force, but a tangible electronic—we used to call it, magnetic-emanation that bombards the dormant atomic structure of the too glibly called *dead* hand. Your presence, then, in the shop was what vitalized its implanted hate force and released it to exhibit its present destructive manifestation."

"Hate! Hate! Hate!" It sobbed from Eula. "And I suppose you mean that this hateful thing is now scuttling along the gutters, coming home; and it somehow wickedly knows that the descendant of the man who cut it off is here and it will exact some horrible vengeance."

DR. HARRIES looked at Jimmy and very soberly nodded. Jimmy asked his question for the third time, and not with any doubting scorn.

"Just what can it do?"

"We have so far," the doctor weighed the possibilities with merciless impartiality, "discussed only the material sources of its potential; and we know from the reports that it can strangle a hunting hound. We must accept the probability, then, that it could also strangle a man. If we are willing to admit the psychic sources of power—as they are today being admitted in studies of the abnormal strength displayed by lunatics—we must face the possibility that it could be deadly dangerous, not only to the object of its vengeance, but to any interference that might stand in the way of its purpose."

To Eula's close shudder against him Jimmy grunted. "Hmm!" But his tight-mouthed expression showed that he was no longer taking this thing as lightly as he once had. "I suppose," he asked, not very hopefully, "it's no use trying to run away? If the cursed thing can run on its fingertips under its own power it could follow anywhere. What's chances of it running out of gas?"

"We have no means of knowing," the doctor said judicially. "Records of our Society show that destructive forces from the mysterious 'other side' have been known to persist for many hundreds of years."

"That would eventually wear me out," Jimmy said. "We may as well stay here and fight it. ...How?"

"There remains," the doctor said hopefully, "yet another consideration. You have observed that it made no attempt to harm *you* that first day of your meeting. It has retaliated only against those who have molested it—the umbrella woman, the poacher's dog. It is just possible, then—if I may offer a slightly embarrassing surmise—that its smuggling of itself into your pocket and the subsequent following may have been induced by motives of affection."

"Good Lord!" Jimmy's eyes boggled. "What d'you mean, affection from a foul thing like that?"

"Well, it might just be, you know, that—er—your branch of the family descended from that illegitimate offspring and that the hand, or rather its original owner, was your ancestor."

"Godamighty!" Jimmy shuddered away from the thought. "And it wants to snuggle up? Crawl out of the dark and hold hands. Get into bed on cold nights and—"

Eula shrieked. Jimmy looked quickly at her, for the moment forgetful of the impending horror. Eula shrank away from so fearful a connection.

"In any event," the doctor said, "the possibilities of this whole manifestation are so intriguing—quite one of our most authentic cases, I'm sure—that, if you would invite me, I would, despite the many dangers, have to consider it my scientific duty to stay and offer such assistance as I may."

Eula caught at him, not to let him go. "Oh, please! We're so helpless and—frightened. We wouldn't know what ever to do." It was not occurring to her that she had no inescapable part in this hideous thing that she could pack and go.

"Would you advise," Jimmy asked, "that we should be armed?"

"By all means, and immediately. We must accept the surmise that the thing is coming here, and a force like that, if not benevolent, could be devastating, since it is a 'walker of the night.' Er, this tall lady in gray whom I have seen hovering in the background, could she be relied upon in a situation of danger involving, we must be prepared to accept, certain aspects of supra-normal horror?"

"She's one of the three Norns," Eula said. "She lives with all the horrors of this house. If she approves of you she will let you stay."

Mrs. Medford did approve of Dr. Harries as being one who could understand her "physic" manifestations. And Dr. Harries approved of her idea of sitting in séance with her friend Mrs. Shaughnessy. "There is always a possibility," he said, "that out of these visualizations impressed upon the subconscious by wandering thought forces—spirits, as the faithful call them— one may obtain useful information, as one does also occasionally from people under hypnosis."

THE séance turned out to be a distressful affair of meanings and shriekings and dire threats. Mrs. Shaughnessy first moaned and shook and went into her trance, out of which she announced that a "dark spirit" filled the room and wanted to "get through," but not through her; it wanted to "control" someone closer to the house. Whereupon Mrs. Medford went through the moans and shudders and sat finally in a rigid coma. Till a ventral voice croaked from her.

"I'm 'ere," it said. "Not 'ere, but in this 'ouse before it was 'ere. I'm a' lookin' out a winder onto the cabbage garden; which they ain't cabbages but mossy cobblestones. And there's people an' soldiers in harmor an' lords in velvet an'—" Suddenly she shrieked. "I see 'im! There 'e comes! Shoved along by soldiers in harmor and all a'draggin' of iron chains. I see 'im! A 'orrid great 'airy man!" She shook and groaned the anguishes of the hairy man.

"It was a horrid great hairy hand," Jimmy fitted into the picture.

Mrs. Medford shouted out of her temporary quiescence. "'E lifts them 'ands in their chains an' rattles 'is fists. A'cursin' 'e is. Eatin' an' drinkin', 'e says. 'Wakin' an' sleepin', Livin' an' dyin', I'll be awaitin' you, Lord of the Auberge. An' the velvet lord laughs and says 'e, 'Let the judgment of the 'igh Justice be carried out.'" And then suddenly she clutched at her wrist and writhed in fearful resistance and shrieked agony again; and then she slumped down in a quivering heap of moaning and muttering semi-consciousness.

Jimmy and Eula came out of the dark room shivering, Eula unconsciously chafing her own wrist. Dr. Harries was not so much impressed. "So many of these manifestations," he evaluated the experiment, "although the faithful insist that they are 'spirit-controlled', can be ascribed to demonstrations of the subconscious. Impressions formed in not too well balanced and sensitive minds out of reading or hearsay are portrayed with fearful reality. This phenomenon is, in fact, the explanation of visions of saints or Madonnas. Although," he was coldly judicious, "we cannot entirely dismiss the possibility that the sensitive medium, the receiving instrument, having been impressed by some wave length from an outside source. We have witnessed, then, either a visualization of subconscious impressions or—" his acceptance of the possibility was frightening, "—a reaching out of the still active hate force. We can do nothing about it until the hand is here."

IT WAS Lady Jane who served notice that it had somewhere furtively arrived. Out of the dusk came the piercing ki-yies of a poodle frightened to the near death and the creature staggered, rather than ran, under a chair, there to continue its shuddering yelpings.

"So all right then," Jimmy said through tight teeth. "What can be done in the way of protection?" He did not say, in the way of offensive fight.

"Ah!" said Dr. Harries, this time signifying meditation. "If we but knew how to immunize you—that is to say, throw some sort of an impervious blanket about you, as is accomplished by lead in our analogy of radioactive force, we might shut off your emanations from continuing to vitalize the thing."

"Well," Jimmy's very impotence flared to anger, "I'm not doing it on purpose!"

"Of course not. Though that, too, may be an unconscious possibility; since we know that such activation can be consciously projected by such people as the so-called wizards of mediaeval history and by African witch doctors in our present. Protection is supposedly supplied by various 'magic circles' and 'holy pentagrams' and so on, although I do not attach much faith in these myself. More credible is another one of the scouted mediaeval beliefs in the potency of cold iron against what they called witchcraft—which accounts for the spiking of the hand to the door with a nail, the spiking of suicides, supposedly dissatisfied and homeless spirits, through their middles, iron coffins, and so on. Which belief has persisted into our own times in the form of iron amulets, iron crosses, whether as medals or over grave stones. Unfortunately we cannot enclose you in an iron coffin; and in order to spike down the hand again we must first catch it."

"Like catching a cobra. How about," said Jimmy grimly, "the cold iron of a gun?"

"The possibility is acceptable. Since, if such a thing could be disintegrated—say, by a shotgun at close range—while the hate force would not necessarily be dissipated, its physical medium of offense would be shattered."

Jimmy drew a long breath of almost relief. But the doctor mercilessly continued. "We might then be rid of the whole business—unless the force might still persist in some telekinetic form that could move other objects so as to, for example, push a brick off a high wall." To Jimmy's hunted bafflement he offered the cold cheer, "The question of exactly why a brick, or even paint, falls upon the 'unlucky' person has never been sufficiently explored."

"Well, I'm going right into town," Jimmy said, "and buy a sawed-off shotgun."

"Or perhaps," Doctor Harries suggested with that chilly acceptance of the worst possible, "you might get two. And perhaps, although it is still daylight, I might accompany you as an escort."

THEY returned with an arsenal and, in addition, two gaunt boxer dogs. "If they catch it scuttling about the house gutters," Jimmy told Eula, "and between them tear it apart; or eat it; I guess it'll be considerably disintegrated."

Eula's face contorted over so sickening a thought. "I suppose they would at least keep it on the run. But that poacher's dogs—"

That first night after the thing's arrival was a bedlam of scurryings and furious barkings that yielded nothing. Stealthy noises sounded in the unkempt garden. The dogs yelped their excitement after whatever it might be and galloped their great feet hither and yon like mad dray horses. At each disturbance Jimmy and the doctor stood alertly at windows that overlooked the dark grounds. They could discern the shadowy forms of the great dogs racing through moon patches, but not a thing else.

"Of course," the doctor suggested, "...It could still be rats."

"Oh, rats!" Eula expressed her English idiom of disbelief.

"Perhaps we'll at least find tracks in the morning," Jimmy hoped, "and then we'll at least be sure."

Such tracks as they found besides those of the dogs were indecipherable smudges.

"Did the thing," Dr. Harries asked, "when you saw it in the shop, have long fingernails?" And he evaluated the situation so far. "We can at all events assume that the thing is nocturnal, as are nearly all of these darker forces. We may, therefore, feel safe during the day—or fairly so—if we do not venture into dark places. We know that it avoids overwhelming weight, as of two ferocious dogs; also that it is cunning enough to do so, and, as in the poacher's case, to segregate them and attack one at a time. And since it has remained furtive, has not shown itself, we must, I am sorry to say, resign ourselves to the ultimate fact that its purpose is definitely malignant and that it is intelligent enough to be deadly."

"If we could hunt it down by daylight then?" Jimmy expressed a hope. "We can't just go on, knowing that a hellish something in the shape of a great hairy hand is skulking somewhere about the grounds, waiting for darkness to jump out at somebody and tear his throat out."

"If we could but find it. Its grizzly advantage is that it is small enough to hide in any of a thousand holes in the ancient tumbled masonry, while the hate force that activates it is powerful enough to be murderous."

Mrs. Medford knew where to find it. "It's livin' in the root cellar!" she told them; and before they asked her, "I seen it!"

"With the 'physic' eye, I suppose," the doctor said. "But let's take our guns and go look."

THE root cellar was a dim vault of great stones behind a massive door, cool and mouldy. Holes where stones had fallen out dripped water. Bins along the walls contained potatoes and the gross turnips that country folk and cattle ate. The doctor with inadequate flashlight scrutiny surmised it to have been one of those sunless guardhouses for prisoners in the old days of brutality and insanitation.

"Hell!" Jimmy swore. All this uncertainty and impending menace was wearing on his nerves. "There's a million hidie holes. If we could rig an extension light from the house perhaps—?"

"We would still not be able to explore all these holes. Who knows how deep they may burrow into the namks. We would need ferrets, as in a rabbit warren." And he could not refrain from adding his inevitable note of warning. "And we know it is vastly more dangerous than a rabbit."

A scuffling noise in a dim corner whirled both of them around. A choked squeak came from Jimmy's throat and spasmodically he blasted both barrels of his gun in that direction. The flash beam showed that he had very thoroughly disintegrated some onions and a rat.

"And we do know," the doctor mused as though studying a continuous theory, "that it immediately retaliates against aggression." His scientific approach, even in the face of danger, was excruciating. Acrid fumes of nitro powder drove them from the enclosed space.

"My God!" Jimmy coughed. "What a pessimist!"

"We cannot afford," the doctor rumbled, "to be optimistic about any force that operates in the darkness. It is not a mere Christian superstition that light and benevolence are compatible. All we can do is be desperately careful." Over the late meal he suggested, "I would advise, Miss Bogue that you sleep in the same room with our so formidable housekeeper."

Eula fluttered her wide spread fingers at the prospect. I'd be more afraid than—"

"And I," the doctor said, "will move in with Mr. Doak. I would also suggest contiguous rooms—in this old chapel wing with the barred windows."

So it came that the four of them foregathered that night to peer down at pandemonium all round the house. A crashing of bushes, a mad galloping of feet and yelping dogs, at times both together, furiously chasing a something; and then again in separate confusion, the one in a hysteria under something too high in a bush to reach, and the other equally convinced that it had something cornered in a drain. And then the watchers witnessed a horror in the moonlight.

One of the great dogs lurched out of the shadows, coughing and choking, and staggered loose-legged across a strip of lawn. In the uncertain light it looked for a moment as though it held a limp something in its jaws and furiously shook it. But as its head writhed from side to side they could see that nothing was in its jaws; but that a something hung from its throat and was not at all limp!

JIMMY and the doctor snatched their guns and raced downstairs and out. But the dog had by that time staggered into the darkness of bush shadows. Calling brought no response. Not even from the other one!

"We had better not venture too far into the shadows," the doctor warned. "Nor leave the women alone."

At the door both stood for a moment shocked back on their heels.

"My God, we left it open!"

Within the house no worse was immediately apparent than that Mrs. Medford was shuddering back out of a swoon, Eula chafing her hands. Water profusely splashed from the old-fashion wash basin indicated the process of revivement.

"Gaw!" Mrs. Medford mumbled. "I seen it."

"Well, you've seen it before," Eula said crossly, "and you didn't go off like this and leave me all alone."

"Ah!" said Mrs. Medford. "But this time I seen it real. A 'orrible 'airy 'and it were."

"She could not," Doctor Harries said precisely, "have identified it in the uncertain light out from these upper windows. However, since the door was momentarily unguarded, we must sit up, and together, for the rest of the night."

Jimmy was furious with everything in the world; particularly with himself for his uncontrolled nerves that had permitted the door to stand wide. "Yeh," he rasped. "Sit up and tell ghost stories." His hand nervously caressed his throat.

Eula sent him a reproachful look. "He was only warning us."

"Perhaps," said. the doctor, "I have not impressed the warning sufficiently, even upon myself. Or we would not have left open that door. We shall know more in the morning."

All that they knew in the morning was that both dogs were dead. Both heavy-jawed faces contorted and tongues hanging out thickly black.

"Ye-es." The doctor hissed it slowly. "Cunning enough to have run them to exhaustion, confused them and taken one at a time. We must, while daylight lasts, make a very thorough search of every room in this house."

"And since dogs are no good," Jimmy said, "I'll go into town and hire a night watchman. Arm him, by God, with a battery of flashlights and a machine-gun."

JIMMY returned late. "Had a helluva job to find anybody who'd take the chore on. Not at old Dockbridge Manor, they popped their eyes. Why not? Well, there were jaunts there. Not relatives, 'black things'; and there were dead men's bones under the house, they had a legend; and so every damned yokel was scared... But I got a great lout finally. He'd been a guard in the Whitehaven prison, he says, and he'd watch a graveyard if he was paid. D'you find anything in the house?"

Dr. Harries shook his head. "We found only uncertainty; more nerve-racking than discovery. There are rat holes by the dozens in the dark corners of closets and cupboards. Holes large enough through broken plaster for cats to pass. I wish to heaven, since dogs are useless, we might hire a leopard or something that could adequately see in the dark."

It was almost a relief of the uncertainty that night to be awakened by Eula's screams from the next room. Rushing in, the two found her hysterical in Mrs. Medford's arms. Mrs. Medford darkly gave the answer.

"This time *she* seen it! I was a'sleepin' peaceful as a babe when I up and 'eard 'er a' screechin', 'There it is!', and I says, where?, and whatever she seen was so 'orrible, she went off like this."

Eula, shuddering back to normalcy, clung to Jimmy, her arms about his neck, "Take me away!" she moaned. "Oh, take me away, Jimmy, from this fearful place."

All the comfort that Jimmy could give was, "I could let *you* go away. But it would be no use my running too. We know it can relentlessly follow. I've got to stick it out here. Isn't that right, Doctor?"

"I'm afraid so. Flight would be only a postponement, and here we at least know the conditions. This thing must be met and—since we don't know how to immunize its power source—it must be destroyed. *If* its power is destructible. Try to tell us, if you can, just what you saw."

Eula pointed shakily to the window. "Out there. I couldn't sleep, of course; and from the bed I could see the silhouette of that tree's branches outside the window. And then suddenly it was there! Its eyes! Its wicked little red eyes. Sitting on a branch and watching."

Puzzled, the doctor looked at Jimmy.

"The umbrella woman," Jimmy reminded him. "She said she saw eyes. Close, like a spider's, as everybody was calling it at that time. And it had a beastly ring, I think I told you, a black flat disk with two red stones."

"Hm-mm? I wonder? I just wonder now, could it be the dark mirror and the red eyes of Amubis?"

"What's the eyes of Amubis?"

"But no." The doctor shook that theory from himself. "That's an ancient Egyptian magic of terrible power. But that cannot apply here. This is black Norman hate—that history has shown to be powerful enough... You, my dear, you must try to get some rest. We can't have a nervous breakdown on our hands at this precarious juncture. Leave your door open. We shall sit up on watch by turns."

"I suppose," Jimmy grumbled, "we can't really blame that fool of a watchman for not spotting something as elusive as a rat climbing up a tree. It couldn't have jumped that distance, could it?"

"Twenty feet or so? I would hardly think so. At any rate there is no tree opposite this window. Have you any preference for first trick?"

"I'll take it," Jimmy said. "I couldn't sleep under drugs. I'll light me a pipe and stay up. I suppose we must definitely take it by now that the thing is not, as you gruesomely suggested, friendly. It's out for revenge."

"I'm afraid so. And I hardly like to tell you how much afraid. So—don't for a second let yourself nod. Wake me if you even hear anything."

JIMMY soon enough did. The doctor was one who had the faculty of being instantly completely awake. "What goes?"

"There's a scrabbling in the ivy outside the window." Jimmy whispered.

Doctor Harries' answer was loud. "I wish we *could* pretend it might be rats or a burglar. It's not *it* that's afraid. It sounds, in fact, to have gained the window sill. Lights! For God's sake, quick! Light!"

The old-fashioned bulb in the ceiling lit the room but not the outside. With the same impulse both men snatched up their guns and rushed to the window, directing their white flash beams through the glass. Whatever had scrabbled was rat quick enough to disappear. Jimmy threw up the window before the doctor, crying, "Good God! No!" could stop him. The bright glare showed nothing. Only a rustle of retreat scuttled though the ivy.

"Ha!" The doctor found a small satisfaction. "As I thought, it functions best in the dark. Light is a certain measure of defense."

"Look!" Jimmy whispered again, hoarsely. His flash beam was directed on the windowsill.

There in the dust was an imprint! Of a hand! Of long, withered fingers and a palm—and the thin scratches of uncut nails!

From below came another flash into their eyes. The watchman's dim form bulked behind it. "Hanythink up?" he called.

"We don't know," the doctor said quickly before Jimmy might blurt out the shocking discovery and perhaps, despite the man's boast, frighten him entirely away. "We heard something in the ivy. If you do, don't wait, but shoot at the sound."

"Hi will that, sir. Though that there ivy is a 'ome for all the vermin, rats an' sparrows an' what not, in the bloomin' county."

"So a watchman, then," Doctor Harries said, "is no better than dogs." He very firmly closed the window down.

"Why?" Jimmy could not break away from the awed whisper normal to a disturbed night. "Why didn't it break through the glass and in? It broke that shop window."

"I wonder." Dr. Harries stood with narrowed eyes. "Those were little *leaded* panes, weren't they? Could it be that it knew we were armed with weapons that could disintegrate it. Or could it be—could it just be on account of the bars of cold iron at the window? We know so little. Heavens, how little, about these darker forces. We know only that this one has a deadly potentiality."

"A dead man's hand!" Jimmy was muttering, his eyes staring out at nothing. "Supercharged with hate! Able to crawl! Able to run—to choke the life out of—"

"Here, here!" The doctor caught and shook him. "Snap out of that. Once let it crack your nerve and you're lost. Don't you see, that's just what it is hellishly trying to do? Like with the dogs; get them confused and hysterical. Come, get hold of yourself."

"*Phe-eew!*" Jimmy let go a long breath. He shook his head. "It's the damned beastliness of it all. The something from some evil portion of the outer dark. With all the advantage on its side."

"Not quite all," the doctor encouraged him. "We have the advantage of the light. Even flash beams. I don't know why. But it has always been that the darker forces function in the dark. Which, of course, is what makes them so frightful."

Jimmy shook himself to shed the shakiness of his nerves that had been creeping up on him. "You're damn right, Doc. We dassent let go. What about the watchman down there? Ought we not perhaps to give him an inkling, at least, of what sort of thing to watch for?"

"Or rather, to watch out for. If that thing should crawl up on him unexpectedly—"

"I'll tell him first thing in the morning," said Jimmy. "Before he goes home—and let's hope then that he'll come back."

JIMMY did not tell the watchman first thing in the morning. Because there was no watchman! A sick feeling of dread crept up the fine hairs of Jimmy's back as he explored the grounds, expecting to find a limp body with a blackened face huddled somewhere under a bush or in some dim corner of tumbled masonry. He found foot tracks. Not—he thanked God—hand tracks. Big flat-footed boot marks. The man had faithfully patrolled. But he himself had completely disappeared.

"Well, the hell thing can't completely dematerialize a man," he reported in. "Or is that something else we don't know?"

The doctor shook his head. "No. I'm sure that our danger is entirely physical."

"Then I suppose he saw it and emigrated out of the country."

Mrs. Medford offered her, "Aa-ah!" And, "You go an' look in the root cellar!"

"Good heavens!" It came from all of them. "You haven't 'seen' any new horror?"

"No, sirs an' ma'am. I ain't 'ad no sights. But I knows the likes of them constable chaps. I'll bet 'e went root cellar a'lookin' for cold beer, as most folks 'ere keeps it there account o' hice bein' irregular. Else why did 'e 'ave to leave 'is fat job at the jail? You tell me that."

"Now be careful, Jimmy." Eula sent a worried look at him, starting up.

"Hold on a minute," said the doctor, "I want to look up an idea I have in one of these old records. It won't take long—you shouldn't go alone."

But Jimmy was too tense and impatient. "I'll carry my little old 'disintegrator'," he said grimly, "and flash light. I'm having an idea myself, and it's that the man may just possibly be needing help."

"Well, if you find anything, call," said the doctor, obviously torn between research and action.

Surely enough, Jimmy found the flat boot tracks leading to the cellar; and, as they came nearer, they seemed to have been walking on tiptoe. The great door stood open. Jimmy peered down the worn, slimy steps. He called. Listened hopefully for drunken breathing. His only answer was the slow grinding creak of the door in a buffety wind. It reminded him of a radio program. He damned it and shoved an old cobblestone under its lower edge. Leaning thus close, he saw a muddy toe mark on the very sill, and, naturally enough, on the next step.

"The fool!" he growled and he stepped on gingerly down, careful against slipping on the smooth, worn old stone slabs. Not a thing was in the cellar. It was the same dimly dank place that he had seen the first time, sourly redolent, not of stale beer, but of stored vegetables. He did not this time hysterically fire at the soft scurry of rats behind the bins. He flashed his light under them and into the darker corners. Nothing.

Though yes. A door again surely. So green and moss-grown in its equally mossy wall that it could easily be missed. The flash beam would, in fact, not have picked it out at all were it not for a lighter line all along its lintel and jambs. Jimmy stepped closer. And sure enough, the scummy growth had been scratched away by some blunt implement, as though to release old in-grown debris and free the opening. And there, by the sill, lay the implement; a sliver of broken lattice from the arbor outside.

"I wonder now," Jimmy muttered out loud. "I wonder if he could have guessed it would be in there?"

A verdigris brass knob invited his hand. The door swung easily out towards him. Within was wet darkness. He stood uncertainly and flashed his beam about. The place contained bins again—or rather, stout oaken shelves; and on the shelves, stout oaken boxes. Long narrow boxes.

A vague intuition was pressing at the back of Jimmy's mind as to what sort of storage this might be. His nose was curling, uncertainly sniffing, when he saw that one of the boxes had had its lid shoved slightly askew, and the pale whitish gleam that thrust out of the slit to reflect his flash could be nothing other than a bone.

"The old crypt, by God!" Jimmy was, with normal impulse, backing away from it when his lowered flash beam picked out the body! It was huddled limply on the floor and was unmistakable.

The watchman!

THE rough homespun sleeve feebly moved. "Good Lord!" Jimmy rushed in and bent to lift the man. He was heavy. Jimmy yelled over his shoulder:

"Help here! I've found him!"

The boisterous wind must have carried his voice away. A gust of it swung the inner door shut with a slam, cutting off even the dimness from the outer one, leaving only Jimmy's flash beam in the pit blackness.

Jimmy damned. And with the hot breath of the word, chilled. Had that been a gust? He had felt no draught. He'd have to get the man out of there in a hurry. To be in a crypt at any time was a creepy enough happening. To find a blacked-out watchman there, whether drunk or wounded, was a shock to anybody's nerves. To have a charnel house's only source of light and ventilation slam shut on one was—Jimmy kept up his courage by furiously swearing.

His light on the stationary snap he bent again awkwardly and in a frenzy of hurry to lift the man. His sawed-off shotgun in the crook of his arm, it was difficult to get a grip on so lumpy a thing as a man. And the man was— The realization came in like a blow over the heart. He was stiff!

How could his sleeve have moved then? Jimmy yelled again, futilely, for help.

And in that instant a something, violent and bone hard, dashed the flash from his hand! For a moment he could trace its spinning arc through the air and then it tinkled into the corner and was out!

Jimmy's breath eeked out in a choked gasp. His stomach fell away, his blood, everything. Pit blackness and pit silence enveloped him. His knees limp, he sank down on the body he had been trying to lift. Even that relic of humanity was a comfort. Only persistence of vision seemed to function. He could see in the blackness a pale green arc of his last light.

And then another function, desperately needed, began to assert itself out of his paralysis. He could fearfully listen. He heard his pulse—like a persistent and useless little rubber hammer. So he wasn't dead of shock. He could still move. He *must* move.

He shoved himself off that dead thing on which he had fallen and hurled himself toward the door. A blow hit him in the face and rocked him dizzily back. He didn't normally curse it. He was prayerfully thankful for it. What had hit him was mouldily damp; it was the side of one of the old coffins. It oriented him, at least in direction.

He plunged to the door. It must be the door. His hands, desperately fumbling, could feel the wet panels, the straight crack of its jamb. He clawed frenziedly up and down the crack, inches on either side. Desperately back and forth and around.

And there was no knob on the inside!

Jimmy lolled limp against the door. He could feel his knees bend against it and his chest sliding slimily down the boards.

An awful sound stabbed at him with galvanizing force. A sound in itself commonplace and harmless. But here, terrifying. A stealthy scuffling.

It came from that grizzly box up there with the opened lid! Where that bone had been sticking out! The sound was a bony scratching of pointed nails!

Breath surged back to Jimmy, absurdly to *whoo-oosh!* And out of his jetty blackness he fired at the sound.

Pit silence again.

A thin hope of desperation trembled through Jimmy. Could it be possible that there was a merciful God in this hell pit and his blast had shattered the—had "disintegrated"—no other word fitted in—the whatever had made that sound up there? Jimmy's drilled consciousness refused to give it the name that it fearsomely knew.

AND then his whole being shrank together once more to hear the scrabbling of fingernails again. Not rats. Rats never sounded like that. Rats softly pattered. They harmlessly scuffled. They cheerfully squeaked. Rats were inoffensive warm creatures of human homes. They were—

The scrabbling noise plopped onto the sodden floor! Jimmy madly fired in that direction. Madly listened. He was shockingly conscious of the gun-blasted air. Conscious of infinitely worse than that. For that was his all! His last defense! Nobody with a sawed-off shotgun ever carried more than the two cartridges in the barrels. With a sawed-off shotgun it was never necessary—not against anything on earth...

And then Jimmy shrieked. Every breath forced fearfully from him as a something scuttled up the outside of his pants leg, over his back, and rushed coldly savagely to tear at his throat!

Jimmy clawed furiously at it. Not his most remotely dragged-in hope could call for God's mercy. This was *it!* Dried flesh and loathly coarse-hair and overgrown nails! They tore at Jimmy with a savage hate.

Jimmy was able, with all the strength of his two hands, to loosen the thing's grip sufficiently so that he could at least suck in a breath to replenish the emptiness of his long-drawn shriek. The thing, quicker than any rat, let go of Jimmy's throat, twisted itself free, and out of the empty dark slammed itself against his neck. Slammed again at his face. It didn't seem to know about the modernly developed technique of a knockout blow to the jaw. It battered at any part of the head. Coming out of the blackness, Jimmy could see nothing to ward. Every advantage was with the pent-up hate that could see in the dark. It could beat a man to a pulp at its vengeful will.

With arms and elbows, like an already beaten fighter, Jimmy tried to protect his face. Then the thing was at his throat again, as though it could tell that Jimmy was gasping from the fumes of his shots.

Jimmy's desperation gave him strength to tear the thing away. He could feel blood oozing. The thing, needing no rest, battered at his face again. It was not floating in air; it seemed to be getting its take-off from his shoulders, from his arms, even up from his chest, any place where it could momentarily settle and spring. At one time it missed its blow. Its own vicious force carried it on to slap hollowly against a coffin. It plopped to the floor.

With mad hope Jimmy jumped, both feet together, thinking to step on it. But there it was, scuttering up his pants again, a devil thing of the dark, vicious with life, savagely bent on death. Jimmy's feet stumbled over that other dead thing on the floor. Its stiff limbs tripped him. He fell. Immediately he felt the scrabbling fingers run onto his chest. His frenzied snatch this time caught it. It was strong enough, crawling on its three loose fingers, to drag his both hands remorselessly up to his throat and to dig those fingers in. Jimmy dizzily thought he could hear voices and a pounding on the door.

Hope brought him strength again. He tore the thing loose. He knew that flesh ripped with its nails. It twisted itself free. Jimmy tried to roll away from it. That was worse. On the floor it could choose any vantage point from which to fling itself at him. Jimmy heaved himself up to his knees. The thing leaped at his throat again. The light flashes of beaten nerves were sparking within Jimmy's head.

BUT there the beast suddenly let go. Jimmy was able to suck in life-saving breaths and to flail wildly with his arms. If it were possible for the thing to be even temporarily disabled by so soft a thing as a human fist—

The light flashes had not been in his head. They were real. White beams of flash lights. The doctor was curbing Jimmy's wild blind swings. Lifting him, hampered by Eula who clung sobbing to him.

The doctor sharply slapped her.

"Snap out! Get hold of him! This place is poisonous with the fumes of all hell."

Jimmy was able to croak, "Look out! It's *it!* Here! It comes from everywhere!"

Eula made tight-bitten noises out of her hysteria. Together the two rushed Jimmy out. The doctor kicked the door behind him. Uselessly, for they had battered the panels in. They hurried Jimmy, slipping and clawing up the slime-green steps to God's open air. The doctor slammed that door shut.

IT WAS Mrs. Medford who first had the courage to propose going back. After washing Jimmy off and bandaging his torn throat and after a stiff stimulant all round—that she stoutly refused—she offered her fearsome thought.

"It's 'ad its fight. It'll never be weaker than now. Lights, you say, is what scares it. If it's got to be destroyed, what I says is the time is now."

The doctor looked at the extraordinary woman. He slowly began to nod. Jimmy, his lips tightly set, nodded. Eula covered her eyes with her hands—and nodded.

They went then, with the one shotgun and a flashlight each. The outer door had remained shut. In the root cellar nothing moved. The inner door stood broken as it had been left.

"You drag it open," the doctor told Jimmy. "I'll stand by with the gun."

Within the crypt nothing moved. The lights showed only the slime puddles where Jimmy had rolled. Those, and indented scratches of fingernails. From Jimmy's throat squeaked a memory and he turned his beam up to the coffin. The white bone that he had indistinctly seen before still protruded from the chink between box and lid.

Eula screamed. The doctor half leveled his gun and then he softly whistled. Mrs. Medford said, "Aa-ah! I should ha' knowed it."

The white thing was the two bones of an arm—and they had no hand!

The doctor looked at the others, round-eyed. He pointed, thrusting with his finger. It was he who was whispering now.

"It's in there! Come home where it belongs!"

Silently, as though stalking a snake, he handed the gun to Jimmy. He made a rush to the coffin, shoved the arm bones in, and dragged the lid over to close the crack.

"Help me now," he shouted. "Help to hold it down! We don't know how strong it is."

All together, swallowing down repugnance, they grappled with the box. "Light!" the doctor panted. "Out into the sunlight."

Inexpertly, getting in one another's way, desperately gripping down the lid, they pulley-hauled the coffin from its shelf. Shoved it sliding up the wet steps. Out into the warm summer sun.

There with an astounding courage the doctor sat his whole weight down on it. Beckoned Jimmy to add his weight.

Beckoned Eula. She came, but would sit no closer to the oaken board than on Jimmy's lap.

Mrs. Medford said, "So now you've catched it. So now tell us 'ow a thing like that is kept catched."

THE doctor frowned away into the distances of his dark knowledge. "I—don't—know," he said. "For the present, in bright daylight, it will not burst out. I must think. My immediate thought is—nails. *Iron* nails. I expect Mrs. Medford must know where there are some. And the next thought is, what about the unfortunate watchman?"

"We can only guess," Jimmy said. "I'd guess he saw something and tiptoed after it; and then down there—" He shivered in the warm sun and put his fingers tenderly to his throat.

"Yes, I suppose so. We must get him out and notify the authorities."

Mrs. Medford came back with a hammer, and nails. "Not that them'll 'old it down for long. Not come dark."

"No. We must think of something better."

Eula, nose wrinkling, watched with a determined vindictiveness the doctor's nailing of the lid. Suddenly she pointed to where his hands smudged off some gray mold.

"Look. It was he, sure enough."

Faint gothic letters showed. "B-n--t d- l- Cein-ure."

"Yes," Doctor Harries said. "It would make a priceless piece for some museum. But the more I've been thinking, the more convinced am I that light—fire light—will destroy this malignant force. And why not now? And here!"

"God knows there's enough of old timbers lying about." Jimmy, without any argument or question, set about collecting. Eula helped with a determined enthusiasm.

"The only thing I like about this dreadful place," she said. "Is its stock of old firewood."

In the bright sunlight, then, they hoisted the gray-mouldy coffin onto the pyre. Eula vindictively lit it, and they stood back.

The dry timbers roared up and quickly made a red furnace in the middle of which the coffin gave off a vast black smoke before its sides began to crack and long lines of fire crept along the slits and ate into its moldy interior. Eula suddenly covered her eyes and screamed. With a grim satisfaction Jimmy watched a gray spidery horror break through the burning side, scrabble madly in the furnace and then fall back. In tight-lipped silence, his every nerve taut, he watched the gray fingers turn black and curl together and glow red and disintegrate in little licking blue fires.

"That," Doctor Harries said, "I think disposes of that."

Jimmy put his arm about Eula. "At all events," he said, "I think it proves that ours was the respectable branch of us Doaks. It took to my pocket in the first place for some sort of revenge. Fancy my going into the very shop it'd been in all these years. From now on, how shall *we* spell our name?"

Eula pushed away from him. "I'll have nothing to do with anything from the past. The plain American way is all we'll ever use," she said firmly.

"Oke-Doak," retorted Jimmy, at last able to get a grin out of the business. "But how are we going to convince Dad?"

THE END

CASKET DEMON

By Fritz Leiber

Have you ever wondered what makes these glamorous movie stars do the scandalous things they do? Why they revel in getting their names in the papers? The reason may be weightier than you think.

THERE's nothing left for it—I've got to open the casket," said Vividy Sheer, glaring at the ugly thing on its square of jeweled and gold-worked altar cloth. The most photogenic face in the world was grim as a Valkyrie this Malibu morning.

"No," shuddered Miss Bricker, her secretary. "Vividy, you once let me peek in through the little window and I didn't sleep for a week."

"It would make the wrong sort of publicity," said Maury Gender, the Nordic film-queen's press chief. "Besides that, I value my life." His gaze roved uneasily across the gray "Pains of the Damned" tapestries lining three walls of the conference room up to its black-beamed 20-foot ceiling.

"You forget, baroness, the runic rhymes of the Prussian Nostradamus," said Dr. Rumanescue, Vividy's astrologist and family magician. "'*Wenn der Kassette-Tuefel*—or, to translate roughly, 'When the casket-demon is let out, The life of the Von Sheer is in doubt.'"

"My triple-great grandfather held out against the casket demon for months," Vividy Sheer countered.

"Yes, with a demi-regiment of hussars for bodyguard, and in spite of their sabers and horse pistols he was found dead in bed at his Silesian hunting lodge within a year. Dead in bed and black as a beetle—and the eight hussars in the room with him as night-guard permanently out of their wits with fear."

"I'm stronger than he was—I've conquered Hollywood," Vividy said, her blue eyes sparking and her face all Valkyrie.

"But in any case if I'm to live weeks, let alone months, I *must* keep my name in the papers, as all three of you very well know."

"Hey, hey, what goes on here?" demanded Max Rath, Vividy Sheer's producer, for whom the medieval torture-tapestries had noiselessly parted and closed at the bidding of electric eyes. His own little shrewd ones scanned the four people, veered to the black gnarly wrought-iron casket, no bigger than a cigar box, with its tiny peep-hole of cloudy glass set in the top, and finally came to rest on the only really incongruous object in the monastically-appointed hall—a lavender-tinted bathroom scales.

Vividy glared at him, Dr. Rumanescue shrugged eloquently, Miss Bricker pressed her lips together, Maury Gender licked his own nervously and at last said, "Well, Vividy thinks she ought to have more publicity—every-day-without-skips publicity in the biggest papers and on the networks. Also, she's got a weight problem."

MAX RATH surveyed in its flimsy dress of silk jersey the most voluptuous figure on six continents and any number of islands, including Ireland and Bali. "You got no weight-problem, Viv," he pronounced. "An ounce either way would be 480 grains away from pneumatic perfection." Vividy flicked at her bosom contemptuously. Rath's voice changed. "Now as for your name not being in the papers lately, that's a very wise idea, my own, in fact—and must be kept up. *Bride of God* is due to premiere in four months—the first picture about the life of a nun not to be thumbs-downed by any religious or non-religious group, even in the sticks. We want to keep it that way. When you toured the Florence nightclubs with Biff Parowan and took the gondola ride with that what's-his-name bellhop, the Pope slapped your wrist, but that's all he did—*Bride's* still not on the Index. But the wrist slap was a hint—and one more reason why for the next year there mustn't be one tiny smidgen of personal scandal or even so-called harmless notoriety linked to the name of Vividy Sheer.

"Besides that, Viv," he added more familiarly, "the reporters and the reading public were on the verge of getting very sick of the way your name was turning up on the front page every day—and mostly because of chasing, at that. Film stars are like goddesses—they can't be seen too often, there's got to be a little reserve, a little mystery.

"Aw, cheer up, Vivo I know it's tough, but Liz and Jayne and Marilyn all learned to do without the daily headline and so can you. Believe an old timer: euphoric pills are a safer and more lasting kick."

Vividy, who had been working her face angrily throughout Rath's lecture, now filled her cheeks and spat out her breath contemptuously, as her thrice removed grandfather might have at the maunderings of an aged majordomo.

"You're a fool, Max," she said harshly. "Kicks are for nervous virgins, the vanity of a spoilt child. *For me, being in the headlines every day is a matter of life or death.*"

Rath frowned uncomprehendingly.

"That's the literal truth she's telling you, Max," Maury Gender put in earnestly. "You see, this business happens to be tied up with what you might call the darker side of Vividy's aristocratic East Prussian heritage."

Miss Bricker stubbed out a cigarette and said, "Max, remember the trouble you had with that Spanish star Marta Martinez who turned out to be a *bruja*—a witch? Well, you picked something a little bit more out of the ordinary, Max, when you picked a Junker."

The highlights shifted on Dr. Rumanescue's thick glasses and shiny head as he nodded solemnly. He said, "There is a rune in the Doomsbook of the Von Sheers. I will translate." He paused. Then: "'When the world has nothing more to say, The last of the Sheers will fade away.'"

AS if thinking aloud, Rath said softly, "Funny, I'd forgotten totally about that East Prussian background. We always played it way down out of sight because of the Nazi association—and the Russian too," he chuckled, just a touch nervously. "'...fade away,'" he quoted. "Now why not just 'die?' Oh, to make the translation rhyme, I suppose." He shook himself, as if to come awake. "Hey," he demanded, "what is it actually? Is somebody blackmailing Vividy? Some fascist or East German commie group? Maybe with the dope on her addictions and private cures, or her affair with Geri Wilson?"

"Repeat: a fool!" Vividy's chest was heaving but her voice was icy. "For your information, Dr. 'Escue's translation was literal. *Day by day, ever since you first killed my news stories, I have been losing weight.*"

"It's a fact, Max," Maury Gender put in hurriedly. "The news decline and the weight loss are matching curves. Believe it or not, she's down to a quarter normal."

Miss Bricker nodded with a shiver, disturbing the smoke wreaths around her. She said, "It's the business of an actress fading out from lack of publicity. But this time, so help me, *it's literal.*"

"I have been losing both *weight and mass,*" Vividy continued sharply. "Not by getting thinner, but *less substantial.* If I had my back to the window you'd notice it."

Rath stared at her, then looked penetratingly at the other three, as if to discover confirmation that it was all a gag. But they only looked back at him with uniformly solemn and unhappy—and vaguely frightened—expressions. "I don't get it," he said.

"The scales, Vividy," Miss Bricker suggested.

The film star stood up with an exaggerated carefulness and stepped onto the small rubber-topped violet platform. The white disk whirled under the glass window and came to rest at 37.

She said crisply, "I believe the word you used, Max, was 'pneumatic.' Did you happen to mean I'm inflated with hydrogen?"

"You've still got on your slippers," Miss Bricker pointed out.

With even greater carefulness, steadying herself a moment by the darkly gleaming table-edge, Vividy stepped out of her slippers and again onto the scales. This time the disk stopped at 27.

"The soles and heels are lead, fabric-covered," she rapped out to Rath. "I wear them so I won't blow over the edge when I take a walk on the terrace. Perhaps you now think I ought to be able to jump and touch the ceiling. Convincing, wouldn't it be? I rather wish I could, but my strength has decreased proportionately with my weight and mass."

"Those scales are gimmicked," Rath asserted with conviction. He stooped and grabbed at one of the slippers. His fingers slipped off it at the first try. Then he slowly raised and hefted it, "What sort of gag is this?" he demanded of Vividy. "Dammit, it does weigh five pounds."

She didn't look at him. "Maury, get the flashlight," she directed.

WHILE the press chief rummaged in a tall Spanish cabinet, Miss Bricker moved to the view window that was the room's fourth wall and flicked an invisible beam. Rapidly the tapestry-lined drapes crawled together from either end, blotting out the steep, burnt-over, barely regrown Malibu hillside and briefly revealing in changing folds "The Torments of Beauty" until the drapes met, blotting out all light whatever.

Maury snapped on a flashlight long as his forearm. It lit their faces weirdly from below and dimly showed the lovely gray ladies in pain beyond them. There he put it behind Vividy, who stood facing Rath, and moved it up and down.

As if no thicker anywhere than fingers, the lovely form of the German film star became a twin-stemmed flower in shades of dark pink. The arteries were a barely visible twining, the organs blue-edged, the skeleton deep cherry.

"That some kind of X-ray?" Rath asked, the words coming out in a breathy rush.

"You think they got technicolor, hand-size, screenless X-ray sets?" Maury retorted.

"I think they must have," Rath told him in a voice quiet but quite desperate.

"That's enough, Maury," Vividy directed. "Bricker, the drapes." Then as the harsh rectangle of daylight swiftly reopened, she looked coldly at Rath and said, "You may take me by the shoulders and shake me. I give you permission."

The producer complied. Two seconds after he had grasped her he was shrinking back, his hands and arms violently trembling. It had been like shaking a woman stuffed with eiderdown. A woman warm and silky-skinned to the touch, but light almost as feathers. A pillow woman.

"I believe, Vividy," he gasped out. "I believe it all now." Then his voice went far away, "And to think I first cottoned to you because of that name Sheer. It sounded like silk stockings—luxurious, delicate...*insubstantial.* Oh my God!" His voice came part way back. "And you say this is all happening because of some old European witchcraft? Some crazy rhymes out of the past? How do you really think about it; how do you explain it?"

"Much of the past has no explanation at all," Dr. Rumanescue answered him. "And the further in the past, the less. The Von Sheers are a very old family, tracing back to pre-Roman times. The runes themselves—"

Vividy held up her palm to the astrologist to stop.

"Very well, you believe. Good," she said curtly to Rath, carefully sitting down at the table again behind the ugly black casket on its square of altar cloth. She continued in the same tones, "The question now is: how do I get the publicity I need to keep me from fading out altogether, the front-page publicity that will perhaps even restore me, build me up?"

LIKE a man in a dream Rath let himself down into a chair across the table from her and looked out the window over her shoulder. The three others watched them with mingled calculation and anxiety.

Vividy said sharply, "First, can the release date on *Bride of God* be advanced—to next Sunday week, say? I think I can last that long."

"Impossible, quite impossible," Rath muttered, still seeming to study something on the pale green hillside scrawled here and there with black.

"Then hear another plan. There is an unfrocked Irish clergyman named Kerrigan who is infatuated with me. A maniac but rather sweet. He's something of a poet—he'd like me light as a feather, find nothing horrible in it. Kerrigan and I will travel together to Monaco—"

"No, no!" Rath cried out in sudden anguish, looking at her at last. "No matter the other business, witchcraft or whatever, we can't have anything like that! It would ruin the picture, kill it dead. It would mean my money and all our jobs. Vividy, I haven't told you, but a majority committee of stockholders wants me to get rid of you and reshoot *Bride*, starring Alicia Killian. They're deathly afraid of a last minute Sheer scandal. Vividy, you've always played square with me, even at your craziest. You wouldn't..."

"No, I wouldn't, even to save my life," she told him, her voice mixing pride and contempt with an exactitude that broke through Maury Gender's miseries and thrilled him with her genuine dramatic talent. He said, "Max, we've been trying to convince Vividy that it might help to use some routine non-scandalous publicity."

"Yes," Miss Bricker chimed eagerly, "we have a jewel robbery planned for tonight, a kitchen fire for tomorrow."

Vividy laughed scornfully. "And I suppose the day after that I get lost in Griffith Park for three hours, next I rededicate an orphanage, autograph a Nike missile, and finally I have a poolside press interview and bust a brassiere strap. That's cheap stuff, the last resort of has-beens. Besides I don't think it would work."

Rath, his eyes again on the hillside, said absently, "To be honest, I don't think it would either. After the hot stuff you've always shot them, the papers wouldn't play."

"Very well," Vividy said crisply, "that brings us back to where we started. There's nothing left for it—I've got to..."

"Hey wait a second!" Rath burst out with a roar of happy excitement. "We've got your physical condition to capitalize on! Your loss of weight is a scientific enigma, a miracle—and absolutely non scandalous! It'll mean headlines for months, for years. Every woman will want to know your secret. So will the spacemen. We'll reveal you first to UCLA, or USC, then the Mayo Clinic and maybe Johns Hopkins... Hey, what's the matter, why aren't you all enthusiastic about this!"

MAURY GENDER and Miss Bricker looked toward Dr. Rumanescue, who coughed and said gently, "Unfortunately, there is a runic couplet in the Von Sheer Doomsbook that seems almost certainly to bear on that very point. Translated: 'If a Sheer be weighed in the market place, he'll vanish away without a trace.'"

"In any case, I refuse to exhibit myself as a freak," Vividy added hotly. "I don't mind how much publicity I get because of my individuality, my desires, *my will*—no matter how much it shocks and titillates the little people, the law-abiders, the virgins and eunuchs and moms—but to be confined to a hospital and pried over by doctors and physiologists... No!"

She fiercely brought her fist down on the table with a soft, insubstantial thud that made Rath draw back and set Miss Bricker shuddering once more. Then Vividy Sheer said, "For the last time: There's nothing left for it—I've got to open the casket!"

"Now what's in the casket?" Rath asked with apprehension.

There was another uncomfortable silence. Then Dr. Rumanescue said softly, with a little shrug, "The casket-demon. The Doom of the Von Sheers." He hesitated. "Think of the genie in the bottle. A genie with black fangs."

Rath asked, "How's that going to give Vividy publicity?"

Vividy answered him. "It will attack me, try to destroy me. Every night, as long as I last. No scandal, only horror. But there will be headlines—oh yes, there will be headlines. And I'll stop fading."

She pushed out a hand toward the little wrought-iron box. All their eyes were on it, with its craggy, tortured surface, it looked as if it had been baked in Hell, the peep-hole of milky glass an eye blinded by heat.

Miss Bricker said, "Vividy, don't."

Dr. Rumanescue breathed, "I advise against it."

Maury Gender said, "Vividy, I don't think this is going to work out the way you think it will. Publicity's a tricky thing. I think—"

He broke off as Vividy clutched her hand back to her bosom. Her eyes stared as if she felt something happening inside her. Then, groping along the table, hanging onto its edge clumsily as though her fingers were numbed, she made her way to the scale and maneuvered herself onto it. This time the disk stopped at 19.

With a furious yet strengthless haste, like a scarecrow come alive and floating as much as walking, the beautiful woman fought her way back to the box and clutched it with both hands and jerked it towards her. It moved not at all at first, then a bare inch as she heaved. She gave up trying to pull it closer and leaned over it, her sharply bent waist against the table edge, and tugged and pried at the casket's top, pressing rough projections as if they were parts of an antique combination-lock.

MAURY GENDER took a step toward her, then stopped. None of the others moved even that far to help. They watched her as if she were themselves strengthless in a nightmare—a ghost woman as much tugged by the tiny box as she was tugging at it. A ghost woman in full life colors—except that Max Rath, sitting just opposite, saw the hillside glowing very faintly through her.

With a whir and a clash the top of the box shot up on its hinges, there was a smoky puff and a stench that paled faces and set Miss Bricker gagging, then something small and intensely black and very fast dove out of the box and scuttled across the altar cloth and down a leg of the table and across the floor and under the tapestry and was gone.

Maury Gender had thrown himself out of its course, Miss Bricker had jerked her feet up under her, as if from a mouse, and so had Max Rath. But Vividy Sheer stood up straight and tall, no longer strengthless-seeming. There was icy sky in her blue eyes and a smile on her face—a smile of self-satisfaction that became tinged with scorn as she said, "you needn't be frightened. We won't see it again until after dark. Then—well, at least it will be interesting. Doubtless his hussars saw many interesting things during the seven months my military ancestor lasted."

"You mean you'll be attacked by a black rat?" Max Rath faltered.

"It will grow," said Dr. Rumanescue quietly.

Scanning the hillside again, Max Rath winced, as if it had occurred to him that one of the black flecks out there might now be *it*. He looked at his watch, "Eight hours to sunset," he said dully. "We got to get through eight hours."

Vividy laughed ripplingly. "We'll all jet to New York," she said with decision. "That way there'll be three hours' less agony for Max. Besides, I think Times Square would be a good spot for the first...appearance. Or maybe Radio City. Maury, call the airport! Bricker, pour me a brandy!"

NEXT day the New York tabloids carried half-column stories telling how the tempestuous film star Vividy Sheer had been attacked or at least menaced in front of the United Nations Building at 11:59 P.M, by a large black dog, whose teeth had bruised her without drawing blood, and which had disappeared, perhaps in company with a boy who had thrown a stink bomb, before the first police arrived. *The Times* and the *Herald Tribune* carried no stories whatever. The item got on Associated Press but was not used by many papers.

The day after that *The News of the World* and *The London Daily Mirror* reported on inside pages that the German-American film actress Vividy Sheer had been momentarily mauled in the lobby of Claridge's Hotel by a black-cloaked and black-masked man who moved with a stoop and very quickly—as if, in fact, he were more interested in getting away fast than in doing any real damage to the Nordic beauty, who had made no appreciable effort to resist the attacker, whirling in his brief grip as if she were a weightless clay figure. The *News of the World* also reproduced in one-and-a-half columns a photograph of Vividy in a low-cut dress showing just below her neck an odd black clutch-mark left there by the attacker, or perhaps drawn beforehand in India ink, the caption suggested. In *The London Times* was a curt angry editorial crying shame at notoriety-mad actresses and conscienceless press agents who staged disgusting scenes in respectable places to win publicity for questionable films—even to the point of setting off stench bombs—and suggesting that the best way for all papers to handle such nauseous hoaxes was to ignore them utterly—and cooperate enthusiastically but privately with the police and the deportation authorities.

On the third day, as a few eyewitnesses noted but were quite unwilling to testify (What Frenchman wants to be laughed at?) Vividy Sheer was snatched off the top of the Eiffel Tower by a great ghostly black paw, or by a sinuous whirlwind laden with coal dust and then deposited under the Arc de Triomphe—or she and her confederates somehow created the illusion that this enormity had occurred. But when the Sheer woman along with four of her film cohorts, reported the event to the Sureté, the French police refused to do anything more than smile knowingly and shrug, though one inspector was privately puzzled by something about the Boche film-bitch's movements—she seemed to be drawn along by her companions rather than walking on her own two feet. Perhaps drugs were involved,

Inspector Gibaud decided—cocaine or mescaline. What an indecency though that the woman should smear herself with shoe blacking to bolster her lewd fantasy!

Not one paper in the world would touch the story, not even one of the Paris dailies carried a humorous item about *Le bête noir et énorme*—some breeds of nonsense are unworthy even of humorous reporting. They are too silly (and perhaps in some silly way a shade too disturbing) for even silly-season items.

DURING the late afternoon of the fourth day, the air was very quiet in Rome—the quiet that betokens a coming storm—and Vividy insisted on taking a walk with Max Rath. She wore a coif and dress of white silk jersey, the only material her insubstantial body could tolerate. Panchromatic make-up covered her black splotches. She had recruited her strength by sniffing brandy—the only way in which her semi-porous flesh could now absorb the fierce liquid. Max was fretful, worried that a passerby would see through his companion, and he was continually maneuvering so that she would not be between them and the lowering sky. Vividy was tranquil, speculating without excitement about what the night might bring and whether a person who fades away dies doubly or not at all and what casket-demons do in the end to their victims and whether the Gods themselves depend for their existence on publicity.

As they were crossing a children's park somewhere near the Piazza dell' Esquilino, there was a breath of wind, Vividy moaned very quietly, her form grew faint, and she blew off Max's arm and down the path, traveling a few inches above it, indistinct as a camera image projected on dust motes. Children cried out softly and pointed. An eddy caught her, whirled her up, then back toward Max a little, then she was gone.

Immediately afterward mothers and priests came running and seven children swore they had been granted a vision of the Holy Virgin, while four children maintained they had seen the ghost or double of the film star Vividy Sheer. Certainly nothing material remained of the courageous East Prussian except a pair of lead slippers—size four-and-one-half—covered with white brocade.

Returning to the hotel suite and recounting his story, Max Rath was surprised to find that the news did not dispel his companions' nervous depression.

Miss Bricker, after merely shrugging at Max's story, was saying, "Maury, what do you suppose really happened to those eight hussars," and Maury was replying, "I don't want to imagine, only you got to remember that that time the casket-demon wasn't balked of his victim."

Max interrupted loudly, "Look, cut the morbidity. It's too bad about Vividy, but what a break for *Bride of God!* Those kids' stories are perfect publicity—and absolutely non-scandalous. *Bride*'ll gross forty million! Hey! Wake up! I know it's been a rough time, but now it's over."

Maury Gender and Miss Bricker slowly shook their heads. Dr. Rumanescue motioned Max to approach the window. While he came on with slow steps, the astrologist said, "Unfortunately, there is still another pertinent couplet. Roughly: 'If the demon be balked of a Von Sheer kill, On henchmen and vassals he'll work his will!'" He glanced at his wrist. "It is three minutes to sunset." He pointed out the window. "Do you see, coming up the Appian Way, that tall black cloud with blue lightening streaking through it?"

"You mean the cloud with a head like a wolf?" Max faltered.

"Precisely," Dr. Rumanescue nodded. "Only, for us, it is not a cloud," he added resignedly and returned to his book.

THE END

THE THIRD SHADOW

By H. Russell Wakefield

Roped together were two mountaineers on the treacherous cone—but three shadows on the snow.

"AND the other man on the rope, Andrew," I asked, "did you ever encounter him?" He gave me a quick glance and tapped the ash from his cigarette.

"Well, *is* there such a one?" he asked, smiling.

"I've many times read of him," I replied. "Didn't Smythe actually see him on the Brenva Face and again on that last dread lap of Everest?"

Sir Andrew paused before replying.

No one glancing casually at that eminent and superbly discreet civil servant, Sir Andrew Poursuivant, would have guessed that in his day and prime he had been the second-best amateur mountaineer of all time, with a dozen first ascents to his immortal fame, and many more than a dozen of the closest looks at death vouchsafed to any man. One who had leaped almost from the womb on to his first hill, a gravity defier by right of birth, soon to revolutionize the technique of rock-climbing and later to write two of the very finest books on his exquisite art. Yet there was something about that uncompromising buttress, his chin, the superbly modeled arête, his nose, those unflinching blue tarns, his eyes, and the high wide cliff of his brow to persuade the reader of faces that here was a born man of action, endowed with that strange and strangely named faculty, presence of mind, which ever finds in great emergency and peril the stimulus to a will and a running to meet and conquer them.

We were seated in my stateroom in the *Queen Elizabeth* bound for New York, he for some recurrent brawl, I on the interminable quest for dollars. The big tub was pitching hard into a nor-west blizzard and creaking her vast length.

I am but an honorary member of the corps of mountaineers, having no head for the game. But I love it dearly by proxy, and as the sage tells us, "He who *thinks on* Himalcha shall have pardon for all sins," and the same is true, I hope, of lesser ranges.

I dined with Sir Andrew perhaps half a dozen times a year and usually persuaded him on these felicitous occasions to tell me some great tale of the past. Hence on this felicitous occasion my "fishing" enquiry.

"Yes, so I remember," he presently said, "but are there not nice, plausible explanations for that? The illusions consequent on great height, great strain? You may remember Smythe, who is highly psychic, saw something else from Everest, very strange wings beating the icy air."

"He isn't the only one," I said, "it's a well-documented tradition."

"It is, I agree. Guides, too, have known his presence, and always at moments of great stress and danger, and he has left them when these moments passed. And if they do not pass, the fanciful might suggest he meets them on the other side. But who he is no one knows. I grant you, also, I myself have sometimes felt that over, say twelve thousand feet, one moves into a realm where nothing is quite the same, or, perhaps, and more likely, it is just one's mind that changes and becomes more susceptible and exposed to—well, certain *oddities.*"

"But you have never encountered this particular oddity?" I insisted.

"What an importunate bag-man you are."

"I believe you have, Andrew, and you must tell me of it!"

"That is not quite so," he replied, "but—it will be thirty-five long years ago next June, I did once have a very terrible experience that had associated with it certain subsidiary experiences somewhat recalcitrant to explanation."

"That is a very cautious pronouncement, Andrew."

"Phrased in the jargon of my trade, Bill."

"And you are going to relate it to me."

"I suppose so. I've never actually told it to another, and it will give me no pleasure to rouse it from my memory. But perhaps I owe it to you."

"Fill your glass, mind that lurch, and proceed."

"I haven't told it before," said Sir Andrew, "partly because it's distasteful to recall, and partly, for the reason that the prudent sea-captain turns his blind eye on a sea serpent and keeps a buttoned lip over the glimpse he caught; no one much appreciates the grin of incredulous derision."

"I promise to keep a straight face," I assured him.

"Yes, I rather think you will. Well, all those years ago, in that remote and golden time, I knew and climbed with a man I will call Brown. He was about my age. He had inherited considerable position and fortune and he was heir, also, to that irresistible and consuming passion for high places, their conquest and company, which, given the least opportunity, will never be denied, and only decrepitude or death can frustrate. Technically, he was a master in all departments, a finished cragsman and just as expert on snow and ice. But there was just occasionally an unmastered streak of recklessness in him, which flawed him as a leader, and everyone, including myself, preferred to have him lower down the rope.

"It was, perhaps, due to one of these reckless seizures that, after our fourth season together, he proposed to a wench, who replied promptly in the affirmative. He was a smallish fellow, though immensely lithe, active, strong and tough. She was not far short of six feet and tipped the beam at one hundred and sixty-eight pounds, mostly muscle. With what suicidal folly, my dear Bill, do these infatuate pigmies, like certain miserable male insects, doom themselves with such Boadiceas, and how piti-lessly and jocundly do those monsters bounce upon their prey! This particular specimen was terribly, viciously, "County," immensely handsome, and intolerably authoritarian. Speaking evil of the dead is often the only revenge permitted us and I have no intention of refraining from saying that I have seldom, almost certainly *never*, disliked anyone more than Hecate Quorn. Besides being massive and menacing to the nth degree, she was endowed with a reverberating contralto which loaned a fearsomely oraculate air to her insistent spate of edicts. Marry for lust and repent in haste, the oldest, saddest lesson in the world, and one my poor friend had almost instantly to learn. Once she'd gripped him in her red remorseless maw, she bullied him incessantly and appeared to dominate him beyond hope of release. Such an old story I need enlarge upon it no more! How many of our old friends have we watched fall prostrate before these daughters of Masrur!

"She demanded that he should at least attempt to teach her to climb, and females of her build are seldom much good at the game, particularly if they are late beginners. She was no exception, and her nerve turned out to be surprisingly more suspect on a steepish slope than her ghastly assurance on the level would have suggested. Poor Brown plugged away at it, because he feared, if she chucked her hand in, he would never see summer snow again. He did his very desperate best. He hired Fritz Mann, the huskiest and best-tempered of all the Chamonix guides, and between them on one searing and memorable occasion they shoved and pulled and hauled and slid her on feet and rump to creditably near the summit of Mt. Blanc. She loathed the ordeal, but she refused to give in, just because she knew poor Brown was longing to join up with a good party, and have some fun. I need say no more, you have sufficient imagination fully to realize the melancholy and humiliating pass of my sad friend. And, of course, it wasn't only in Haute-Savoie and Valais she made his life hell, it was at least purgatory for the rest of the year; she was eternal punishment one might say. A harsh sentence for a moment's indiscretion!"

"What about those occasional feckless flashes?" I asked; "had she quenched and overlaid those, too?"

"Permit me to tell this story my own way and pour me out another drink. In the second summer after their marriage the Browns had preceded me by a few days to the Montenvert, which, doubtless you recall, is a hotel overlooking the Mer de Glâce, three thousand feet above Chamonix. When I arrived there late one evening I found the place in a turmoil and Brown, apparently almost out of his mind. Hecate had fallen down a crevasse that morning and, as a matter of fact, her body was never recovered. I took him to my room, gave him a stiff drink, and he blurted out his sorry tale. He had taken her out on the Mer de Glâce for a morning's training, he said, determined to take no risks whatsoever. They had wandered a little way up the glacier, perhaps further than he'd intended. He'd cut some steps for her to practice on, and so forth. Presently he'd encountered a crevasse, crossed by a snow-bridge, which he'd tested and found perfectly reliable. He'd passed over himself, but, when she followed, she'd gone straight through, the rope had snapped—and that was that. They'd lowered a guide, but the hole went down forever and it was quite hopeless. Hecate must have died instantly; that was the only assuaging thought.

"'Should that rope have gone, Arthur?' I asked. 'Can I see it?'

"He produced it. It was poor stuff, an Austrian make, which had once been very popular but had been found unreliable and the cause of several accidents. There was also old bruising near the break. It wasn't a reassuring bit of stuff. 'I realize,' said Brown hurriedly, 'I shouldn't have kept that piece. As you know, I'm a stickler for perfection in a rope. But we were just having a little easy work and, as that rope's light and she always found it so hard to manage one, I took it along. I'd no intention of actually having to trust to it. We were just turning back when it happened. I swear to you that bridge seemed absolutely sound.'

"'She was a good deal heavier than you, Arthur,' I said.

"'I know, but I made every allowance for that.'

"'I quite understand,' I said. 'Well, it's just too bad,' or words to that effect. I was rather at a loss for appropriate expressions. He was obviously acting a part. I didn't blame him, he had to. He had to appear heavy with grief when he was feeling, in a sense, as light as mountain air. He got a shade tight that evening, and his efforts to sustain two such conflicting moods would have amused a more cynical and detached observer than myself. Besides, *I* foresaw the troubles ahead.

"THE French held an enquiry, of course, and inevitably exonerated him completely, then I took him home to face the music, which, as I'd expected, was strident and loud enough. How far was it justified, I asked myself. He should, perhaps, not have taken Hecate up so far. Even if that rope hadn't gone, he'd never have been able to pull her up by himself—it would have taken two very strong men to have done that. He could merely have held her there, and she would, I suppose have died of slow strangulation, unless help had quickly come. Yet there is always risk, however prudently you try to play that game; it is the first of its rules and nothing will ever eliminate it. You must take my word for all this, which is rather outside your sphere of judgment. All the same the condition of that rope—and I wasn't the only one to examine it—didn't help things. Still, all that wouldn't have mattered nearly so much if he'd been a happily married man. I needn't dwell on that. Anyway the dirty rumor followed him home and resounded there."

"What was your candid opinion, Andrew?" I asked.

"I must ask you," he replied, "to believe a rather hard thing, that I had and have no opinion, candid or otherwise. It *could* have been a pure accident. All could have happened exactly as he said it did. I've no valid reason to suppose otherwise. He may have been a bit careless; I might have been so myself. One takes such practice mornings rather lightly. There is risk, as I've said, but it's miniscule compared with the real thing. The expert mountaineer develops an exquisitely nice and certain "feel" for degrees of danger, it is the condition precept of his survival—

and adjusts his whole personality to changing degrees. He must take the small ones in his stride. The errors of judgment, if any, that Brown committed were petty and excusable. His reason for taking that rope was sensible enough in a way."

"Yes," I put in, "I can more or less understand all that, but you actually knew him well and you're a shrewd judge of character. You were in a privileged position to decide."

"Was I? A very learned judge once told me he'd find it far easier to decide the guilt or innocence of an absolute stranger than of a close friend; the personal equation confuses the problem and pollutes the understanding. I think he was perfectly right. Anyway I am shrewd enough to know when I am baffled, and I have always felt the balance of probability was peculiarly nicely poised. In a word, I have no opinion."

"Well, I have," I proclaimed. "I think he had a sudden fearful temptation. I don't think it was exactly premeditated, yet always, as it were, at the back of his mind. He realized that bridge would go when she had her weight on it, knew a swift, reckless temptation, and let it rip. I think he'd kept that rotten rope because he'd always felt in a vague half-repressed way, it might, as they say, 'come in handy one day.'"

Sir Andrew shrugged his shoulders. "Very subtle, no doubt," he said, "and you may be right. But I know I shall never be able to decide. Perhaps it is that personal equation, for I was always fond of him, and he saved my life more than once at the greatest peril to his own; and since his marriage, that ordeal of thumbscrew and rack, I had developed profound sympathy for him. Hecate was far better dead. I greeted his release with a saturnine cheer. We will leave that point.

"Well, he had to face a very bad time. Hecate's relatives were many and influential and they pulled no punches, no stabs in the back, rather. No one, of course, actually cried, 'Murder!' in public but such terms as 'Darned odd!', 'Very happy release!', 'Accidents *must* happen!' and so on, were in lively currency.

"Very few people comprehend the first thing about mountaineering, just sultry celluloid visions of high-altitude-and-octane villains slashing ropes, so this sepsis found receptive blood-streams. I did my best to foster antibodies and rallied my fellow climbers to the defense. But we were hopelessly out-numbered and out-gunned, and it was lucky for poor Brown he had more than sufficient private means to retire from public life to his estate and his farming, and insulate himself to some extent against the slings and arrows which were so freely and cruelly flying about.

"I spent a weekend with him in April and was shocked at his appearance: even life with Hecate had never reduced him to such a pass. His nerves were forever on the jump, he had those glaring insomniac eyes, he was drinking far more and eating far less than was good for him; he looked a driven haunted man."

"Haunted?" I asked.

"I know what you mean," he said, "but I don't think I can be more definite. I will say, however, I found the atmosphere of the house unquiet and was very glad to quit it. Anyway, something had to be done.

"'You must start climbing again, Arthur,' I said.

"'Never! My nerve's gone!' he replied.

"'Nonsense!' I said. 'We'll leave on June third for Chamonix. You must conquer all this and at the very place which tests you most starkly. You will be amongst friends. It will be a superb nerve tonic. This tittle-tattle will inevitably die down—it has started to do so already, I fancy. There is nothing to fear, as you'll discover once you're fit again. Come back to your first, your greatest, your only real love!'

"'What will people say?' he muttered uncertainly.

"'What say they, let them say! Actually I think it'll be very good propaganda; no one'd believe a guilty man would return to the scene of such a crime. My dear Arthur, you're a bit young to die, aren't you! If you stay moping here you'll be in the family vault in a couple of years. I'll get the tickets and we'll dine together at the Alpine Club on June the second at eight p.m. precisely.'

"To this he promptly agreed and his fickle spirits rose. So the fourth of June saw us entering the Montenvert, where our reception was cordial enough.

"IT TOOK him over a week, far longer than usual, to get back to anything like his old standard, but I'd expected that. On the ninth day I decided it was time for a crucial test of his recovery. It was no use frittering about, he'd got to face the hard thing, something far tougher than the practice grounds.

"After some deliberation I chose the Dent du Géant for the trial run. It was an old friend of ours, and the last time we'd done it, four years before, we'd simply raced to the aluminum Madonna that more or less adorns its summit. The Géant, I will remind you, is a needle, some thirteen thousand feet high, situated towards the southern rim of that great and glorious lake of ice, part French, part Swiss, part Italian, from which rise some of the most renowned peaks in the world, and of those the acknowledged monarchs are the Grandes Jurasses, the Grèpon Aiguilles and, of course, the Mont Blanc Massiv itself. It is sacred ground to our fraternity and the very words ring like a silver peal. The Géant culminates in a grotesque colossal tooth or rock, some of which is in a fairly advanced state of decay. These things are relative, of course, it will almost certainly be standing there, somewhat diminished, in five thousand years time. It provides an interesting enough climb, not, in my view, one of the most severe, but sheer and exposed enough. Nowadays, I understand the livelier sections are so festooned with spikes and cords that it resembles the fruit of the union of a porcupine and a puppet. But I have not revisited it for years and, for very sure, I never shall again.

"Brown agreed with my choice, which he declared himself competent to tackle, so off we went late on a promising morning and made our leisurely way up and across the ice to the hat. He seemed in pretty good shape, and once, when a most towering and displeasing sèrac fell almost dead on our line, he kept his head, his footing and his life. Yet somehow I didn't quite like the look of him. He didn't improve as the day wore on and to tell the truth, I didn't either."

HERE Sir Andrew paused, lit a cigarette, and continued more slowly. "You are not familiar with such matters, but I will try and explain the cause of my increasing preoccupation. We were, of course, roped almost all day, and from very early on I began to experience those *intimations*—it is difficult to find the precise, inevitable word—which were increasingly to disturb and perplex me on that tragic expedition. It is extremely hard to make them plain and plausible to you, who have never been hitched to a manila. When merely pursuing a more or less untrammeled course over ice it is our custom to keep the rope neither trailing nor quite taut, but always—I speak as leader—of course, one is very conscious of the presence and pressure of the man behind. Now—how shall I put it? Well, over and over again it seemed to me as if that rope was behaving oddly, as though the pull I experienced was inconsistent with the distance Brown was keeping behind me, as though something else was exercising pressure nearer to me. Do I make myself at all plain?"

"I think so," I replied. "You mean, as though there was someone tied to that rope between you and Brown."

"Nothing like so definite and distinct as that. Imagine if you were driving a car and you continually got the impression the brakes were coming on and off, though you knew they were not. You would be puzzled and somewhat disconcerted. I'm afraid that analogy isn't very illuminating. It was just that I was conscious of some inexplicable anomaly connected with our roped progress that day. I remember I kept glancing around in search of an explanation. I tried to convince myself it was due to Brown's somewhat inept, sluggish and erratic performance, but I was not altogether successful in this attribution. To make it worse a thick mist came on in the afternoon and this increased our difficulties, delayed us considerably, and intensified my somber and rather defeatist mood.

"Certain pious, but, in my view, misguided persons, profess to find in the presence, the atmosphere, of these doomed Titans, evidence for a benevolent Providence, and a beneficent cosmic principle. I am not enrolled in their ranks. At best these eminences seem aloof and neutral, at worst, viciously and virulently hostile—I reverse the pathetic fallacy. That is, to a spirited man, half their appeal. Only once in a long while have I been lulled into a sense of their good will. And if one must endow them with a Pantheon, I would people it with the fickle and malicious denizens of Olympus and Valhalla, and not the allegedly philanthropic triad of heaven. In no place is the working of a ruthless, blind causality more starkly shown. And never, for some reason, have I felt that oppressive sense of malignity more acutely than during the last few hours of our climb that day, as we forced our groping way through a nightmare world of ice-pillars, many of them as high and ponderous as the Statue of Liberty, destined each one of them, soon to fall with a thunder like the crack of doom. And all the while I was bothered with that rope. Several times, as I glanced round through the murk, I seemed to sense Brown almost at my heels, when he was thirty feet away. Once I actually saw him, as I thought, near enough to touch. It was a displeasing illusion."

"Were you scared?" I asked.

"I was certainly keyed-up and troubled. I am never scared, I think, when actually on the move. It was just that there was a noxious puzzle I couldn't solve. We were in no great danger, just experiencing the endemic risks inherent in all such places. But I was mainly responsible for the safety of us both and my mode of securing that safety was impaired."

"I imagine," I said, "that the rope establishes, as it were, some psychic bond between those it links."

"An unexpectedly percipient remark," replied Sir Andrew. "That is precisely the case. The rope makes the fate of one the fate of all; and each betrays along its strands: his spiritual state; his hopes, anxieties, good-cheer, or lack of confidence. So I could feel Brown's hesitation and poor craftsmanship, as well as this inexplicable interruption of my proper connection with him.

"When we eventually reached the hut I had in no way elucidated the problem. I didn't like the look of Brown; he was far more tired than he should have been and his nerves were sparking again. He put the best face he could on it, as good mountaineers are trained to do, and declared a night's rest would put him right. I hoped for the best."

"Did you mention your trouble with the rope?"

"I did not," said Sir Andrew shortly. "For one thing, it might have been purely subjective. For another, what was there to say? And the first duty of the mountaineer is to keep his fears to himself, unless they are liable to imperil his comrades. Never lower the psychic temperature if it can possibly be avoided. Yet somehow, I cannot define precisely how, I gained the impression he had noticed something and that this was partly the cause of his malaise.

"The hut was full, but not unpleasantly so, with young Italians for the most part, and we secured good sleeping places. Then we fed and lay down. It was a night of evil memory. Brown went to sleep almost at once, to sleep and to dream, and to tell of his dreams. He was, apparently, well, beyond all doubt, dreaming of Hecate and—how shall I put it?—in contact, in debate with her. And what made it far more trying to the listener, he was mimicking her voice with perfect virtuosity. This was at once horrible and ludicrous, the most pestilential and disintegrating combination of all, in my opinion. He was, it seemed, pleading with her to leave him alone, to spare him, and she was ruthlessly refusing. I say 'it seemed,' because the repulsive surge of words was blurred, and only at times articulate; just sufficient to give, as it were, the sense of the dialogue. But that was more than enough. The sleep-hungry Italians were naturally and vociferously infuriated, and I was compelled to rouse Brown over and over again, but each time he relapsed into that vilely haunted sleep. Once he raised himself and thrust out blindly with his arms. And Hecate's minatory contralto spewed from his throat, while the Italians mocked and cursed. It was a bestial pandemonium.

"The Italians left early, loud in their execrations of us. One of them, his black eyes wide with fear and anger, shook his lantern in my face and exclaimed 'Who is this woman!' 'What woman?' I replied. He shrugged his shoulders and said: 'That is for you to say. I do not think I would climb the Geant with him if I were you! Good luck, Signore, *I think you will need it!*' Then they clattered off, and at four o'clock we followed them.

"I KNOW now I should have taken that Italian's advice and got Brown back by the easiest and quickest route to the hotel, but when I tentatively suggested it, he almost hysterically implored me to carry on. 'If I fail this time,' he said, 'I shall never climb again, I know it! I *must* conquer it!' I was very tired, my judgment and resolution were at a disgracefully low ebb, and I half surrendered. I decided we would go up some of the way to a ledge or platform I remembered, at about the twelve thousand-foot level, rest, eat, and turn back.

"We had a tiresome climb up the glacier, Brown in very poor form, and that nuisance on the rope beginning again almost at once. We crossed the big crevasse where the glacier meets the lower rocks and began to ascend. There was still some mist, but it thinned as the sun rose. I led and Brown, making very heavy weather, followed. The difference between his performance this time and that other I have mentioned, was gross and terrifying. I remember doubting if he would ever be a climber again and realizing I had made a shocking error in going on. I had to nurse him with the greatest care and there was always that harassing behavior of the rope. Only those with expert knowledge of such work could realize the great and deadly difference it made. I could never be quite sure when I had it properly firm on Brown, and he was climbing like a nervous novice. My own standard of the day was, not surprisingly, none too high. I'd had a damned bad, worried night and my mind was fussed and preoccupied. Usually one climbs half-subconsciously, that is the sign-manual of the expert, a rhythmic selection and seizure of holds, with only now and again a fully controlled operation of will and decision. But now I was at full stretch all the time and ever ready for Brown to slip. Over and over again I was forced to belay the rope to some coign of vantage and coax and ease him up, and there was forever that strong interruption between us. The Géant was beating us hands down all the time and I hadn't felt so outclassed since my first season in the Alps. The light became most sinister and garish, the sun striking through the brume, creating a potent and prismed dazzle. So much so that more than once I fancied I saw Brown's outline duplicated, or rather revealed at different levels. And several times it seemed his head appeared just below me when he was still struggling far down. And then there were our shadows, cast huge on the snow-face across the gulf, vast and distorted by those strange rays.

"That there were *three* such shadows, now stationary, now in motion, was an irresistible illusion. There was mine, there was the lesser one of Brown, and there was another in between us. What was causing it? This fascinating and extraordinary puzzle served somewhat to distract my mind from its heavy and intensifying anxiety. At last, to my vast relief, I glanced up and saw that hospitable little platform not more than sixty feet above me. Once there, the worst would be, I thought, over, for I could lower Brown down more easily than get him up.

"I shouted down to him, 'We're nearly there!' but he made no reply. I shouted again and listened carefully. And then I could hear him talking, using alternatively *his* voice and Hecate's.

"I cannot describe to you the kind of ghostly fear which then seized me. There was I fifteen hundred feet up on a pretty sheer precipice with someone whose mind had clearly gone, on my rope. And I had to get him, first to the ledge, then try and restore him to a condition in which descent might be possible. I could never leave him there; we must survive or die together. First, I must reach that platform. I set myself to it, and for the time being he continued to climb, clumsily and mechanically, and carrying on that insane dialogue, yet *he kept moving!* But for how much longer would that mechanism continue to function and bring him to his holds? I conquered my fear and rallied again that essential detachment of spirit without which we were both certainly doomed.

"So I set myself with the utmost care to reach that ledge. Between me and it was a stretch of the Geant's rottenest rock, which I suddenly remembered well. It is spiked and roped now, I believe. When that gneiss is bad, it is very, very evil indeed. Mercifully, the mist was not freezing or we should have been dead ere then. How I cursed my insensate folly, the one great criminal blunder of my climbing career! This rush of rage may have saved me, for just when I was struggling up that infamous forty-five feet I got a fearful jerk from the rope. I was right out, attacking a short overhang, exposed a hundred percent, and how I sustained that jerk I shall never know. I even drove my teeth into the rock. It was one of those super-human efforts only possible to a powerful, fully trained man at the peak of his physical perfection, when he knows that failure means immediate death. Somehow then he draws out his final erg of strength and resilience.

"At last I reached the ledge, belayed like lightning, gasped for breath and looked down. As I did so, Brown ceased to climb, screamed, and then a torrent of wild, incoherent words spewed from his mouth. I yelled at him encouragement and assurance, but he paid no heed. And, though he was stationary, clawing to his holds, the rope was still under pressure, working and sounding on the belay. No explanation of that has ever been vouchsafed me. For a moment my glance flickered out across the great gulf on to the dazzling slope opposite; and there were my shadows and Brown's, and another which seemed still on the move and reaching down towards him.

I COULD see his body trembling in every muscle and I knew he must go at any second. I shouted down wildly again and again, telling him I had him firm and that he could take his time, but again he paid no heed. I couldn't get him up, I must go down to him. There was just one possible way which, a shade technical, I will not describe to you. Nor is there need or point in doing so, for suddenly Brown relinquished all holds and swung out. As my eye followed him, once more it caught those shadows, and now there were but two, Brown's hideously enlarged. For a moment he hung there screaming and thrashing out with his arms, his whole body in violent motion. And then he began to spin most horribly, faster and faster, and almost it seemed, in the visual chaos of that whirl, as though there were two bodies lashed and struggling in each other's arms. Then somehow in his writhings he worked free of the rope and fell two thousand feet to his death on the glacier below, leaving my shadow alone gigantic on the snow.

"That is all, and I want no questions, because I know I should have no answers for them and I am off to bed. As for your original question, I've done my best to answer it. But remember this, perchance such questions can never quite be answered."

THE END

THE LAST THREE SHIPS

By Margaret St. Clair

*Fifteen deserted ships at night might give off a graveyard, eerie effect;
but it was all right if one kept away from those last three hulls.*

THE best of it was that it wasn't really stealing. Everybody
knew that the ships had been moored in the estuary because
mooring them was cheaper than rutting them up for scrap would
have been. There was a guard and a patrol at night, of course, but
both were perfunctory and negligent. Evading them was so easy
that it was no wonder Pickard thought of his thefts as a sort of
praiseworthy salvaging.

Night after night he scrabbled in the bowels of the rotting
Liberty ships and came up with sheets of metal, parts of
instruments, and lengths of brass and copper pipe. He had a friend
in the boat-building business who bought most of what he
appropriated, and at prices which were only a shade below normal.
Now and then Pickard had moments of uneasiness—fifteen or so
deserted ships at night give an eerie, graveyard effect—but he
always dismissed the moments as due to imagination and nerves.
The ships were just ships, and there wasn't anything to worry
about, provided you had sense enough to stay away from the last
three hulls. Pickard had worked on these one night, and he wasn't
so sure they *were* just ships.

Business was good. After the first month he hired a helper, a
tall, gangling youth named Gene, whom he duly warned to avoid
the last three ships. Gene took over with no difficulty at all
Pickard's belief that his occupation was legitimate salvage, not
theft, and he suggested a number of worthwhile improvements in
the salvaging technique. When they were put into practice, Pick's
receipts increased by nearly forty percent.

Pickard shared the excess fifty-fifty with Gene, and for two
months all went well. Pick's wife got the Persian lamb greatcoat
she had been talking about and made two payments on it. Pickard

liked the way it looked on her. Then Bert, Pickard's friend in the boat-building business, began to complain that the salvage they were bringing in didn't amount to much.

Pick and Gene had a conference. Gene suggested they see what they could get from the last three ships, which were untouched, but Pickard vetoed the idea emphatically. They decided they might be able to make up for the lack of quality in their salvage by increasing its quantity. They worked like beavers all week, and Pick's motorboat had to make two trips to get all the stuff to Bert. But when Bert saw it, he shook his head; they got five dollars less than they had last time.

An argument started on the way back from Bert's shop. Gene didn't see any reason why they shouldn't salvage on the last three hulls, and said so repeatedly. Pick opposed him, formally at first and then with increasing bitterness. It irked him to be forced by his conscience to oppose Gene's doing something that he wished he would do. "All right, then," Pickard said at last. "Try it yourself t'morra night. Don't say I didn't warn you. Stay there a coupla hours. See how you like working around on them last three ships."

Gene pushed his felt skullcap to a defiant angle. "O.K., pop, O.K." He knew Pickard detested being called pop. "You can just bet I will."

IT WAS getting along toward daylight before Gene came back to where they had moored the motorboat. Pick waited for him anxiously, chipping at his fingernails. He ought to've known better than to let a dumb kid like that go on them last three ships. But when Gene came back every pocket was crammed with loot and he was staggering under the weight of a gunnysack he had slung over his shoulder. He showed the stuff to Pick, and Pick had to admit that it was good.

"How was it?" Pickard asked after a minute. "I mean, how was it on them ships?"

"Oh, nice," Gene answered. There was an odd, almost dreamy note in his voice. "Lots of stuff. I didn't like it at first. But after I got used to it, it was nice."

"But—" Pickard checked himself and peered as closely at Gene as he could in the still faint light. As far as he could see, the kid was smiling. Maybe Pickard had been a dope. That one night he'd tried to work on them hulls—there couldn't have been anything following him. Gene was a smart boy, and he seemed to like it on the hulls.

Gene came back the next night with an even better load, but the night after that he didn't come back at all. Pickard waited for him as long as he dared and then, though it was asking for trouble with the patrol, made a hurried, nervous search of the last three ships. What could have happened to the kid? Pick would have heard the noise if the patrol had got him. Had he fallen and hurt himself?

Pick's search, though hasty, was thorough. No Gene. Only, on the last hull, he found the boy's felt skullcap floating brim up in a sheet of filthy bilge.

Pickard was so upset he couldn't sleep when he got home. He got up at noon and sat around morosely with his hands between his knees. Estelle noticed his worry and kept at him until he told her about it. At the end of his account, she laughed.

"He was a jerk, Pick," she said comfortingly. "What happened was he got scared and ran and then was ashamed to come back and tell you about it afterwards."

"Yeh. But what scared him?" Pickard swallowed. "I remember hearing," he said with some difficulty, "about how there was a welder got welded up in one of those ships when they was building them. They launched the ship with him in it. And then there was a man down in the double bottom and his air hose caught fire. And all like that. Maybe I ought to look for a private job. Them last three hulls—they're funny at night."

Estelle snorted. "That's a lotta horsehair, Pick, and you know it. I sure never thought you'd be chicken. There ain't nothing there. But if you don't like them last three ships, don't go on them. Get yourself another helper, and have him do it."

The new helper quit about four hours after he had been hired, saying he didn't like night work. Pick didn't argue with him. He paid him his time and then (Estelle's remark about being chicken had stung him) went on the last hull by himself.

He stayed there less than an hour. He was a good deal more sensitive than Gene had been. What drove him away was nothing visible, but an emotion so complex as to be quite beyond his powers of analysis.

He felt tired and a little feverish when he got home, as if he was coming down with something. He must have taken cold or something on the ship. He had supper with Estelle and then went to bed. It was about eleven a.m. when he had his dream.

IT STARTED out mildly enough. He was hunting through one of the last three hulls for a highly saleable chunk of everdur he knew was somewhere about. As he hunted he began to have a feeling, faint and then stronger, that something pretty unpleasant was lurking on the edge of his vision. Two or three times he turned around abruptly, hoping to surprise it, but it moved faster than he could.

He kept on looking for the everdur, up and down ladders and in the crew's quarters and the engine room. At last, in the bilge of number two hold, he saw the half-submerged chunk of metal.

As soon as he saw it, he forgot he had been hunting it. By the strange equivalence of dreams, it was the bilge, the filthy stinking bilge, which became the object of his desire. He knelt down beside it, scooped it up in his hand, sick with disgust and self-loathing, and began to drink.

Pick's heart was beating violently when he woke. Of all the dumb dreams! What did a thing like that mean? His heart was still pounding abnormally when the noon whistle blew. But after a while, lying with his head resting on his arms, he began to smile unconsciously.

He got up around three and read the paper while Estelle used the vacuum on the Venetian blinds. She kept looking at him and frowning while she worked. As they were eating, she said. "You going on them three ships tonight, Pick?"

"Yeah."

"I—" Estelle ran her tongue over her clotted lipstick. "Don't do it, Pick."

"Why not?" Pickard answered. His face wore a dim remote smile. "You said yourself there wasn't nothing there."

"Yeah, I know. But—" Estelle worked a patch of polish loose from one fingernail, "—it's different when it's you, Pick. You ain't

183

acting like yourself. We can get along somehow, and I don't care about the coat. Please don't go."

Pickard got up and kissed her. He reached for his cap. "Don't worry about it, Es," he said from the door. He gave her a look, bland and composed, which she was to remember afterward. "It's O.K. I ain't scared."

AND the funny part of it was, he wasn't. He never was scared again. He liked it fine on the hulls. Even when Gene came up behind him two nights later in the hold of the *M. S. Trajan* and pawed at him with his rotting hands, Pick wasn't scared. He screamed and screamed, of course, and tried to fight Gene off, but that was more or less a reflex action. Part of him, deep inside, was delighted.

This was a good thing, because it would not have helped him to be scared. He hit Gene over and over again, but he couldn't hurt Gene; Gene was already dead. And then Pick was floundering around in the bilge—the sickening stinking loathsome wonderful bilge—and screaming automatically, while Gene stood over him making soft blubbering noises with his oozing lips. The other one came forward from where he had been lurking and proceeded with what he had to do. He didn't stop until Pickard was one of them permanently.

Estelle never did finish the payments on her fur coat. After a considerable interval of mourning she set up housekeeping with a man named Saddler, who had long admired her. The ships went back to their slow job of rusting at their moorings without bothering the taxpayers. And nowadays, if one is so indiscreet as to go poking at night among the decaying hulls as they roll quietly at anchor in the estuary, he will find that the last three are populated by a small, happily-rotting company, a company consisting of Pickard, Gene, and the welder, who has the honorable position of Oldest Inhabitant.

THE END

THE HOUSE

By Rog Phillips

The town folk hated the house, so they set fire to it and burned it down.
But the ghosts inside laughed.

THERE was a speck of blood on Mary's lower lip where she had bitten it, trying to hold herself in. I noticed it while I kept my eyes on the road. And I groaned inwardly. It would be nip and tuck now whether we could make it to the next town before the baby came.

The highway took a sudden dip and then turned sharply. A difficult road after dark. Blacktop, just wide enough for two cars to pass each other, and with no center line to get your bearings from. The edge blended into the shoulder so that it took real concentration to keep out of the ditch.

The headlights didn't help much. The road ate up the light instead of throwing it back.

Mary swayed back and forth, and groaned. The pains were coming faster now. I cursed myself for a fool. I had thought we could make it back home before the baby came; and home was still two hundred miles away. We'd never make it.

I glanced up at the sky. The black storm clouds had blotted out all the stars now. Any minute the storm would break. Just another thing to add to our troubles.

Aunt Martha had certainly picked a fine time to die. Of course we had had to go to the funeral. Hadn't she left us all her money? The baby wasn't due for another two weeks yet. We had thought we could make it easy. But we hadn't reckoned with the effects of a long trip in the car. The baby was going to come a week early.

Any minute now. I watched Mary as much as I could, ready to slam on the brakes at a moment's notice.

Something loomed across the road up ahead. It was a detour sign pointing to the left. I slowed down to a crawl and turned off the highway. The headlights revealed a one way, rutty dirt road.

185

We hadn't gone a block when it started to rain. It started easy. Just a few drops now and then. But the car picked that time to act up. The motor would hesitate just a little, and then pick up; go a little ways, and then do it all over again. I glanced at the gas gauge. It showed half full.

It was raining in earnest now. Pouring down in almost solid sheets. And the car slipped from one rut to another in lurches that were tearing the heart out of Mary. I crawled along at twenty miles an hour, trying to make it as easy on her as I could.

And every minute or so the motor would hesitate a little, then pick up again. It was getting worse each time.

A LONG hill loomed ahead, with black trees coming right to the edge of the road. The water was pouring down the ruts in the road. I switched to intermediate at the foot of the hill and gunned the motor. The hind end slipped and skidded in and out of the ruts all the way to the top.

Just as we slid over the hump the motor stopped altogether. I shut off the headlights and stepped on the starter. It ground out hopelessly. The motor was dead.

Down at the foot of the hill ahead of us one lonely light blinked. It must be a house. I turned the headlights back on and let off the brakes. The car coasted downhill, bouncing from side to side.

It came to a stop about three hundred yards from the light.

"Do you think you could make it to that house?" I asked my wife.

"I don't know, Fred," she replied, "but I'll try."

I shut off the lights and climbed out. The mud came up around my shoes as I walked around the front of the car to the other side.

Taking the flashlight out of the glove compartment and turning it on, I helped Mary get out. As she stepped from the running board a flash of lightning lit up the surroundings as bright as daylight. I could see the look of suffering in her eyes, and no doubt she could see the look of worry on my face, because she said, "Don't worry, darling. Everything will turn out all right."

Her voice was so calm and soothing I could almost believe her. I didn't say anything because—well, dammit, it was thundering so much she couldn't have heard me anyway!

With my arm around her waist and the flashlight turned to the ground just ahead of her, Mary made it down the road until we were even with the light, which came from about thirty feet off the road.

The flash of lightning had shown it to be an old style, three story, gable house. Half the shutters were gone from the windows, and half of those that remained hung at crazy angles from one hinge.

The wind wasn't too strong. It moaned through the trees quietly, and creaky noises came from the direction of the house. As we stood there and looked at it from the road for a minute, while Mary was resting, and it jumped out of the darkness with each flash of lightning, I thought that some movie producer would give a million dollars to have this setting, just as it was, to produce a movie horror picture.

The lightning flashes revealed a winding path going from the road through the grass and weeds to the front porch of the house. I had given up trying to keep my feet out of puddles. They were sopping wet. And the rain soaked into my suit and shirt, and had even gone through my hat now so that the sweatband was wet and clammy.

I kept my arm around Mary and walked off the path in the weeds so that I could keep her from falling. It seemed like ages before we reached the bottom step to the porch.

As we set foot on the porch the front door swung open. Sometimes the thing you should expect is so startling that it is stupefying.

In spite of the storm and the lightning, in spite of the broken, creaking shutters, and the air of mysterious unearthliness of the house, I had expected a normal, cheerily dressed farmer's wife to meet us at the door. Or even the farmer himself, in dirty overalls, maybe with a beard, a pipe stuck in his mouth, perhaps.

Perhaps, subconsciously, I had feared it would not turn out that way. But my wife needed help. Sane help, of a normal standard, understandable woman, if not of a doctor.

So when I looked at the figure standing in the dimly lighted doorway, almost silhouetted, something died in me. From that instant on, the sense of unreality of this night dominated everything.

HE WOULD have been big if he had stood straight. But even humped over, with his vacant face stuck out a foot farther than it seemed possible it could be, his head was level with mine.

Edgar Bergen must have met him sometime, or he could not have made Mortimer Snerd's voice so exactly like his. He stood in the doorway, silently watching us creep across the porch, until we were only two feet from him.

Then he opened his mouth and chuckled in what he thought was a friendly manner and said only one word. "Hello." It was then I instinctively looked behind him for Bergen. But he wasn't around. I didn't blame him. Right then I would have given five years salary to not have been around myself.

"Hello," I answered, forcing myself to sound friendly and unconcerned. "Our car broke down, and the storm…"

He didn't answer, but stepped back into the house. We took that to be an invitation to enter, and followed him. I sized him up quickly as we stepped through the door. He was about twenty years old, with the strength of two men, from the width and thickness of his shoulders, stooped until he looked like an ape. His face was large, coarse, and completely lacking in any trace of intelligence. His lips were thick, and his mouth hung open all the time, except for an occasional, momentary closing, probably due to involuntary swallowing.

He had on a baggy pair of faded overalls and a worn out pink plaid shirt. His arms hung limply at his sides, the hands thick hams with short trunks for fingers.

As I closed the front door behind us he half turned, and raising his voice a little, said, "Oh, ma. Some folks are here to see you."

"What's that?" a sharp female voice came from the direction of the stairs.

"Hello up there," I called, putting all the friendliness in my voice I could. I knew that if someone human didn't show up soon I would drag Mary out of there and go back to the car.

A white blob appeared over the banister of the upper landing of the stairs. It jerked back, and then a figure started down the steps.

It was obviously the mother of the thing that had let us in. There was a family resemblance in the stooped over posture. But the rest made me think of New England witches. A coal black dress that hung on her like a sack. A black shawl over her head. Slim blue veined hands. Pasty, wrinkled face. Long nose and protruding chin.

"This does it," I muttered to my wife. She nodded her head in silence.

"How do you do," she greeted, bobbing her head. Then she cackled, just as I knew she would.

"Hello," I said, smiling sickly. "The storm caught us, and my wife is going to have a baby any minute. Do you have a phone so we could get a doctor?"

"Oh, isn't that nice," she remarked inanely. Then, as if realizing the gravity of the situation she started toward the dirty cot against the wall that served for a davenport, saying over her shoulder, "Bring her over here where she can lie down."

Then, to her son, "Alvin! Go into the kitchen and put a dishpan of water on to heat."

"Yes, ma," he said obediently. Then, with a friendly look at me, and another Snerd chuckle, he turned and disappeared into the kitchen.

I HALF carried Mary over to the cot. She sank onto it as if she never expected, nor wanted to ever get up again. Then she looked up at me with a wan smile that pulled at my heartstrings.

"Do you have a car? Or are there any neighbors near that I could get in touch with a doctor through?" I asked the old woman anxiously.

"No neighbors," she hacked. "But I can take care of your wife just the same as a doctor. Many's the time I've brought little ones into the world." She pointed vaguely toward the kitchen. "Brought him into the world all by myself!" She cackled proudly.

I shuddered at the prospect of having a son like that. But if I lived out the night I would probably lose my own mind and wander around with a vacuous expression on my face the rest of my life.

"I'll see how Alvin is coming with the water," the old lady muttered aloud to herself, darting toward the kitchen.

I took Mary's hand in mine, not bothering to answer the old lady. Mary squeezed my hand and smiled. Then she bit her lip again and gripped my hand spasmodically.

Finally she relaxed and opened her eyes. "It will come in a little while now," she remarked dreamily.

I ground my teeth with a feeling of helplessness. There was nothing I could do except pray, of course. I didn't dare leave her to work on the car. I had an idea what was wrong with it now, but even if I got it fixed it was too late to get her into a hospital. It would be better for her to have it here than in the car.

The old lady came back finally with a pan of hot water; her son following with a handful of yellowish white rags that had once been towels. She set the water on a rickety chair and took the towels from her son.

"You two boys go into the kitchen," she hacked in what *she* thought was a motherly tone of voice. "You'll only be in the way here, and I don't want you under foot."

I forgave her mentally for putting me in the same class with her son, and followed him through the door to the kitchen. The lamp in the kitchen was smoking and the chimney had darkened so that its light came out in streaked shadows that projected weird pictures on the dirty, plastered walls.

I glanced around curiously. The nine-foot ceiling had a large section of plaster missing over the sink, and cracks spread from it like martian canals in all directions, to form an intricate network over the entire ceiling.

The walls had fared better, and aside from an occasional crack, were in good condition. The large bucket of water by the sink gave the lie to the two faucets. If there had ever been hot and cold running water it was now a part of the ancient history of the house. The floor was of first grade oak and the woodwork and doors of solid mahogany.

"I used to have a dog," Alvin broke in on my silent inspection. "He hasn't come home for two weeks. I can't understand it." He started to sob and rubbed at his eyes with fists so huge they did little more than rub his cheek.

I WAS instantly sorry for him. Despite the danger of life and limb that lay in his frame, if he were ever aroused, inside he was just like a child. Patting him gently on the shoulder I said, "Would you like to have another dog, Alvin? I'll get you one if you do."

"Would you?" he asked wonderingly. "Gee!" He choked back his tears and leered at me in what he seemed to think a friendly and pleasing manner.

With great effort I kept from shuddering and tiptoed to the door. Opening it a mere crack, I peeked into the front room. The old witch was busy over Mary. Mary's eyes were closed, and her lower lip was sucked in, her teeth clamped on it.

"Would you like to come upstairs and see what *I* got?" asked Alvin eagerly.

"Not now," I shrugged him off.

"Aw, come on," he pleaded, and took my arm.

I looked at his hand and arm, and a picture of what they could do to me made me give in without a struggle.

Chuckling sobbingly, Alvin took my hand and led me to a door that opened up on the back stairs.

"What about taking the lamp?" I asked.

"Oh, we won't need that," he said with a friendly leer. "I know the way."

Without resistance I gave in. My hand was completely lost in his as I stumbled up the steps in absolute darkness. After what seemed an hour to my feverishly active brain we reached the second floor landing. Alvin's breathing was loud in the quiet darkness. And I could feel my heart beating against my ribs as I stumbled down the hall, led by this mindless hulk.

We started to ascend another stairway. I tried to pull back, but Alvin kept climbing, apparently oblivious of my terror and eager to show me what he had. And now my overworked imagination began to paint pictures of something sinister. A room full of skeletons, a beautiful girl in chains, held prisoner by this halfwit and his witch mother for some sinister reason, an insane father in a padded room—all the crazy things I had read about in horror stories crowded into my mind to torture me.

By the time we reached the third floor landing I was pulling back with all my strength. But Alvin kept a firm grip on my hand and ambled along in the total darkness unmindful of my struggles.

He pulled me through a doorway. We were in a small room with one window, against which the rain beat violently. A flash of lightning lit the room dimly for a second. The dark hulk of Alvin's form was bending over something.

I TURNED in terror to dash out of the room. Instead, I bumped against the door and it slammed shut with a loud bang that shook the floor. Frantically I searched for the doorknob. My hand encountered nothing but flat surfaces. I opened my mouth to cry for help, but no sound came out.

And then Alvin struck a match. The room lit up and I turned around, dreading to look, and yet compelled to see what horror this room contained.

Alvin replaced the chimney on the lamp he had just lit. On the table beside the lamp was a pan of water. He pointed proudly to a small, crudely made, toy sailboat, floating in the pan.

"See?" he said in a very proud voice. "I made it all by myself!"

I leaned weakly against the closed door. Glancing around I saw that the room contained only the table upon which the lamp and the pan of water rested, a rickety chair with the legs wired together, and a cot on which dirty blankets were piled. The wall in which the window was set slanted up to meet the ceiling in the middle of the room. Bare rafters formed the ceiling, and the dim light from the lamp went past them to cast vague shadows on the under side of the roof.

I pulled out my handkerchief and wiped my damp face. Then I drew in a long, shuddering breath. "That's fine, Alvin," I said with forced enthusiasm. "You made it all by yourself? Well, you certainly did a fine job."

Alvin's chest expanded in pride.

"But I think we'd better get downstairs now," I added. "Your mother might need us any minute now."

"Yes, that's right," he said slowly. "I forgot about *her.*" He hesitated in such a way that I knew he was referring to Mary.

IN the kitchen again, I went to the door to the front room and started to open it. As my fingers touched the knob a sound came from the other room. It was the sound of a *baby* crying!

I threw the door open and rushed in. The old witch was holding a small baby in her hands. *MY* baby! It was yelling lustily. A glance told me it would be all right, so I ran over to Mary's side. Her eyes were closed, her breathing heavy and uneven.

I looked up at the old lady fearfully. Her eyes were worried.

"Your wife is pretty bad off," she said. "She might not live through it."

"Now that the baby's come I don't need to stay with her," I said. "I'll go out and see if I can find out what's wrong with the car. I've got to get Mary to the hospital."

I dashed toward the front door, taking the flashlight out of my pocket. As I opened the front door I mentally kicked myself for being so terrified on the stairs that I had not remembered it. There had been no need for that horrible journey upstairs to have been made in darkness!

I stumbled down the path to the road through the rain, thunder and lightning rolling across the black sky. Twice I stumbled and fell in the mud.

Finally I reached the car and lifted the hood. It took only a moment to find the broken wire and fix it. Climbing in, I stepped on the starter and the motor took at once.

With a clash of gears I started along the road. The wheels spun, and the car slid all over the road, but I finally came to a stop even with the path to the house.

Leaving the motor running, I ran down the path, bounded up the front steps and opened the front door. Mary's eyes were still closed.

Picking her up gently, I carried her down the steps and back along the slippery path, placing her in the back seat of the car. Then I ran back for the baby.

The old witch had wrapped it in a dirty blanket. I took it out of her arms and ran out of the room throwing a hasty thanks over my shoulder and a muttered promise to return the blanket as soon as Mary was safely in the hospital.

WITH the baby on the front seat beside me I put the car in low, slowly let out the clutch so that the wheels would take instead of spinning. As the car moved slowly forward I glanced in the direction of the house. At that moment a flash of lightning brighter than any before lit up the scene so that it was as bright as day.

That instant flash photographed every detail of the house on my mind so strongly that I knew I would never forget it. There were now two lighted windows. Alvin had forgotten to blow out the lamp in his room on the third floor.

It was an old style mansion. Two full stories with a high roof. Three gables were set into the roof slope in the front. Light was flowing feebly from the window in the one to the right.

The front porch was a wide, ornate affair, the fancy frill work falling away, some of it gone. The narrow lap siding of the walls was split in many places, pulled out in some.

Several dead trees were scattered about in the weed covered front yard. From their arrangement it was obvious the yard had once, long ago been beautifully landscaped.

The architecture of the house, wrecked and paintless as the house itself was, spoke eloquently of a glorious past. As I topped a rise in the road and glimpsed the lights of a city in the distance I thought, "The house is a ghost. A spirit of something that was long ago. And the people in it, that halfwitted but childishly friendly giant and his slightly mad old witch of a mother, aren't really people. Just the spirit of the house. The mindlessness of the man, the emptiness of the house. His hulking frame, the giant body. His vacant eyes, its empty future. And the little old lady in black was the spirit of all the people who had lived there."

Then I shook myself, as if waking from some nightmarish dream, and, with my eyes on the lights of the distant city, shifted into high and gathered speed on the long downgrade.

The rain had stopped now. And the sky, drained clean of the ugly black clouds that had covered it, almost imperceptibly grew light with the early rays of dawn.

MARY'S pale face was framed by a clean, white pillow. The hospital sheets were pulled up under her chin so that all that showed was her face and hair. Her eyes were closed, the lids dark.

I stood wet and miserable beside the bed. Wet and shivering, but with thankfulness in my heart. The baby was a boy, safely in the care of a competent nurse now. And my wife would live.

The doctor was putting away his stethoscope and bottles. He was a typical country doctor. Average height, around fifty, his stocky body draped in a tweed suit.

"You are very lucky, Mr. Johnson," he said to me. "Your wife has gone through this remarkably. Wet to the skin, with no doctor in attendance, it's a wonder she lived at all. Where did you say she had the baby?"

"It was an old three-story house on the detour toward Springfield. You probably know the place, in a kind of a gully. A little old lady lives there with her son. He's a halfwit, about twenty years old. He must weigh well over two hundred."

The doctor looked at me with a queer look in his eyes. For some reason I could not fathom I started to tremble violently. I put my shaking hand up to get a firm grip on my jaw to keep my teeth from rattling.

The doctor just kept looking at me. Then he turned to the nurse and said quietly, "Do you know the place, Miss Walters?"

"Why—why yes, doctor. Isn't that the place—"

"Certainly. Certainly," he shut her off. Then he turned his piercing eyes on me again.

"Suppose, Mr. Johnson," he said softly, "we take that blanket back to the old lady. Your wife will be all right now. Let's take the blanket back, and then you can get a room in the hotel and get some sleep."

"Fine," I answered, somewhat relieved. But there was still something I couldn't lay my finger on. Something, deep in my very soul, it seemed.

The doctor's face was straight ahead, his eyes on the road. I sat beside him in his car as it purred along, the damp, dirty blanket on my lap. I was still trembling, and I wasn't saying anything because that deep, fearful something inside of me made me afraid to talk.

The doctor's calm silence was slowly unnerving me.

Just before we reached the crest in the road that hid the house from view he turned his head slightly and said, "If it wasn't for that old blanket—"

"What do you mean, doctor?" I asked hoarsely.

"You can see for yourself in just a minute," he answered and relapsed into silence.

The doctor's car dipped gracefully downward as the crest of the long hill was passed. Ahead through the trees would be the house. I strained my eyes to catch a glimpse of it.

I couldn't see it. "I guess it must be over the next rise," I said.

The doctor didn't answer. His eyes were on the road. He had slowed the car down to a crawl, craning his neck to see every inch of the road. Suddenly he stopped the car and pointed to a spot on the road.

"Is that one of your footprints?" he asked.

I looked wonderingly. Then I climbed out of the car and looked at it closely. There were others like it along the side of the road. Some had a deep imprint as of a woman's heel. Some were made by a man's shoes.

I turned and looked at the doctor. He stared at me intently, his face expressionless.

SUDDENLY some unknown emotion shook me. I started to follow those footprints frantically. I glanced wildly about, looking for the house.

The footprints turned off the road onto a path that wandered crookedly through the weeds. *That* was the same path!

I looked up. The house *had* to be there. The path led up to a broken, stone foundation. Piled around the foundation were heaps of charcoal and half-burned boards. "The house had burned after we left. Alvin's lamp had set it on fire," I thought.

But again that unknown emotion gripped me. I ran and stumbled down the path. My eyes searched out every footprint in the mud. I followed until they reached the place where the front steps were lying, crumbled and charred.

Then I surveyed the scene, expecting to see wisps of steam rising from the hot coals, the remains of what, a few short hours before had been the house. There were no wisps of steam.

I stumbled into the charred ruins. They were cold. Wildly I looked around. My brain was screaming, "You are mad! You are *mad!*"

My aching eyes came to rest on the cot. It was inside the end foundation wall; its legs sunk in ashes. There were blankets and a mattress on it. Dirty. Streaked with black and grey. Sodden.

Slowly I took the blanket from under my arm where I had put it unconsciously when I climbed out of the doctor's car. It too was streaked with black and grey. It too was heavy with the rain. The memory of my mad dash to the car with the baby came up before my eyes. *There had not been time for it to become even damp!*

Wonderingly, I stepped through the piles of ashes and stood beside the cot. My eyes took in its every detail. The depression on it, showing that someone had lain on it recently. The signs of childbirth.

My brain began to spin. I swayed. A firm hand on my shoulder steadied me. I turned my head and looked into the sympathetic eyes of the doctor. I tried to speak but my lips trembled.

He gripped my shoulder reassuringly. I sucked in a deep breath and slowly let it out. Then I turned back to the cot. Reverently, if one who is mad can be reverent, I laid the blanket on the cot.

Then I looked up in the direction where, the night before, the second floor landing had been. I seemed to see it. And again I seemed to see the white blob of the old lady's face peering over the rail. Wordlessly I thanked her. Then I turned and made my way back to the path.

I kept my eyes on the doctor's car. It was my goal. It was sanity, which I must reach or perish. And as I walked firmly through the mud of the path I seemed to hear a deep, pathetic voice crying out to me.

"Come back. Come back. Don't you want to see my sailboat again? I made it all by myself."

THE END

If you've enjoyed this book, you will not want to miss these terrific titles…

ARMCHAIR SCI-FI & HORROR DOUBLE NOVELS, $12.95 each

D-51   **A GOD NAMED SMITH** by Henry Slesar
WORLDS OF THE IMPERIUM by Keith Laumer

D-52   **CRAIG'S BOOK** by Don Wilcox
EDGE OF THE KNIFE by H. Beam Piper

D-53   **THE SHINING CITY** by Rena M. Vale
THE RED PLANET by Russ Winterbotham

D-54   **THE MAN WHO LIVED TWICE** by Rog Phillips
VALLEY OF THE CROEN by Lee Tarbell

D-55   **OPERATION DISASTER** by Milton Lesser
LAND OF THE DAMNED by Berkeley Livingston

D-56   **CAPTIVE OF THE CENTAURIANESS** by Poul Anderson
A PRINCESS OF MARS by Edgar Rice Burroughs

D-57   **THE NON-STATISTICAL MAN** by Raymond F. Jones
MISSION FROM MARS by Rick Conroy

D-58   **INTRUDERS FROM THE STARS** by Ross Rocklynne
FLIGHT OF THE STARLING by Chester S. Geier

D-59   **COSMIC SABOTEUR** by Frank M. Robinson
LOOK TO THE STARS by Willard Hawkins

D-60   **THE MOON IS HELL!** by John W. Campbell, Jr.
THE GREEN WORLD by Hal Clement

ARMCHAIR SCIENCE FICTION CLASSICS, $12.95 each

C-16   **THE SHAVER MYSTERY, Book Three**
by Richard S. Shaver

C-17   **GIRLS FROM PLANET 5**
by Richard Wilson

C-18   **THE FOURTH "R"**
by George O. Smith

ARMCHAIR SCIENCE FICTION & HORROR GEMS SERIES, $12.95 each

G-5   **SCIENCE FICTION GEMS, Vol. Three**
C. M. Kornbluth and others

G-6   **HORROR GEMS, Vol. Three**
August Derleth and others

If you've enjoyed this book, you will not want to miss these terrific titles…

ARMCHAIR SCI-FI, FANTASY, & HORROR DOUBLE NOVELS, $12.95 each

D-1   **THE GALAXY RAIDERS** by William P. McGivern
        SPACE STATION #1 by Frank Belknap Long

D-2   **THE PROGRAMMED PEOPLE** by Jack Sharkey
        SLAVES OF THE CRYSTAL BRAIN by William Carter Sawtelle

D-3   **YOU'RE ALL ALONE** by Fritz Leiber
        THE LIQUID MAN by Bernard C. Gilford

D-4   **CITADEL OF THE STAR LORDS** by Edmund Hamilton
        VOYAGE TO ETERNITY by Milton Lesser

D-5   **IRON MEN OF VENUS** by Don Wilcox
        THE MAN WITH ABSOLUTE MOTION by Noel Loomis

D-6   **WHO SOWS THE WIND...** by Rog Phillips
        THE PUZZLE PLANET by Robert A. W. Lowndes

D-7   **PLANET OF DREAD** by Murray Leinster
        TWICE UPON A TIME by Charles L. Fontenay

D-8   **THE TERROR OUT OF SPACE** by Dwight V. Swain
        QUEST OF THE GOLDEN APE by Ivar Jorgensen and Adam Chase

D-9   **SECRET OF MARRACOTT DEEP** by Henry Slesar
        PAWN OF THE BLACK FLEET by Mark Clifton.

D-10   **BEYOND THE RINGS OF SATURN** by Robert Moore Williams
        A MAN OBSESSED by Alan E. Nourse

ARMCHAIR SCIENCE FICTION CLASSICS, $12.95 each

C-1   **THE GREEN MAN**
        by Harold M. Sherman

C-2   **A TRACE OF MEMORY**
        By Keith Laumer

C-3   **INTO PLUTONIAN DEPTHS**
        by Stanton A. Coblentz

ARMCHAIR MASTERS OF SCIENCE FICTION SERIES, $16.95 each

M-1   **MASTERS OF SCIENCE FICTION, Vol. One**
        Bryce Walton—"Dark of the Moon" and other tales

M-2   **MASTERS OF SCIENCE FICTION, Vol. Two**
        Jerome Bixby: "One Way Street" and other tales

If you've enjoyed this book, you will not want to miss these terrific titles…

ARMCHAIR SCI-FI, FANTASY, & HORROR DOUBLE NOVELS, $12.95 each

D-21   **EMPIRE OF EVIL** by Robert Arnette
THE SIGN OF THE TIGER by Alan E. Nourse & J. A. Meyer

D-22   **OPERATION SQUARE PEG** by Frank Belknap Long
ENCHANTRESS OF VENUS by Leigh Brackett

D-23   **THE LIFE WATCH** by Lester Del Rey
CREATURES OF THE ABYSS by Murray Leinster

D-24   **LEGION OF LAZARUS** by Edmond Hamilton
STAR HUNTER by Andre Norton

D-25   **EMPIRE OF WOMEN** by John Fletcher
ONE OF OUR CITIES IS MISSING by Irving Cox

D-26   **THE WRONG SIDE OF PARADISE** by Raymond F. Jones
THE INVOLUNTARY IMMORTALS by Rog Phillips

D-27   **EARTH QUARTER** by Damon Knight
ENVOY TO NEW WORLDS by Keith Laumer

D-28   **SLAVES TO THE METAL HORDE** by Milton Lesser
HUNTERS OUT OF TIME by Joseph E. Kelleam

D-29   **RX JUPITER SAVE US** by Ward Moore
BEWARE THE USURPERS by Geoff St. Reynard

D-30   **SECRET OF THE SERPENT** by Don Wilcox
CRUSADE ACROSS THE VOID by Dwight V. Swain

ARMCHAIR SCIENCE FICTION CLASSICS, $12.95 each

C-7   **THE SHAVER MYSTERY, Book One**
by Richard S. Shaver

C-8   **THE SHAVER MYSTERY, Book Two**
by Richard S. Shaver

C-9   **MURDER IN SPACE** by David V. Reed
by David V. Reed

ARMCHAIR MASTERS OF SCIENCE FICTION SERIES, $16.95 each

M-3   **MASTERS OF SCIENCE FICTION, Vol. Three**
Robert Sheckley, "The Perfect Woman" and other tales

M-4   **MASTERS OF SCIENCE FICTION, Vol. Four**
Mack Reynolds, "Stowaway" and other tales

2139780R00116

Made in the USA
San Bernardino, CA
16 March 2013